Bannon heard something burst through the vegetation...

A second later a hand clamped over his mouth. He raised his hands to defend himself and saw the blade of a knife gleam in the filtered moonlight.

Bannon reached upwards frantically for the wrist that held the knife. His fingers closed around the wrist, as the Japanese soldier behind him tried to drive the point of the knife into Bannon's throat. Bannon lurched to the side, spinning around and pulling the Japanese soldier's arm downwards, throwing him over his shoulder.

The Japanese soldier flew through the air and landed on his back, but he bounded around and jumped to his feet quickly, the knife still in his right hand, blade up and pointed at Bannon...

Go Down Fighting

by
John Mackie

A JOVE BOOK

Excepting basic historical events, places, and personages, this series of books is fictional, and anything that appears otherwise is coincidental and unintentional.

The principal characters are imaginary, although they might remind veterans of specific men whom they knew. The Twenty-third Infantry Regiment, in which the characters serve, is used fictitiously—it doesn't represent the real historical Twenty-third Infantry, which has distinguished itself in so many battles from the Civil War to Vietnam—but it could have been any American line regiment that fought and bled during World War II.

These novels are dedicated to the men who were there. May their deeds and gallantry never be forgotten.

GO DOWN FIGHTING

A Jove Book / published by arrangement with
the author

PRINTING HISTORY
Jove edition / January 1986

ISBN: 0-515-08444-1

Jove books are published by The Berkley Publishing Group,
200 Madison Avenue, New York, N.Y. 10016.
The words "A JOVE BOOK" and the "J" with sunburst
are trademarks belonging to Jove Publications, Inc.

PRINTED IN THE UNITED STATES OF AMERICA

Go Down Fighting

ONE . . .

It was two hours before dawn on July 19, 1944. A three-quarter moon floated in the sky, but its light didn't penetrate the thick vegetation of the New Guinea jungle. Beneath the vines, flowers, and jagged leaves, crouching in holes hacked into the ground, was the Twenty-third Regiment's reconnaissance platoon, waiting for the attack to begin.

Buck Sergeant Charlie Bannon from Pecos, Texas was in charge, and he looked at his watch. The luminous hands glowed at 0345 hours, and the attack would commence at 0500 hours. He wiped his mouth with the back of his hand and looked around.

The jungle was silent except for the calls of night birds and the howling of wild dogs. Bannon's men were lined up on both sides of him, their M 1 rifles locked and loaded and their bayonets fixed. It'd be a sneak attack with no artillery preparation to tip off the Japs that it was coming. The GIs would come out of their holes and rush the Japanese soldiers opposite them, hurling them back from the positions the Japanese had captured during the previous night.

The night had been a disaster. Bannon had been trapped behind enemy lines for eight hours and fought his way back alone, hiding like an animal, stabbing Japs whenever they got in his way. Lieutenant Breckenridge had been wounded seriously and was in the division medical headquarters. Casualties had been heavy, and now Bannon commanded the recon platoon because he was the ranking man.

He never commanded the entire platoon before. His greatest

responsibility thus far in the war had been command of the first squad, but the roulette wheel of fate had spun around and his number fell into the slot. He had to give the orders instead of take them. He was twenty-four years old and responsible for the lives of twenty-six men.

He wished he could puff a cigarette, but he couldn't because the lit end could be seen by the Japs. Pulling his canteen out of its case, he unscrewed the lid and raised the tin container to his lips, drinking down some lukewarm water. The tension was almost unbearable. He had a cramp in his stomach and a headache.

Bannon was six feet tall and lanky, with sandy hair beneath his steel pot. He had a rawboned face with more lines in it than a man his age should have. He'd enlisted in the Army on the day after Pearl Harbor and hit the Guadalcanal Beach with the first wave of GIs. He'd been fighting for his life and his country ever since. He'd been wounded many times and carried a steel plate in his head.

He looked at his watch again. Only two minutes had passed since the last time he checked the time. He sucked in air between his clenched teeth.

"Calm down," said Pfc. Frankie La Barbara, who was sharing the foxhole with him. "If that bullet comes with your name on it, there's nothing you can do except fall on your fucking face."

Bannon looked at Frankie La Barbara, who was from New York City's Little Italy. Frankie also was a six-footer, but huskier and swarthier than Bannon. Frankie had black hair and a broken nose that still was healing. The stitches hadn't been taken out yet and his nose hurt like hell. Frankie chewed gum frantically, switching it from one side of his mouth to the other, making it crack and snap every time his jaws closed. Bannon and Frankie had been together ever since Basic Training at Ford Ord, California. They'd had good times and bad times, but mostly bad times.

"I just don't give a fuck anymore," Frankie said, snapping the gum. "I got a feeling my number is coming up in this attack."

2

"Your number isn't coming up in this attack," Bannon said. "Only the good die young."

"Oh yeah?" Frankie asked. "Well I seen a lot of young rotten fucks get killed, so that's bullshit."

Bannon shrugged. "I'm gonna go see how the others are doing. You hold down the fort here."

Bannon climbed out of the foxhole. He slung his rifle over his shoulder and looked south into the jungle where the Japanese were. That jungle had belonged to the American Army at six o'clock yesterday evening, but then the Japanese attacked suddenly and unexpectedly, pushing the GIs back. Now it would have to be recaptured, and Bannon knew that Frankie was right: In ten years this entire part of the world would be forgotten, and the men who died here would be remembered only by their families and friends, and there'd be another war going on someplace else, probably.

He turned to his right and headed toward the next foxhole.

"Halt—who goes there!" shouted a voice inside the foxhole.

"Bannon!"

"Oh," said the voice of Pfc. Billie Jones, known as "the Reverend" because he'd been an itinerant preacher in Georgia before the war.

Bannon approached the foxhole and looked inside. Beside the Reverend Billie Jones was Private Victor Yabalonka, the former longshoreman from San Francisco.

"How's everything going in here?" Bannon asked.

"Okay," said the Reverend Billie Jones.

"What about you?" Bannon said to Yabalonka.

"I'm okay too."

"We're gonna jump off in a little while," Bannon told them. "When I say go, move it out, but don't get too far ahead of the rest of us and don't fall back. We'll wanna keep the lines straight, understand?"

The men grunted.

"As you were," Bannon said.

Bannon walked away, heading toward the next foxhole. The jungle was hot and humid and Bannon's uniform was plastered against his skin. His feet itched inside his boots. He wished he could take a bath and drink a cold glass of beer.

"Halt!" yelled the voice in the next foxhole. *"Who goes there!"*

"Bannon!"

"Advance to be recognized!"

Bannon walked closer to the foxhole. "You didn't recognize my voice?"

The big gnarled face of Private Joshua McGurk looked up at him. McGurk was the giant of the recon platoon, seven feet tall and tipping the scales at three hundred and ten pounds. Before the war he'd been a lumberjack in Maine.

"Yuh," McGurk said, "I knew your voice, but I wanted to make sure. Them Japs is sneaky, y'know."

"I know." Bannon looked down at McGurk, who was very sensitive and not too bright. Everybody tried not to antagonize him because he had a ferocious temper. Bannon had learned that the best way to deal with him was treat him like a child. "You did the right thing," he said to McGurk. "If you're not sure, make sure."

McGurk nodded and blinked his eyes. "Yuh."

Bannon looked at Private Randolph Worthington, who'd hunted big game in Africa for sport before the war. "How're *you* doing?"

"I'm all right, Sergeant. When things settle down, I'd like to have permission to talk with the C.O."

"Ask me when things settle down."

"Okay."

Bannon dropped down to one knee beside the foxhole. A mosquito landed on his neck and jabbed its prong in, and Bannon raised his hand, smashing the mosquito into goop.

"We'll move out in a little while," he said, beginning the same sermon he'd just delivered to the Reverend Billie Jones and Private Yabalonka. He told McGurk and Worthington to stay lined up with everybody else and not to stop for anything.

"Keep firing your weapons," Bannon said. "That's the most important part. Even if you can't see anything, fire anyway. Your bullets'll make the Japs keep their heads down. Got it?"

4

The men nodded, and the leaves festooned to their helmets trembled in the moonlight.

"Any questions?" Bannon asked.

"Nope," said McGurk.

Private Worthington shook his head.

Frankie La Barbara was all alone on his knees in the bottom of his foxhole. Bannon hadn't returned from his inspection yet and Frankie's hands were clasped together in prayer. His eyes squinched shut and his lips moved like two squirming worms as he whispered: "Oh Lord, I don't know if I believe in you or not, but if you're there, please get me through the next attack in one piece, okay? If you do, I promise I'll go to confession right after the attack, and then I'll go to Mass every Sunday for as long as I live. I won't gamble or use bad language anymore, and I won't fuck any more nurses whether they're married or not. Okay?"

Frankie listened for the voice of God, but heard nothing except the nightbirds and monkeys. He clasped his hands tighter and was about to pray more, when he heard the crack of a twig nearby. He dived onto his M 1 rifle and pointed it in the direction of the sound.

"Halt—who goes there!" he shouted.

A rotund figure emerged out of the darkness. "What the hell were you doing in there, praying?"

The voice was deep and hoarse, and Frankie La Barbara would know it anywhere. It was the voice of Colonel Bob Hutchins, the commanding officer of the Twenty-third Infantry Regiment. Frankie looked up at him, amazed to see the colonel so close to him.

Colonel Hutchins carried a Thompson submachine gun in his right hand, and wore his helmet low over his eyes. His big pot belly hung over his cartridge belt and his eyes gleamed out of the darkness.

"I just asked you a question, young soldier," Colonel Hutchins said in his Arkansas drawl. "I asked if you were praying down there."

"Yes sir, I was," Frankie admitted.

5

"What the hell were you praying for?"

Frankie was embarrassed to have been caught in the act of praying. "I dunno," he said.

"You don't know what you was praying for?"

"Well yeah, I mean yes sir, I know what I was praying for."

"Well what in the hell was it?"

Frankie thought for a few moments. "I was praying for good luck, I guess, sir."

Colonel Hutchins spat a lunger onto the ground and then dropped down to one knee beside Frankie's foxhole.

"Waal," said Colonel Hutchins, "you can pray for good luck if you want to, but I'd say that it's the Japs over there who ought to be praying for good luck, because they're the ones who're gonna need it most. Do you wanna know why?"

"Why sir?"

"Because they're gonna have to face murderous sons of bitches like you in only one more hour. I almost feel sorry for the Japs, because you're not gonna be nice to them, are you now?"

"No sir."

"You're gonna really fuck 'em up, ain'tcha?"

"Yes sir."

"You're gonna stab 'em with your bayonet and kick 'em in the balls, ain'tcha?"

"Yes sir."

Colonel Hutchins shook his head sadly. "Boy, I'd hate to be one of them poor hungry skinny Japs over there, because they ain't gonna have a chance against a big mean feller like you. If I was a praying man, which I ain't, but if I was I'd pray for the souls of them poor Japs that're gonna run into you this morning, because they're gonna die, ain't they, young soldier?"

"Yes sir."

Colonel Hutchins leaned closer to Frankie and winked. "Wanna drink?" he asked, licking the left side of his upper lip.

"Yes sir," replied Frankie.

Colonel Hutchins reached behind him and pulled his canteen out of its case. He handed the canteen to Frankie and Frankie unscrewed the top eagerly, because he knew what was inside. Frankie raised the canteen to his lips and threw his head back.

"Take it easy, now," Colonel Hutchins said gently. "Save some for me."

The fiery sweet liquid burned its way down Frankie La Barbara's throat. It was the famous white lightning brewed in the Headquarters Company mess hall by one of Colonel Hutchins's cooks, based on a recipe belonging to the legendary Sergeant Snider, a former moonshiner from Kentucky who recently had been shipped back to the States with his million-dollar wound.

"Thanks sir," said Frankie La Barbara, handing the canteen back.

Colonel Hutchins took a swig for himself and dropped the canteen back into its canvas case. He looked at the watch on his wrist.

"The attack'll begin pretty soon," Colonel Hutchins said. "I expect you to give it your best, young soldier."

"Yes sir," Frankie replied.

"Don't let me down."

"No sir."

Colonel Hutchins stood up, turned around, and walked away. In seconds he merged with the blackness of the night and was gone. Frankie La Barbara dropped back into the foxhole, sweating profusely from the sudden influx of alcohol.

He's just a loudmouth and a drunk, Frankie La Barbara thought. *Why do I love that old son of a bitch so much?*

In the next trench, by the light of the moon, the Reverend Billie Jones read his handy pocket Bible. His eyes squinted because the light was piss poor, and he ran his fingers across the sentences so he could keep track of where he was.

Opposite him sat Private Victor Yabalonka, the former longshoreman from San Francisco, and he had mixed feelings about Bibles. He'd been an atheist and a member of the Communist Party before the war, but two strange events had happened to him during the past week and he still wasn't sure of how to handle them.

7

It began when Billie forced him to take one of the handy pocket Bibles that he carried around in his knapsack. Yabalonka had buttoned the Bible into his shirt pocket and forgot all about it, but later that day he'd been shot, and the Bible stopped the bullet.

At first Yabalonka had been astounded by the strange event, but then realized it was no more than a coincidence. He'd heard tales of bullet-stopping Bibles ever since Basic Training, and now realized that the tales probably were all true. Tons of lead in the form of bullets or shrapnel flew around battlefields when things got hot and heavy, and it was inevitable that some of it would hit Bibles, because there were many Bibles on battlefields too. Lots of men carried them in their shirt pockets. Religious organizations back in the States shipped Bibles to the front by the carload.

Just when Yabalonka had rationalized the incident, he'd been shot again the next day, and his handy pocket Bible had stopped the second bullet too! That one really scrambled his brains, but now he'd rationalized it away just like the first one. It was just another coincidence, not the intervention of any supernatural being. Strange things happened in the world. Anybody who ever read Ripley's *Believe It or Not* would know that. If people could be born with two heads and four arms, why couldn't a Bible stop two bullets?

The Reverend Billie Jones looked at his watch. "Well, it won't be long now."

"Sure won't," Yabalonka replied.

"Don't you think you'd better talk with God before we charge on out of here?"

"I don't believe in God, Billie. I don't wanna hurt your feelings or anything like that, but I just don't."

"Even after he saved your life!"

Yabalonka regretted telling Billie about the first incident, but he had the sense not to tell him about the second. "It was just a coincidence," Yabalonka said. "I was lucky."

The Reverend Billie Jones stared at him. "You can't even see the hand of God when it's right in front of your face!"

"Calm down."

"I am calmed down. You're just too stubborn for your own good. If Jesus Christ himself jumped into this foxhole right now, you wouldn't believe it was him."

A boot scraped against the dirt on the edge of the foxhole, and a second later somebody jumped into the foxhole! The Reverend Billie was ready to drop down on his knees and pray to Jesus Christ, and Yabalonka's jaw dropped open, his heart beating wildly.

It was Captain Phil Mason, the commanding officer of Headquarters Company, a husky dark-complected man with black hair showing underneath his helmet.

"What the hell's going on in here?" he asked.

"Nothing sir," said the Reverend Billie Jones, who'd been on his way down to his knees, but raised himself now.

"That's just the goddamn trouble!" Captain Mason said. "There's nothing but bullshit going on here, instead of two soldiers keeping their eyes open! If I was a Jap I could've killed the both of you!"

The Reverend Billie Jones swallowed hard, because Captain Mason was right. Yabalonka looked like a little boy who'd been caught with his hand in the cookie jar.

"You two had better wake the fuck up!" Captain Mason said. "You know that this jungle is crawling with Japs! Keep your eyes open and knock off the horseshit! You're lucky I'm not Sergeant Butsko, because if he was here he'd kick both of your asses all over this jungle, understand?"

"Yes sir!" they said in unison.

Captain Mason climbed out of the foxhole and walked away. In seconds he was out of sight. The Reverend Billie Jones looked at Private Yabalonka. "I guess we'd better do what he said."

"Guess so," Yabalonka replied.

In another part of the jungle, Buck Sergeant Bannon headed back to his foxhole. A bird screeched in the tree above his head and made him jump three inches off the ground, but then he realized it was just a bird, and continued to trudge through the greasy muck that was the floor of the jungle.

His uniform was soaked with his sweat and his boots felt as if somebody had poured warm soup into them. Yet this was the coolest part of the day. The heat would really become intense in another hour or two when the sun came up. At noon it'd be over a hundred degrees in the shade.

Bannon felt a moment of dizziness, and came to a stop on the trail. He was in a thick part of the jungle, with bushes and trees on both sides of him, and long skinny vines hanging down like ropes over the trail. Visibility was poor and crickets chirped in the bushes.

He took a deep breath and tried to steady himself. *Maybe I'm coming down with malaria,* he thought. He knew that many men had been felled by malaria already. Even Frankie was laid out by malaria periodically. Frankie had caught it on Guadalcanal and suffered recurring episodes ever since.

Bannon took off his helmet and wiped the sweat off his forehead with the back of his forearm. He'd torn his sleeves off his shirt for cooling, and his shirt was unbuttoned down to his navel. He reached back for his canteen, when he heard something rustle in the leaves behind him.

Before he could turn around he heard something burst through the vegetation, and a second later a hand clamped over his mouth. He raised his hands to defend himself and saw the blade of a knife gleam in the filtered moonlight.

Bannon reached upwards frantically for the wrist that held the knife. His fingers closed around the wrist and he pushed against it, as the Japanese soldier behind him tried to drive the point of the knife into Bannon's throat. The Japanese soldier grunted and Bannon lurched to the side, spinning around and pulling the Japanese soldier's arm downwards, throwing him over his shoulder.

The Japanese soldier flew through the air and landed on his back, but he bounded around and jumped to his feet quickly, the knife still in his right hand, blade up and pointed at Bannon.

Bannon had his own G.I. issue Ka-bar knife out now. He'd drawn it while the Jap was flying through the air, and now was ready to roll.

10

"I got a Jap over here!" Bannon shouted. *"Somebody gimme a hand!"*

The Japanese soldier knew Bannon was calling for help, and realized he had to make his move. He didn't dare run away, because he knew Bannon would get him from behind. All he could do was try to kill Bannon quickly and make a fast getaway.

The Japanese soldier shifted his weight from his left foot to his right foot. Bannon watched him like a hawk. He knew the Japanese soldier was under pressure, and Bannon was going to wait to see what he'd do.

"Let's go!" Bannon yelled. *"I got a Jap over here!"*

The Japanese soldier wore a soft cap on his head, a tattered pale green uniform, and leggings. He lunged forward as the last word came out of Bannon's mouth, and Bannon was waiting. The Japanese soldier thrust his knife toward Bannon's heart, and Bannon dodged to the side, holding out the blade of his Ka-bar knife. The point of the blade went into the Japanese soldier's wrist, and the Japanese soldier's forward motion caused the blade to tear an angry red line up his arm. The Japanese soldier howled and pulled his knife backwards, stunned by the suddenness of the pain, and Bannon plunged the blade of his knife to the hilt in the Japanese soldier's stomach. Pulling back the knife, Bannon raised his arm and slashed the Japanese soldier's throat.

The Japanese soldier collapsed at Bannon's feet, blood gushing out the crack in his neck. Bannon took a step backwards, knelt down, and wiped the blade of his knife on the pant leg of the dead Japanese soldier. He stood when the blade was clean, and heard footsteps thundering on the trail. A few seconds later American soldiers came onto the scene.

"You the guy that called for help?" one of them said.

"Yeah," Bannon replied.

"Whatsa matter?"

Bannon looked down at the dead Japanese soldier, which the others hadn't seen yet because of the darkness.

"Nothing's the matter now," Bannon said, stuffing the knife back into its sheath.

TWO . . .

Tall, lean, Major General Shunsake Yokozowa stood at his map table, looking down at prominent terrain features. He was in a tent near the foot of the Torricelli Mountains, approximately eight miles from the bivouac of the recon platoon.

He drank hot instant coffee stolen from an American storehouse during General Adachi's attack of July 9, and it filled General Yokozowa with nervous energy. He had plenty to be nervous about, because his division was scheduled to attack the Americans at dawn that very morning.

It would be a crucial attack, and if it didn't roll back the American left flank, the Japanese Army on New Guinea would be finished.

General Yokozowa's Twentieth Division was part of the Eighteenth Japanese Army, commanded by General Adachi, and it was on its last legs. The Americans and Australians, aided by natives, had been slashing it to ribbons since 1942, and now only approximately seven thousand men were left. Of that number, four thousand were combat effectives.

The supply situation was nonexistent. The Eighteenth Army was cut off by the American Navy and the various American air forces, which controlled ocean approaches and the air. The Eighteenth Army was subsisting on supplies it captured during the attack of July 9, and those supplies had been costly. The Eighteenth Army lost nine thousand men during that one night, but managed to punch a hole in the American line on the east bank of the Driniumor River, a hole that had since been repaired.

Last night at sunset the Twentieth Division had attacked the American left flank near Afua, and shattered it. General Adachi hoped that the flank would collapse, causing the entire American line to destabilize, but the flank hadn't collapsed. It had been reinforced and finally solidified 250 yards north of the village of Afua.

Last night General Yokozowa had persuaded General Adachi to give him reinforcements. He'd argued that one more determined push would break the American south flank, and General Adachi relented, sending General Yokozowa the Third Battalion from the Seventy-eighth Infantry Regiment and the Second Battalion from the Eightieth Infantry Regiment.

Those units were taken from the main Japanese defense line on the west bank of the Driniumor River. It was a gamble to thin out the lines, but General Adachi took the chance. He knew that his situation was desperate and a bold stroke was required. General Yokozowa's dawn attack would be that bold stroke.

General Yokozowa smiled as he looked down at the map, but he didn't smile like other people. He raised his upper lip and showed his front teeth when he smiled. The corners of his lips didn't turn up the way normal people's lips did. General Yokozowa had a strange smile, and he was a strange man.

He was five feet eight inches tall and he'd gained several pounds since July 9, thanks to the American supplies his men had captured. His uniform was raggedy and drenched with sweat, and he wore a pair of American combat boots that he'd taken from a dead American soldier, because his own boots had rotted to shreds in the humid jungle.

But that wasn't what made him strange. He was strange because he had American blood in his veins, and he didn't want it there. He considered his American blood a disgrace. His only consolation was that nobody knew about it except some members of his family, and they weren't about to tell anybody.

But General Yokozowa knew, and the knowledge made him hate Americans even more than the average Japanese hated

13

Americans. General Yokozowa's great-grandfather had been an American naval officer who'd seduced his great-grandmother, made her pregnant, and then sailed away without marrying her. General Yokozowa's grandfather had been born a bastard, although a husband was soon obtained for General Yokozowa's great-grandmother. The Yokozowas were a wealthy mercantile family and thank goodness they could buy whatever they needed.

General Yokozowa despised his American blood. He considered it the source of all his bad habits and weaknesses. He was especially aggressive in attacking Americans because he thought, on a subconscious level, that by defeating Americans he could defeat his own cowardly American blood.

He took out an American cigarette and lit it, while continuing to gaze at the map. In only an hour and fifteen minutes the attack would begin. The future of the great Japanese Eighteenth Army would be decided during the next few hours. General Yokozowa puffed his cigarette nervously.

His plan was simple. He'd attack at dawn, and he was sure he'd take the Americans by surprise. He doubted whether they'd expect another attack so soon after the last one. If all went well he'd break through their flank and it would fall apart. Meanwhile, General Adachi's remaining units on the Driniumor River would hit the center of the American line. General Yokozowa and General Adachi were gambling that the American lines would melt away at that point. Then all Japanese units would charge toward the main military objectives in the area: the Tadji airstrips and the port of Aitape. The Japanese Eighteenth Army would capture those objectives, wipe out all Americans in the vicinity, replenish their stores with American supplies, and then move west through the jungle to the American installation at Hollandia, where the American supreme headquarters on New Guinea was located.

It was an ambitious plan. General Yokozowa figured the odds were about fifty-fifty for its success. General Yokozowa looked at his watch. The attack would begin soon. All the plans were made and there was nothing more he could do at his headquarters. Now it was time for him to leave for the front, because he wanted to lead the attack personally. A general

14

leading his men could give those men that extra bit of inspiration that could spell the difference between victory and defeat.

"Lieutenant Higashi!" he shouted.

The tent flap was swept to the side and young Lieutenant Higashi entered the tent. He was five feet two inches tall and his head was shaved smooth. "Yes sir!"

"We're leaving for the front. Notify the others."

"Yes sir."

Lieutenant Higashi saluted, performed a snappy about-face, and marched out of the office. General Yokozowa walked to his desk and lifted his potlike helmet off it, placing it on his head. He tied the strap underneath his chin so that the helmet wouldn't wobble and make him appear foolish if he had to run.

Fastened to the left side of his waist was his samurai sword, and on the right side of his belt was his Nambu pistol. A pouch affixed to his belt carried ammunition for the pistol.

He stopped in front of his small four-inch mirror and looked at himself. He thought he looked stalwart and brave, the very model of a modern Japanese major general, a leader of men, a warrior of the Emperor. As he walked toward the tent flap, he was aware that he was crossing the stage of history. He believed that the upcoming battle would be crucial for Japan, and he was playing the leading role. If he won he'd be draped in glory, and if he lost there would be his hara-kiri knife.

He passed through the opening and saw his staff officers waiting in the outer office, their faces flashing in the light of the kerosene lamp. Their mouths were set in grim lines and their eyes were narrowed with determination. Everybody knew that the stakes were high and the odds were against them. Everybody knew it would be do or die from that moment on.

"We're all ready?" General Yokozowa asked.

"Yes sir!" they replied in unison.

"Let us bow our heads and ask the gods to bless our great enterprise."

The officers inclined their heads downward and closed their eyes. Some prayed to Izanagi who, according to legend, stuck his spear into the water and made the islands of Japan out of the drops that fell from his spear. Others prayed to Isanagi's daughter, Amaterasu, who became the Sun Goddess and the mother of Japan. A few prayed to Jimmu, Japan's first emperor, believed to be the great-great-great-grandson of Amaterasu. General Hokozowa prayed to Hirohito, the current Emperor, a man and a god at the same time, the leader of the Japanese people. General Yokozowa asked for strength, courage, clearness of thought, and the victory that would save the great Japanese race from her vicious ruthless enemies.

"Are we finished?" General Yokozowa asked.

His staff officers raised their faces and opened their eyes. Not one dared to say he wasn't finished.

"Excellent," General Yokozowa said. "Let us go now and defeat the enemies of our land."

He strode toward the front exit of the tent and stepped outside into the night. Stars twinkled overhead and the moon floated in the sky. His officers followed him as he strode purposefully toward the front lines.

Not far away, Colonel Hutchins also walked through the hot bug-infested jungle. Mosquitoes and gnats stung his skin but he barely felt them because a substantial quantity of white lightning was surging through his veins.

He passed foxholes where men crouched with their M 1 rifles, waiting for the order to attack. Soldiers in machine-gun nests broke down their .30 and .50 caliber machine guns, so they could carry the pieces on their backs and set them up quickly when they got to where they were going. Other soldiers packed and repacked their knapsacks, trying to keep busy, trying not to think about what it'd be like to be impaled on the ends of Japanese bayonets.

Colonel Hutchins knew what was going through their minds. He'd been a private in the infantry himself. It'd been during the First World War, and he'd served in the famous Second Division under General LeJeune. He'd fought in Belleau Wood and the Argonne Forest. On the second of October, 1918, he'd charged up the side of Mont Blanc Ridge and saw his friends get shot to shit all around him. He remembered the famous words of General Lejeune:

*To be able to say, when this war is finished, "I belonged
to the Second Division, and I fought with it at the Battle
of Mont Blanc Ridge," will be the highest honor that
can come to any man.*

Colonel Hutchins would never forget those words, and he
still believed every one of them was true. He still believed that
he'd won the highest honor that could come to any man, and
that's why he was arrogant at times, and why he often wasn't
respectful of higher-ranking officers who'd never belonged to
the Second Division and never fought with it at the Battle of
Mont Blanc Ridge.

Walking through the jungle, his submachine gun in his right
hand, he remembered what it was like to be an ordinary soldier
in the trenches before a big attack. He knew the fear and
desolation every man felt, and how every man would think of
death and the hereafter, because those subjects couldn't be
avoided in the hour before the attack. Reflection on those subjects often made soldiers mystical and drove them into the arms
of the Almighty.

Colonel Hutchins knew what it meant to those soldiers to
see their regimental commander out there with them, sharing
the same hardships they shared, and facing the same dangers.

Colonel Hutchins stopped beside a foxhole and knelt down.
The two young GIs in it stared at him with a mixture of fear
and awe.

"How're you doing, gennelmen?" Colonel Hutchins asked.

"Fine sir," said one of them nervously.

"Okay sir," added the other.

"Good," said Colonel Hutchins, "glad to hear it. You know
what you got to do this morning, don'tcha?"

"Yes sir."

"You know which way the Japs are, don't you?"

"Yes sir."

"Which way is that?"

The soldiers pointed to the south.

"That's right," Colonel Hutchins replied. "When you get
the order to move out, that's the way you go. And you'll utilize

17

your marching fire. When you see Japs, shoot the dirty yellow bastards down, and if you get close to them, stick them with your bayonets. Get my drift?"

"Yes sir."

"I'm not gonna wish you good luck," Colonel Hutchins said, "because you're Americans, and that's the best luck a man can have. Just remember your training and follow your orders, and you'll be fine. Carry on."

"Yes sir!"

Colonel Hutchins stood at the edge of the foxhole, and the two young infantry soldiers inside saluted him. He saluted back, turned around, and walked away, transferring his submachine gun to his right hand.

When he reached the first bush he ducked into it and took out his canteen. Unscrewing the lid he raised the canteen to his mouth and took a swig of white lightning. It went down like drops of fire, and he sucked in air through his teeth. He returned the canteen to his back pocket and looked at his watch. Only approximately one hour before jump-off. The shit was about to hit the fan.

He sidestepped out of the bush and continued walking until he came to his field command post, set up just behind headquarters. It was closer to the front than many of his staff officers wanted, but Colonel Hutchins was the boss and Colonel Hutchins always got his way.

His command post was a bunker dug into the ground. The roof was made of logs covered with a layer of rocks over a layer of sandbags. Colonel Hutchins lowered his head and entered the bunker from the rear.

"Ten-hut!" said Major Cobb, his operations officer, who saw him first.

The other officers snapped to attention.

"As you were!" Colonel Hutchins said, taking off his steel pot and hanging it on a peg. "Anything happen while I was gone?"

"General Hawkins called, sir," Major Cobb said. "He was most anxious to speak with you."

"Get him for me."

"Yes sir."

Colonel Hutchins walked to the map table and looked down. Illumination was provided by a kerosene lamp suspended over the map table. The windows of the bunker that faced south were covered with fabric, so the Japs couldn't see the light of the lamp.

Colonel Hutchins glanced at the troop dispositions. His regiment was part of the Eighty-first Division, commanded by Major General Clyde Hawkins, and it had been reinforced during the night by the 114th Regimental Combat Team. The division had been thrown for a minor loss last night, but the Japs were on their last legs. The division would attack the tired hungry Japs and wipe them out. That was the plan, anyway.

"The call is going through, sir," said Major Cobb, a stout man who wore wire-rimmed glasses on the end of his tiny pug nose.

Colonel Hutchins stepped back from the map table and made his way to the telephone switchboard, lifting the receiver from the hand of the operator and holding it against his ear.

He heard mild static but nothing compared to what he'd hear if he was communicating by radio transmission. Several seconds later he heard the voice of General Hawkins.

"Where the hell have you been?" General Hawkins asked.

"Inspecting my front lines."

"You should always stay close to communications."

"Yes sir."

"Any problems?"

"No sir."

"Hit them Japs hard, Hutchins. Don't take any shit from them."

"Yes sir."

"I expect you to be in Afua by ten hundred hours."

"Yes sir."

"Any questions?"

"No sir."

"Over and out."

The connection went dead in Colonel Hutchins's ear. Colonel Hutchins handed the receiver to the telephone operator, then turned to Major Cobb.

"I want you to stay in touch with the general throughout the attack, got it?"

"Where are you going to be?"

Colonel Hutchins pointed south. "Thataway."

"You're going to lead the attack personally?"

"That's right."

"But sir . . ."

Colonel Hutchins interrupted him. "Don't but me. Just do as I say. Got it?"

"Yes sir."

"Good. I'll take you, Lieutenant Harper, and Pfc. Bombasino with me."

Lieutenant Harper swallowed hard. The last place he wanted to be was at the front with Colonel Hutchins.

Colonel Hutchins looked at Lieutenant Harper. "You look like you just swallowed a dead rat, son. Are you all right?"

"Yes sir."

"Round up Bombasino and tell him to put my field radio on his back."

"Yes sir."

Lieutenant Harper dashed out of the bunker. Colonel Hutchins reached behind him and pulled his canteen out of its case. He raised it to his lips and gulped down some white lightning. Slipping the canteen back into its case, he noticed everybody staring at him.

"What the hell are you people looking at!" he hollered. "If you-all don't have any work to do, I'll give you some!"

The officers scurried around the bunker, trying to appear as though they were busy. Colonel Hutchins walked to the peg and lifted his helmet off it, dropping it onto his head. He didn't tie the strap because if a bomb landed near him, the concussion wave could tear his head off along with the helmet. He raised his submachine gun and opened the bolt to make sure a round was in the chamber.

20

"I'm ready to roll!" he declared, heading toward the exit. "Everybody out of my way!"

General Yokozowa arrived at the front just as the first faint glow of dawn appeared on the horizon. The morning sun still was out of sight, and untrained eyes probably couldn't detect that glow, but General Yokozowa had been living in the outdoors for more than two years, and he knew the first glimmer of dawn when he saw it.

He glanced at his watch, and it was four forty-three. His attack was scheduled to begin at five-fifteen. Surrounded by his staff and aides, he proceeded toward the front row of foxholes. Soldiers poked their heads over the rims of the foxholes and saw the strange procession pass through their midst. It was seldom that they saw generals this close to no-man's-land. They stood at attention and saluted, and General Yokozowa saluted them back.

"Soon the attack will begin!" he declared. "Fight hard for your Emperor, and remember that your ancestors will be watching you!"

He looked at his men as he passed them by, and was sickened by what he saw. Their clothes were rags, and some wore fragments of American Army uniforms. Many were ill, their eyes sunken deep into their faces. They were bearded and filthy, and General Yokozowa could feel their fatigue.

The men had slept little for weeks. They'd been fighting and climbing mountains, carrying heavy equipment through thick jungles, and staging commando raids at night. Prior to the attack of July 9, these frontline units had been subsisting solely on a diet of sago palm starch. Since then they'd been eating captured American food, but it had made many of them ill. American food was greasy, and the Japanese soldiers weren't used to it.

General Yokozowa had faith in his men despite all that had happened to them, because they were Japanese and they carried within them that ineffable but precious substance known as Japanese Spirit. They may have been weak and tired, but they

21

were still the best soldiers in the world, General Yokozowa believed. They would fight fiercely and the gods would smile on them. They would not fail, General Yokozowa thought, even though he knew very well that they'd failed in the past.

General Yokozowa didn't want to dwell on the negative. He only wanted to think about the positive. It didn't make sense to him to be a defeatist before the battle had even begun.

He stood between two foxholes and placed his fists on his hips, moving one foot ahead of the other, staring into the jungle ahead. That's where the Americans were, and in that direction lay the Tadji airstrips and the port of Aitape, the principal military objectives in the area.

"I think you'd better get down, sir," said Lieutenant Higashi, his aide-de-camp.

"That won't be necessary," General Yokozowa said.

"But the Americans are just over there."

"They can't see me," General Yokozowa replied. "The Americans are very poor night fighters."

Ka-pow!

A bullet zapped over General Yokozowa's head, and General Yokozowa dived toward the ground. So did all his staff officers and aides, and embarrassment fell like a truckload of dirt over them. No one knew what to say, because General Yokozowa had been proven wrong. He had lost face. It was a most awkward situation for General Yokozowa and his staff officers.

General Yokozowa's face smarted with humiliation. He believed that the American portion of his being had caused him to make that remark just before the bullet was fired. Now he had to think of something to say to sweep the embarrassment away.

"It was just a wild shot," he said finally. "Nothing to worry about."

To prove his point, he stood up boldly.

Ka-pow!

General Yokozowa dived to the ground again. Now the embarrassment and humiliation were even worse. General Yokozowa realized that the only thing to do was come clean and admit everything.

"I was wrong," he said. "It *is* much too dangerous to stand up here. Let's move back a short distance."

He scratched around on the muck and turned around, crawling toward the next treeline. His staff officers and aides crept behind him, and all the soldiers in the vicinity were spooked, because they thought a terrible bad omen had just been revealed to their horrified eyes. Their commanding general had fucked up, and commanding generals weren't supposed to fuck up, at least not in view of their troops.

Bannon looked down into the foxhole. "What the hell were you firing at!" he demanded.

"A Jap," McGurk replied, unable to look Bannon in the eye.

"What Jap!"

McGurk pointed south. "A Jap out there."

"You saw a Jap out there?"

"Yes Sergeant."

"I think you're pulling your prick too much, McGurk. You didn't see anything out there."

"Yes I did, Sergeant."

"All you did was tell the Japs that we're here."

"You think they don't know we're here, Sergeant?"

"Don't fire that rifle of yours anymore unless you see a Jap coming right at you, got it?"

"I did see a Jap, but he wasn't coming at me."

"Well I just told you not to fire at one unless he was coming right at you."

"Okay."

Bannon looked at Private Worthington. "You didn't see anything, did you?"

"No, but I wasn't looking, either."

"What were you doing?"

"I was cleaning my rifle."

"Was it dirty?"

"No."

"Then what were you cleaning your rifle for?"

"Because I didn't have anything else to do."

23

"Well I'm gonna give you something to do right now. Keep your fucking eyes open and make sure McGurk doesn't fire at any more Japs that aren't there."

McGurk scowled. "I saw a Jap out there," he said.

"Yeah sure."

"I did!"

"Oh, yeah?" Bannon said. "Well tell me something, McGurk. If you could see a Jap from here, why is it that no Jap can see me from there?"

"I dunno," McGurk replied.

"You want me to tell you why?"

"Go ahead."

"Because the Japs can't see us at this distance at night, just like we can't see them."

"I saw one," McGurk said.

"Bullshit!"

Ka-pow!

A bullet zipped over Bannon's head, and he dived into the foxhole with McGurk and Private Worthington. He landed at their feet, and they dropped beneath the rim of the foxhole. It was tight in there for two big men, but now three were in there and they jostled each other as they tried to get up.

Bannon was embarrassed. He also was shaken up. "I guess some people can see better than others," he said.

"Guess so," McGurk replied.

Worthington didn't say anything. He didn't want to make matters worse. Bannon wondered how old Sergeant Butsko would've handled the situation. He thought about that as he put his helmet back on and realized Butsko would've toughed it out, without any apologies. Old Butsko would say only assholes made apologies.

"Stay awake in here," Bannon said. "Keep your eyes open. If you shoot at something, you'd damn well better make sure something's there."

"There *was* something there," McGurk replied.

Bannon was going to tough it out. He scowled as he climbed out of the foxhole, and kept his head low as he walked back to his hole, using bushes for cover and concealment, moving quickly across open clearings. Somehow he felt that he wasn't being a very effective platoon sergeant. He thought he was nothing compared to Butsko, who ran the platoon with an iron grip and punched out anybody who defied him.

But Butsko was gone now. He'd been wounded during the night of July 9 and they'd put him in for the Congressional Medal of Honor. Last thing Bannon heard was that Butsko was on his way back to the States to be awarded the medal. Bannon couldn't imagine what Butsko would be like back in the States. He figured Butsko would wind up in jail before long. He'd killed an Australian in a bar in Brisbane before shipping out for Guadalcanal and always tended to get in trouble in civilian situations, but he was one hell of a soldier.

Bannon wished he could be more like Butsko. He wished he had that same inner strength and that same gut intelligence. Butsko knew more about small unit tactics than most officers, and kept the lunatics and criminals in the recon platoon in line through sheer physical intimidation. Butsko had been Bannon's idol.

Bannon arrived at his foxhole and saw Frankie pointing his M 1 rifle at him.

"It's only me," he said, jumping into the foxhole.

"What was all the shooting about?"

"McGurk shot at a Jap, and then a Jap shot at me."

"Too bad the Jap missed."

Bannon gave Frankie a dirty look. "I'm getting sick of your bullshit. I think I need another runner. Go down to that next foxhole and tell Worthington that he's gonna be my runner from now on. You buddy up with McGurk. Get going."

"I don't wanna stay in that foxhole with McGurk. He's practically a moron."

"So are you."

"Fuck you, Bannon."

"Get going, La Barbara."

"Make me."

"What do you mean—make you?"

"Just what I said—make me."

Bannon groaned. He was in no mood to duke it out with

Frankie La Barbara, but what else could he do?

"Okay," he said. "Let's go."

"I'm gonna kick your ass," Frankie replied.

Bannon climbed out of the trench. So did Frankie La Barbara. They laid down their weapons and took off their helmets. Raising their fists, they advanced toward each other. Frankie had a wicked gleam in his eyes. Bannon wanted to beat the shit out of Frankie quickly and then get back in that foxhole.

Suddenly they heard the rattle of a machine gun. Bullets whistled all around them and they dived back into the foxhole, bumping heads on the way down.

"You dumb fuck!" Bannon said. "You almost got me killed!"

"Your mother's pussy!" Frankie replied.

Bannon was so tired of Frankie's backtalk that he thought his brains would explode out of his ears. There wasn't much room inside the trench but Bannon found space for a short uppercut to the point of Frankie's chin, snapping Frankie's head back. Frankie fell against the wall of the trench and Bannon delivered a short chopping right to Frankie's left temple. Bannon followed up with a left hook, but Frankie blocked it and elbowed Bannon in the nose. Bannon dug a jab to Frankie's kidney and Frankie punched Bannon in the mouth with a right cross.

Bannon fell against the far wall of the foxhole and Frankie dived on him, taking Bannon's throat in his hands and squeezing his thumbs against Bannon's Adam's apple. Bannon coughed and sputtered and tried to kick Frankie in the balls, but Frankie dodged out of the way. Bannon joined his hands together and shot them straight up in the air, breaking Frankie's hold on his throat. He slammed Frankie in the gut, hooked up to his head, whacked him on the side, and jabbed him on the nose.

Frankie's nose was the most sensitive part of his body because it'd been broken recently and the stitches still were in. Frankie howled in pain and Bannon brought one up from the bottom of the foxhole, smashing Frankie on the nose again.

Frankie's nose shattered and he fell on his back, his knees sticking up in the air. He was out cold. Bannon took a deep breath and felt like stomping on Frankie's face, but held himself back because he figured he'd need Frankie in the attack that was soon to begin.

Bannon crawled out of the foxhole and gathered together the two M 1 rifles and helmets that he and Frankie had left there. He dragged them back into the foxhole and looked at Frankie, who was still out cold at the bottom, blood streaming from his nostrils, irrigating his five-day-old beard.

The shit you gotta do to keep these lunatics in line, Bannon thought, shaking his head. *I can't stand this son of a bitch anymore, and I don't care what we went through together.*

Bannon cupped his hands around his mouth and shouted: *"Worthington!"*

"Yo!"

"Get your ass over here!"

Bannon took his o.d. green handkerchief out of his back pocket and wiped his face with it. Then he pulled his canteen out of its case and took a drink. He needed a cigarette badly, but couldn't smoke. Glancing toward the horizon, he saw the faint pink color of dawn. He could see the stars fading in the sky.

Worthington crawled to the rim of the foxhole. "You wanted me for something, Sergeant?"

"Yeah. You're my new runner. Drag this son of a bitch here to McGurk's foxhole and throw him in."

Worthington's eyes widened as he looked at Frankie out cold at the bottom of the trench. "What happened to him?"

"He talks too much—that's what happened to him. Get him the fuck out of here."

Worthington slid into the foxhole, picked Frankie up, and threw him out. The jolt of landing woke Frankie up. He opened his eyes to half-mast and saw the trees dancing around in the darkness.

"What happened?" he asked.

Bannon tossed Frankie's helmet and rifle out of the foxhole. "I just assigned you to McGurk's foxhole. Get going."

"Huh?" Frankie said.

"Do I have to draw you a picture?"

Frankie touched his nose and said: "Ouch!" Then he remembered what had happened. "You son of a bitch!" he said to Bannon, and then jumped back into the foxhole.

"Get the fuck out of here!" Bannon said. "I'm sick of looking at you."

Blood ran over Frankie's upper lip and into his mouth. He spit a gob of it out. Bannon glared at him.

"I gotta see a medic," Frankie said.

"There's no time."

"I'll make time."

Bannon's body seemed to explode, and his right fist smashed Frankie on the nose. Frankie didn't see the punch coming because it was a sucker punch, and Frankie went down for the count.

"Get him out of here," Bannon said. "Then come back and listen to that damned walkie-talkie."

Worthington dragged Frankie out of the foxhole and crawled away, his hand grasping the back of Frankie's collar. Bannon sat down in the foxhole. He raised the walkie-talkie to his ear and listened to it, in case any important messages were being broadcast. He glanced at his watch. The attack was scheduled to begin in only fifteen minutes.

THREE . . .

Colonel Hutchins glanced at the watch on his wrist. It was 0450 hours. He turned to Lieutenant Harper. "Pass the word along. Tell everybody to get ready."

"Yes sir."

Lieutenant Harper lifted the receiver from the backpack radio carried by Pfc. Nick Bombasino from South Philly. He spoke into it, repeating Colonel Hutchins's order to all the battalion commanders, and Colonel Hutchins unslung his .45 caliber Thompson submachine gun.

It was his favorite jungle weapon, because those big fat .45 caliber bullets could stop anything under the size of elephant. They made a small hole when they went in, and a big hole when they came out. Colonel Hutchins thought a Thompson submachine gun was the best weapon to use in close quarters. He was too old to fuck around with bayonets. All he wanted to do was blow the Japs away and keep moving on.

He opened the bolt of the submachine gun to make sure a round was in the chamber. All the GIs in the vicinity locked their eyes on him and watched his every move. He was the most important person in their lives just then, and he was well liked in his regiment. The men considered him tough but fair, and they knew he cared about them. They'd follow him anywhere, even if he was a drunk and a loudmouth.

The sky had gone from black to gray. The horizon was pink and the stars were bleaching out. It was dawn on the island of New Guinea and the temperature was eighty-eight degrees. The time had come to go to war.

Colonel Hutchins reached for his canteen and took one last drink of white lightning. He wiped his mouth with the back of his wrist and dropped the canteen back into its case. Turning around, he said to Major Cobb: "You're in command as of right now, and you'll remain in command until you see me again."

"I don't think you should go out there, sir."

"I don't care what you think."

Colonel Hutchins faced south again, where the Japanese soldiers were. He carried his Thompson submachine gun in his right hand and walked toward his front line of foxholes. The men in the foxholes saw him coming and knew the attack would begin momentarily. They checked the clips in their M 1 rifles and made sure their bayonets were affixed properly.

Colonel Hutchins licked his lips as he advanced toward no-man's-land. He couldn't help thinking of the day he charged up Mont Blanc Ridge with the good old Second Division. He felt the same tension, the same sense of great purpose. He knew that the Japanese Army on New Guinea was at the end of its resources. A good kick in the ass might send it reeling backwards for good.

Colonel Hutchins reached the front row of foxholes at the edge of no-man's-land. The men in the foxholes looked up, wondering how he could just stand there in full view of the enemy. The white lightning crackled in Colonel Hutchins's veins. He looked toward the Japanese lines, narrowed his eyes, and bared his teeth.

"You slant-eyed cocksuckers," he said, "I'm coming to get you now."

Three hundred yards away, General Yokozowa drew his samurai sword out of its sheath. It was a *taichi*-type sword, 750 millimeters long, and was over a hundred years old. His father had bought it for him when General Yokozowa graduated from the military academy. It had belonged to an impoverished old officer who had inherited it from his father, another old officer.

The blade and handle formed a long continuous shallow curve, the handle comprising one-third the length of the entire sword. It lacked a handguard, like most Japanese swords, but had a brass disc guard, a *tsuba*, at the juncture of blade and handle.

General Yokozowa held the sword in his right hand and admired the balance. He considered the sword an excellent weapon, and he'd killed many Chinese, Korean, and American soldiers with it. Today he'd kill more, bathing the blade in American blood. This is what he thought as he raised the sword high over his head.

"The time has come to attack," he said to the officers assembled around him. "The sun is rising on the horizon, look at it now. That rising sun is the symbol of our great nation, in its ascendancy over the world. Soon you will feel the rays on your faces. Know that those rays are the rays of the gods in heaven, and they will give you the strength to do what you must on this great day. When I give the order to attack, I want you to rip into the Americans and annihilate them totally. You must never stop and you certainly never must step backwards. Your orders are to move forward constantly and destroy every American who stands in your way. Today we will cover ourselves with glory, and tonight we will drink sake together in the port of Aitape and reminisce about the great deeds we have performed. Are we all ready?"

The officers nodded and grunted that they were ready.

"Excellent," General Yokozowa said. "Follow me and let us take our attack positions."

General Yokozowa stepped forward, his samurai sword in his right hand, and his retinue of officers followed him. Soldiers in foxholes gazed in awe at their general and his famous antique sword. They knew that the big attack was about to begin, and they knew how crucial it was. If they won they'd have American food and medical supplies, but if they lost they faced starvation in the New Guinea jungles, being tracked down like animals by the Americans.

The Japanese soldiers knew that they had to win. They held Arisaka rifles or captured M 1s in their hands tightly and waited for the order to attack.

• • •

31

Colonel Hutchins looked at his watch. It was ten minutes before jump-off. He looked to his left and right, and saw all faces on him. The men were waiting for him to give the order to go.

A bullet cracked over his head. Another snapped by his ear. The Japs had seen him. It was light enough now. He should get down, but Colonel Hutchins knew it'd look bad if he flopped onto his big fat belly just then in front of his men.

Besides, he didn't much give a damn about what happened to him anyway. He had a snootful of white lightning and nothing special to live for. He had no wife and no kids that he knew about. He was married to the Army and his soldiers were his kids. He had to inspire them, and he wouldn't be very inspiring if they saw him fall down on his big fat belly.

Moreover, if the Japs killed him, it'd be good for morale within the regiment. It would make the men aware that their commanders faced the same dangers they faced, and spilled their blood on battlefields too. Then the men would know that their officers were their comrades-in-arms, and not just their bosses.

A Japanese bullet hit the dirt near his foot, and he flinched slightly. Calmly he raised his wrist and looked at the face of his watch. The men's eyes were fixed on him as he read the time. The sweep second hand ticked toward the number 12. It was only twenty seconds away. A Japanese machine gun opened fire and the bullets whistled all around Colonel Hutchins. He grit his teeth and raised his Thompson submachine over his head.

"This is it!" he hollered. *"Follow me!"*

Colonel Hutchins brought his Thompson submachine gun down to his chest level and held it at high port arms. He threw his left foot forward and began his headlong charge.

On the other side of no-man's-land, General Yokozowa led his staff to the front row of his division's fortifications. He looked at his watch and saw that the time had come for the big attack. Gripping his samurai sword in his right hand, he held it high over his head, the blade pointing straight up at the heavens.

All the Japanese soldiers in the vicinity saw the point of that blade. They crouched in their foxholes and held their rifles and bayonets tightly, ready to jump out. General Yokozowa glowered at the American lines and uttered a quick final prayer. He couldn't wait to get into the American lines and start slashing the Americans to shit. Somewhere deep in his pysche he thought it would be the same as cutting and ripping the American part of him out, expunging himself from its contamination.

General Yokozowa lowered his samurai sword and pointed it directly at the American lines. He narrowed his eyes and set his jaw. A shot rang out and a bullet flew over his head, but he didn't falter. Another bullet hit Captain Kenji, standing to his right, but no one moved to help Captain Kenji as he toppled to the ground.

All the officers stared with great intensity at the American lines, as if the energy in their brains could pass through their eyes like death rays and destroy the Americans. The Japanese officers and soldiers heard shouting coming from the American lines, but it didn't faze them. Nothing could alter their course now. They were committed to the destruction of the Americans or to their own deaths. There could be no compromises.

General Yokozowa leapt forward suddenly.

"Banzai!" he screamed. *"Tenno heika banzai!"*

"Banzai!" replied his staff officers. *"Banzai!"*

They flashed their samurai swords over their heads as they followed him into the thick dark jungle. Behind them, the Japanese soldiers jumped out of their holes and joined the charge. They bellowed *Banzai* and shook their rifles and bayonets, anxious to close with the Americans and cut them up. Like a huge wave they swept through the thick tangled foliage, as the first sliver of the morning sun dawned on the horizon.

Colonel Hutchins jogged through the jungle, holding his submachine gun tightly in his hands. Behind him he heard his men sounding off with rebel yells, Bronx cheers, Arizona cattle calls, and you name it. Their combat boots thundered on the jungle floor as they followed him into battle. The index finger of Colonel Hutchins's right hand was poised against the trigger of his submachine gun, and the safety was off, ready to open fire. Ahead of him he saw dark figures moving through the jungle in the dawn light. Then he heard the cries of *Banzai*, and he realized that the Japs were counterattacking right off the bat. Both forces would collide against each other in the jungle. It was going to be a big fucking mess.

"They're coming at us!" Colonel Hutchins hollered. *"Hit the bastards on the run!"*

Colonel Hutchins leapt over a fallen log and dodged around a tree. He barged through a bush and on the other side saw a Japanese soldier running toward him with a rifle and bayonet in his hands. Colonel Hutchins aimed the Thompson submachine gun at him and pulled the trigger. The submachine gun kicked in his hands and hot lead spit out the barrel, striking the Japanese soldier in the head and blowing it apart.

The Japanese soldier collapsed onto what was left of his face and Colonel Hutchins jumped over his fallen body. As soon as he hit the ground he pulled the trigger of his submachine gun and mowed down three Japanese soldiers running toward him. A fourth Japanese soldier vaulted over his fallen comrades and thrust his rifle and bayonet at Colonel Hutchins's heart. Colonel Hutchins parried the rifle and bayonet to the side with his submachine gun and batted the Japanese soldier in the chops with its butt. The eyes of the Japanese soldier rolled up into his head and he dropped to his knees. Colonel Hutchins kicked him in the face and stepped to the side, holding his Thompson submachine gun parallel to the ground and pulling the trigger. The submachine gun roared and mowed down three more Japanese soldiers who'd been headed toward Colonel Hutchins.

The air was filled with gunsmoke, and Colonel Hutchins couldn't see a damn thing. He took a step backwards and coughed. Then, through the smoke, he saw a Japanese officer rush toward him, holding his samurai sword over his head. Colonel Hutchins aimed his submachine gun at him and pulled the trigger.

Click!

The submachine gun was empty. The Japanese officer swung his samurai sword down. Colonel Hutchins raised his submachine gun to block the blow. The samurai sword struck the submachine gun and sparks flew into the air. Colonel Hutchins

34

lashed out with his foot and kicked the Japanese officer in the balls. The Japanese officer screeched horribly and let go his sword. He cupped his hands around his mangled family jewels, and Colonel Hutchins smashed him in the face with the butt of his submachine gun. The Japanese officer was thrown onto his back by the force of the blow, and Colonel Hutchins dropped to one knee, reloading the submachine gun.

His hands trembled because he wasn't a kid anymore and on top of that he drank too much. Opening his ammo pouch, he removed a long clip of .45 caliber bullets. Soldiers struggled and battled all around him, cursing and burping, trying to stab each other, trip each other up, and gouge out each other's eyes. Colonel Hutchins pushed the clip into the slot on the bottom of the submachine gun, but it wouldn't go. Something was blocking it. He tried again, his hands shaking more than ever, and then something told him to look up.

His eyes bulged out of his head at the sight of a Japanese sergeant aiming a Nambu pistol at him. Colonel Hutchins couldn't run and he couldn't hide. He couldn't shoot back because his submachine gun wasn't loaded. The Japanese sergeant pulled the trigger, and the Nambu pistol fired. The bullet grazed Colonel Hutchins's left bicep muscle so closely he could feel its heat. For a moment Colonel Hutchins thought he'd been shot, but then he realized it wasn't so. He was still alive, but it didn't appear that he'd be alive for long.

The Japanese sergeant took aim again, and pulled the trigger.
Click!
He was out of ammunition too! Colonel Hutchins sprang forward with whatever strength he had left in his fifty-year-old legs. The Japanese sergeant saw him coming and swung the Nambu pistol wildly at Colonel Hutchins's head. Colonel Hutchins still wore his helmet and the pistol smacked against it, knocking the helmet off his head. Colonel Hutchins saw stars for a moment but that didn't stop him from wrapping his arms around the Japanese sergeant's torso. His forward momentum knocked the Japanese sergeant on his ass, and Colonel Hutchins landed on top of him. They rolled over and around on the ground, trying to gain leverage on each other. The

Japanese sergeant was twenty-three years younger than Colonel Hutchins, which meant he had more stamina, but Colonel Hutchins was stronger. Colonel Hutchins dug his elbow into the ground to prevent himself from rolling over again, and held the Japanese sergeant against the ground underneath him. He raised his left hand and punched the Japanese sergeant in the mouth, splitting his lip, but that only opened the Japanese sergeant's energy reverve. He bucked like a wild horse, and Colonel Hutchins fell off him. The Japanese sergeant scrambled to his feet and looked around for a weapon, it could be anything, and he saw a rock. He bent over to pick it up but Colonel Hutchins sprang to his feet and kicked him in the nose.

The Japanese soldier bent backwards and fell onto the ground. Colonel Hutchins jumped onto his face with both combat boots, and that closed down the Japanese sergeant's energy reserves. The Japanese sergeant shut his eyes and went limp on the ground. Colonel Hutchins stomped him a few more times to make sure he'd never get up again, and then looked around for his submachine gun.

His hair bristled on his neck when he saw two Japanese soldiers running toward him, aiming their rifles and bayonets at his heart. Colonel Hutchins had nothing to fight with. He even had trouble catching his breath. *I'm getting too old for this shit,* he thought. *I'm not the man I used to be.*

The Japanese soldiers rushed closer. Colonel Hutchins wasn't the kind of man who'd run away. He flashed on that day he'd charged up Mont Blanc Ridge with the good old Second Division. Lunging toward the Japanese soldiers, he hollered at the top of his lungs.

All he had to fight with were his bare hands. The Japanese soldiers pushed their rifles and bayonets toward Colonel Hutchins's heart. He dodged to the left at the last moment and kicked the Japanese soldier nearest him in the ass. The force of the kick caused the Japanese soldier to collide with the one beside him. They tripped over each other's feet and fell to the ground. Colonel Hutchins picked up a rock and threw it at both of them. Then his eyes fell on an M 1 rifle and bayonet in the hands of a dead American soldier lying in a puddle.

Colonel Hutchins picked up the rifle and bayonet, just as the two Japanese soldiers raised themselves up off the ground. Colonel Hutchins waited for them to charge, so he could counter off their moves, when suddenly three American soldiers got in the way. The Japanese soldiers were surprised to see them there. They'd thought they were going to make mincemeat out of an old American colonel, but the deck had been shuffled and new cards had been thrown at them. They stood their ground and raised their rifles and bayonets as the American GIs slammed into them.

Colonel Hutchins looked around and saw no Japanese soldiers nearby. He spotted his Thompson submachine gun lying on the ground and staggered toward it, kneeling and picking it up. Reaching into his ammo pouch, he pulled out one of those long clips full of fat .45 caliber bullets. He jammed the clip into the bottom of the submachine gun, worked the bolt, aimed the barrel into the air, and hit the trigger.

The submachine gun barked viciously, and Colonel Hutchins was pleased to find it working properly. Holding the submachine gun tightly, he looked around, still trying to catch his breath. He gasped and felt a pain in his chest. It was a terrible pain, as if his chest were being split open with a wooden stake.

What's this? he thought. *Am I getting a fucking heart attack?*

He took a step and his chest hurt more. He grit his teeth and wished he'd stayed back in his bunker. He realized he wasn't anything like the kid who'd charged up Mont Blanc Ridge twenty-six years ago. That kid was long gone, and he was a fifty-year-old man who smoked and drank too much.

He looked around, and the battlefield undulated before his eyes. His legs gave out underneath him and he dropped to his knees. Through the smoke and mist he saw Japanese soldiers running toward him. He raised his submachine gun and pulled the trigger. The submachine gun chattered, but somehow the Japs kept coming. His aim was off. Something told Colonel Hutchins that he was going to die.

He didn't want to die. He had things to do and whisky to drink, whores to screw and dice to throw. Gritting his teeth, he aimed the submachine gun carefully. The Japs were only fifteen feet away. Colonel Hutchins pulled the trigger and the submachine gun shook and stuttered in his hands. Bullets flew out of the stubby barrel, and the Japanese soldiers tripped over their feet. They spun through the air as the stream of bullets tore flesh off their bodies, and their blood made graceful red spirals in the air.

They fell to the ground, and Colonel Hutchins burped like a bullfrog. The pressure in his chest suddenly was relieved. He realized that the pain had been caused by gas, not a heart attack. He wasn't as bad off as he'd thought.

He looked around and saw men clashing everywhere. Half of the copper sun was above the horizon now, and the jungle was bathed in a red glow. Soldiers elbowed, kicked, stabbed, and shot each other. Both sides were at a standstill, unwilling to retreat and unable to advance.

Colonel Hutchins reached down into his guts for his deepest loudest voice. *"Forward Twenty-third!"* he hollered. *"Push the cocksuckers back!"*

Japanese soldiers nearby turned to him; his voice attracted their attention. Colonel Hutchins took a deep breath and charged forward, holding the butt of his submachine gun between his elbow and his waist. Japanese soldiers converged on him, and he pulled the trigger of the submachine gun.

It rocked and bucked in his arms, but he held it tightly and bared his teeth. Hot lead shot out of the barrel and gunsmoke billowed in the air. The stream of bullets hit a Japanese soldier in the head and shredded it beyond recognition. Colonel Hutchins pulled the barrel down, and the next burst caught a Japanese soldier in the throat, ripping it apart. The Japanese soldier dropped to the ground, his head attached to his body by only a few tendrils. Again Colonel Hutchins leaned on the barrel of his submachine gun, because the firing tended to make it rise, and he shot a burst into the chest of the next Japanese soldier, mashing his lungs, heart, and esophagus. That Japanese soldier toppled to the dirt, and Colonel Hutchins ran out of ammunition again.

Japanese soldiers came at him from all angles. *Me and my*

38

big mouth, he thought. He raised his submachine gun to parry bayonet thrusts, when suddenly, out of the corner of his eye, he saw a huge shadow enter the picture.

This huge shadow was none other than Private Joshua McGurk from Skunk Hollow, Maine. He'd lost his M 1 rifle somewhere along the way, and now carried a long thick branch, wielding it in both hands like a club. He swung the club down with all his strength, and struck a Japanese soldier on top of his helmet. The helmet dented into a big V, and the top of the Japanese soldier's head caved in. Blood and brains squirted out of the Japanese soldier's eyes, nose, and mouth as the force of the blow hurled him to the ground.

McGurk swung sideways and hit a Japanese soldier on his upper arm, cracking the bone. The Japanese soldier shrieked in pain and jumped up and down. McGurk swung again and whacked the Japanese soldier in the face, fracturing countless bones, knocking the Japanese soldier cold.

The Japanese soldier fell to the ground and McGurk jumped over him, a murderous gleam in his eye. He swung to the left and right, clobbering the Japanese soldiers in the vicinity of Colonel Hutchins. The Japanese soldiers fell like flies, and Colonel Hutchins stared goggle-eyed at all the incredible mayhem.

I'm gonna put this soldier in for a medal, he thought.

McGurk swung the club low and broke a Japanese soldier's leg. He swung high and fractured a Japanese soldier's ribs. He swung down and smacked a Japanese soldier's head into his chest cavity. Lashing out with his foot, he kicked a Japanese soldier's balls into his intestines. Winding up and taking a deep breath, he slammed a Japanese officer on the shoulder, nearly dismembering it. On his backswing, he aimed at a Japanese soldier's head. The Japanese soldier had the presence of mind to lean back, but he wasn't fast enough. The end of McGurk's club took off the Japanese soldier's nose. Blood spurted out and the Japanese soldier didn't know what hit him. He staggered two steps to the left, and then two steps to the right, as blood poured down his face into his mouth and onto his uniform shirt.

McGurk narrowed his eyes and swung again, connecting with the Japanese soldier's ear, shattering his skull. The Japanese soldier was thrown to the ground and didn't move a muscle.

That finished off the Japanese soldiers who'd surrounded Colonel Hutchins. The full light of morning illuminated the jungle, as McGurk walked up to Colonel Hutchins, whose trembling hands loaded his Thompson submachine gun.

"You all right, sir?" asked McGurk, breathing heavily.

"I'm fine."

"I think you'd better get back where it's safe, sir."

"Go back hell!" Colonel Hutchins replied. "I just got here!" Colonel Hutchins raised his submachine gun over his head and lurched forward into the thick of the fighting. *"Push 'em back!"* he bellowed. *"Kick their fucking asses!"*

His voice traveled all across the battlefield; they didn't call him "Hollerin' Hutchins" for nothing. Buck Sergeant Charlie Bannon from Pecos, Texas heard the command, but he was in the thick of the fighting and didn't even know what direction the Japs should be pushed back to. A Japanese soldier pushed his rifle and bayonet toward Bannon's heart, and Bannon parried it to the side, smashing the Japanese soldier in the mouth with his rifle butt. The Japanese soldier collapsed, and Bannon stepped forward, slashing down with his rifle and bayonet, ripping the next Japanese soldier from the right side of his neck to the left side of his beltline. He stabbed his rifle and bayonet forward, burying the bayonet to the hilt into the chest of the next Japanese soldier, and then he pulled back on his rifle and bayonet, but the damned thing wouldn't disengage.

The blade was stuck in the ribs of the Japanese soldier's chest. Bannon tugged again, but the blade wouldn't come loose. The Japanese soldier fell onto his back, and Bannon placed his foot on the Japanese soldier's chest to get some leverage.

Soldiers fought and clawed all around Bannon, and a Japanese soldier named Machi saw Bannon trying to pull his bayonet out of the chest of the Japanese soldier on the ground, who was a friend of Machi's.

"No!" yelled Machi, running toward Bannon.

Bannon didn't understand what he said, but he heard Machi coming. He pulled his rifle and bayonet once more, but it still was stuck in the Japanese soldier's chest. Machi came closer, and Bannon didn't have time to bend over and pick up the Japanese soldier's rifle and bayonet. Machi already was on top of Bannon.

"*Yaaaahhhhhhhh!*" screamed Machi, plunging his rifle and bayonet toward Bannon's heart.

Bannon danced out of the way and looked around frantically on the ground for a weapon. Much stuff was there, but Machi had altered his course and charged Bannon again.

"*Yyaaaaahhhhhhhhhhhh!*"

Machi thrust his rifle and bayonet toward Bannon's stomach, and Bannon pounced on the rifle and bayonet with both his hands, while dancing to the side and sucking in his stomach.

The blade missed Bannon's stomach by a half inch. Bannon tried to yank the rifle and bayonet out of Machi's hands, but Machi wouldn't let go. Machi leaned backwards, to pull the rifle and bayonet away from Bannon, but Bannon wouldn't let go.

The two soldiers snorted and grunted as they tried to gain possession of the weapon. They were so close they could look into each other's eyes and smell each other's nasty morning breath. Bannon was taller and huskier than Machi, but Machi had muscles like steel belts. They twisted and tugged at the rifle and bayonet, but nothing worked for either of them.

Machi tried to kick Bannon in the balls, but Bannon turned sideways and received the blow on his hip. Bannon tried to snake his leg around Machi, to trip him up, but Machi wouldn't fall. Bannon was caught standing on one leg for a moment, and Machi pushed. Bannon fell backwards, but he wouldn't let the rifle and bayonet go. He dropped onto his back, and Machi fell on top of him.

The rifle and bayonet was sandwiched between them. Machi reached up with his right hand and tried to jab his thumb into one of Bannon's eyes. Bannon raised his left hand and grabbed Machi's wrist. Machi punched Bannon in the mouth with his

41

left hand, and Bannon was dazed momentarily. He grabbed Machi's throat with his right hand and squeezed Machi's Adam's apple.

Machi had the worst sore throat in his life. He coughed while clawing wildly at Bannon's face. Machi had long dirty fingernails and they made four red lines across Bannon's cheek. One of his fingernails came within a quarter of an inch of Bannon's left eye.

Bannon continued to squeeze Machi's throat, and Machi pounded his fists on Bannon's face, smashing Bannon's nose. Bannon was forced to loosen his grip on Machi's face. Machi punched Bannon again, and Bannon lost consciousness for a few moments.

Machi jumped to his feet, looked around on the ground for something to bash Bannon with, and saw a rock. He picked it up with both of his hands, raising it into the air. Bannon opened his eyes and saw the rock about to be launched toward his head. Then he saw something flash in the middle of the Japanese soldier's chest. It was the end of a bayonet. The rock dropped out of the Japanese soldier's hands. Bannon struggled to get to his feet. The Japanese soldier was pulled backwards as Frankie La Barbara yanked his bayonet out of the Japanese soldier's back.

"Ya owe me one!" Frankie La Barbara shouted to Bannon.

He turned around and was whacked in the face by the butt of a Japanese rifle. Frankie was knocked cold and went flying onto his back, where he didn't move a muscle.

Bannon picked up the nearest rifle and bayonet. A Japanese soldier stood over Frankie and prepared to run him through, when Bannon charged.

Blood dripped from Bannon's broken nose as he thrust his rifle and bayonet toward the Japanese soldier's chest. The Japanese soldier tried to parry it out of the way, but he'd been taken by surprise and couldn't do it. The tip of the bayonet tore through the Japanese soldier's shirt and pierced his skin. It burrowed into the Japanese soldier's soft belly, and the Japanese soldier's eyes rolled up into his head. He heaved his last sigh and dropped to his knees. Bannon pulled back his bayonet. The Japanese soldier fell onto his face, and a pool of blood widened underneath him.

Bannon turned around and saw Frankie La Barbara getting up off the ground.

"We're even!" Bannon hollered.

On another part of the battlefield, General Yokozowa chopped up American soldiers with his samurai sword. He swung to the left and right, lopping off arms, legs, and heads. American soldiers tried to stab him with their rifles and bayonets, and he parried the thrusts easily to the side. General Yokozowa was a master swordsman, and he knew all the dirty tricks too. He advanced steadily, cutting down Americans the way a man with a machete cuts saplings and branches. His nostrils were flared with anger and his eyes were wide with delight.

General Yokozowa was enjoying himself. He felt as if every American he killed helped to purge the foul American blood in his veins. His fanaticism over this gave him extra strength, and no American could stand for long in front of him. Some Americans were bigger than he, and he cut them down to size. The smaller ones he dispatched easily. Americans fired wild shots at him but missed. He whacked off the hands that held their pistols and rifles. He screamed *Banzai!* at the top of his lungs and moved forward inexorably against the Americans.

In the press of battle, it was difficult to see General Yokozowa until he was right on top of you, and by then it was too late. He slashed and ripped, chopped and hacked, leaving a trail of blood and broken limbs behind him. He held his famous antique samurai sword in both his hands and brought it down with all his strength, cleaving apart the skull of the American soldier in front of him. The American soldier dropped to the ground, and behind him was Private Victor Yabalonka, the former longshoreman from San Francisco.

Yabalonka looked up and saw the Japanese officer in front of him. The Japanese officer had a gleam in his eyes and a triumphant smile on his lips. Yokozowa raised his samurai sword over his head and swung down. Yabalonka held up his rifle and bayonet to defend himself, and the blade of the samurai sword came down on top of it.

Sparks flew into the air and the *clang* echoed across the battlefield. Yabalonka's hands stung and he knew that the Japanese officer in front of him was a strong son of a bitch. General Yokozowa reared back his sword to swing at Yabalonka from the side, and Yabalonka held out his rifle again to protect himself.

Clang!

The samurai sword struck the M 1 rifle with such force that Yabalonka lost his grip, and the M 1 rifle went flying through the air. The grin on General Yokozowa's face broadened as he raised his samurai sword for the death blow.

Fuck this! thought Private Yabalonka. He spun around and ran away, colliding with the back of an American fighting with a Japanese, dancing around both of them, continuing to steamroller through the thick mauling battle. He ducked and dodged, receiving cuts on his arms from stray bayonets, but managed to get away from the deadly sword of General Yokozowa, who had plenty of American victims nearby whom he didn't have to chase.

Yabalonka continued to flee but finally was stopped cold by the sight of a Japanese soldier in front of him. The Japanese soldier had been following his progress and maneuvered to get in his way. Before Yabalonka could change direction, the Japanese soldier charged, angling his rifle and bayonet toward Yabalonka's heart.

Yabalonka didn't have enough time to get away. All he could do was stand his ground and try to do something spectacular. The Japanese rifle and bayonet came closer and Yabalonka stepped forward, batting the barrel out of his way with a sweep of his left forearm, and punching the Japanese soldier flat in the mouth with his right fist.

It was a haymaker, and the Japanese soldier went down for the count. Yabalonka snatched the rifle and bayonet out of the Japanese soldier's hands, and spun around. Another Japanese soldier attacked him from behind. Yabalonka parried the thrust out of his way, but he'd started his parry a split second too late. The Japanese soldier's bayonet tore across Yabalonka's left bicep muscle. Yabalonka bellowed like an angry wild animal as he bashed the Japanese soldier in the mouth with his rifle butt.

The Japanese soldier fell down. Yabalonka looked straight ahead and saw a Japanese sergeant aiming a pistol directly at him. Yabalonka decided that his only hope was to charge the Japanese sergeant and somehow confuse his aim.

Yabalonka snarled and threw his left foot forward, charging the Japanese sergeant, and the Japanese sergeant pulled his trigger its final eighth of an inch.

Blam!

Yabalonka felt as if somebody hit him on the chest with an ax. He was knocked off his feet and fell flat on his back. The Reverend Billie Jones happened to be standing in the vicinity, and saw him go down. Billie Jones pulled his bayonet out of the chest of the Japanese soldier he'd just stabbed and ran toward the Japanese sergeant who'd shot Private Victor Yabalonka.

The Japanese sergeant heard him coming and spun around, firing his pistol. The bullet zipped through the material of Billie Jones' shirt, but missed his flesh, and then Billie Jones was on top of the sergeant. He thrust his rifle and bayonet toward the Japanese sergeant's chest, and the Japanese sergeant tried to parry the bayonet with his pistol, an inadequate weapon for the job.

The bayonet smashed into the Japanese sergeant's chest, and the pistol dropped out of his hand. Billie Jones raised his big foot, placed it against the sergeant's chest, and pulled his bayonet out. Then he turned around and ran toward Victor Yabalonka, kneeling beside him.

Yabalonka's chest was covered with blood. It welled out of a hole near his breastbone, and Yabalonka's face was pale as snow. Billie Jones reached for Yabalonka's wrist, to feel for his pulse, but there wasn't much pulse to feel. Yabalonka was nearly dead.

"Medic!" the Reverend Billie Jones shouted.

There was no medic around. The Reverend Billie Jones wanted to bandage Yabalonka's wound, but heard the rustle of footsteps in front of him. He looked up and saw a Japanese officer advancing toward him, holding a samurai sword over his head in both his hands.

The Japanese officer's eyes glittered with delight; a fiendish smile spread across his face. His samurai sword dripped blood, and he was General Yokozowa himself, still on his gory rampage.

Japanese and American soldiers struggled against each other, stabbing and kicking, as General Yokozowa measured the Reverend Billie Jones. Billie Jones was a big man, and General Yokozowa considered him worthy of his steel. He stepped toward the Reverend Billie Jones, and Billie stood up over the body of Victor Yabalonka, his friend although they'd disagreed about nearly everything.

Billie Jones's rifle and bayonet was in his hands, and bad intentions shone in his eyes. His closest friend was dying, and Billie Jones was in the full rush of violent emotions. Sorrow mixed with rage in his heart. He wanted to kill every Jap in the world.

General Yokozowa took another step toward the Reverend Billie Jones, and the Reverend Billie Jones took a step toward General Yokozowa. Both knew they were in the preliminaries of a fight to the death. General Yokozowa was confident that he'd win, because he'd killed countless American soldiers already that morning. The Reverend Billie Jones wasn't certain that *he'd* win, but he was definitely going to try and put the tall Japanese officer away.

"Banzai!" screamed General Yokozowa, and he charged toward the Reverend Billie Jones, the beautiful antique samurai sword held high over his head.

The Reverend Billie Jones charged also, angling his rifle and bayonet toward General Yokozowa's heart. General Yokozowa swung the samurai sword down, and Billie Jones realized he'd better block that blow. At the last moment he raised his rifle and bayonet into the air, and General Yokozowa's famous samurai sword crashed down into it. Orange sparks flew into the morning sky, and Billie Jones took a step backwards.

General Yokozowa swung sideways, and Billie Jones jumped back. The tip of the sword passed an inch in front of Billie Jones's G.I. belt buckle. General Yokozowa leaned forward and swung from his other side. Again the Reverend Billie Jones had to retreat suddenly.

Billie Jones realized that his M 1 rifle and bayonet was no match for the Japanese officer and his samurai sword. The Japanese officer had too much reach, and there was no way to overcome it.

Then the Reverend Billie Jones thought of a way to overcome the reach advantage, and was surprised that he hadn't thought of it before. He turned around and ran away from General Yokozowa, while ramming a round into the chamber of his M 1 rifle and clicking the safety off.

General Yokozowa leapt after him, but Billie had a lot of running room. The battlefield had thinned out considerably since the fight had begun, and Billie leapt over corpses littering the ground. General Yokozowa was right behind him, because General Yokozowa wanted to demolish the big American soldier.

Finally Billie stopped and spun around. General Yokozowa was only ten feet away. Billie aimed quickly and pulled the trigger of his M 1 rifle. *Blam!* The hot bullet twirled through the barrel and blasted out the end. It zapped through the air and slammed into General Yokozowa, knocking him onto his ass.

General Yokozowa sat on the ground and blinked. One moment he'd been charging the Reverend Billie Jones, and the next moment he was on his ass. At first he didn't know what had hit him. His samurai sword still in his hand, he looked down and saw blood drenching his uniform shirt. Then his lights went out and he fell onto his back.

The Reverend Billie Jones stepped forward to put a bullet through General Yokozowa's head, but several Japanese officers and men in the area had seen their commanding general get shot, and rushed to his aid. Some dropped down next to him, to see if they could help, and the others rushed toward the Reverend Billie Jones.

Billie fired his M 1 rifle from the waist, shooting a few of the Japanese soldiers, but the rest fired back. The air filled with bullets, and Billie Jones dived toward the ground.

Private Randolph Worthington was nearby, and he saw the Reverend Billie Jones hit the dirt. He stabbed the Japanese soldier in front of him with his rifle and bayonet, to get him out of the way, and then dropped down to one knee, bringing the butt of his rifle to his shoulder, aiming at the Japanese soldiers advancing toward Billie Jones.

The former big-game hunter lined up his sights and squeezed his trigger. *Blam!* One of the Japanese soldiers collapsed onto the ground. Worthington aimed and fired again. *Blam!* The legs of the next Japanese soldier gave out underneath him. *Blam!* The third Japanese soldier received the bullet in the chest, and the impact knocked him over onto his back.

More Japanese soldiers in the vicinity rallied to the aid of General Yokozowa. They dropped to their bellies and fired at Private Worthington, who got closer to the ground too. The Japanese soldiers pinned him down with steady volleys of fire, while other Japanese soldiers carried General Yokozowa away. The battlefield had thinned out to the point where other GIs could see Worthington taking fire, and Sergeant Bannon was one of the GIs. Bannon threw a hand grenade at the Japanese soldiers, and blew several of them into bits. Then he and the other GIs charged the Japanese soldiers who'd survived.

The Japanese soldiers rose to their feet, but they were badly demoralized. They wouldn't run away or surrender, but the sight of their fallen commanding general had taken the starch out of them. Bannon, Worthington, and several other GIs tore into the Japs, kicking, bashing, and stabbing, until the Japanese soldiers were lying on the ground, bleeding and twitching.

Bannon looked around and saw GIs advancing through the jungle. The Japanese soldiers were retreating, and when Japanese soldiers were retreating the only thing to do was stay on their asses and make them retreat more.

"Let's go!" Bannon hollered, waving his arm forward. *"The*

fucking war isn't over yet! Kill them fucking Japs!"

He ran after the retreating Japanese soldiers, and the other GIs followed him. They plowed through the jungle, jumping over the bodies of dead Japanese and American soldiers. Ahead of them, through the green leaves and knotted branches, they saw Japanese soldiers withdrawing. The GIs fired their rifles as they advanced into no-man's-land, and the Japanese soldiers continued to fall back.

FOUR . . .

Colonel Hutchins emerged out of the jungle like a bloody monstrous apparition. His uniform was torn and splotched with blood. He'd lost his helmet and run out of ammunition. Blood oozed from cuts and nicks all over his body.

"My God!" said Major Cobb when his eyes fell on Colonel Hutchins. "Medic!"

Colonel Hutchins staggered closer. He carried his Thompson submachine gun in his right hand and really dragged his ass. Major Cobb didn't think Colonel Hutchins could walk another five paces, and he rushed forward to help him.

"Are you all right, sir?" asked Major Cobb.

"Is there any news?" Colonel Hutchins replied in a hoarse voice.

"All commanders are reporting that the Japs are falling back, sir."

"Issue the order to pursue."

"I've already done that, sir. I think you'd better lie down."

"Have you notified General Hawkins yet?"

"Not yet."

"Bombasino!"

"Yes sir."

"Lemme use that radio."

"Yes sir."

Bombasino turned around so that Colonel Hutchins could make a transmission from the radio he carried on his back. Colonel Hutchins reached for the headset, when suddenly the jungle spun around him. He dropped to his knees and shook his head like the old wardog that he was.

"I think you'd better lie down, sir," Major Cobb said.

"I'll lay down in a minute."

Colonel Hutchins managed to get to his feet. He wavered to the left and right, then put in a call to General Hawkins at division headquarters. He waited while the call went through, and felt as though he was on a merry-go-round. A few times he thought he'd pass out, but he was a stubborn man. He didn't want to lie down in front of his men until he'd made his report. He didn't want to sit down either. He refused to believe he was as tired and weak as he felt.

Finally General Hawkins's voice came over the airwaves.

Colonel Hutchins took a deep breath. "We pushed them back," he said weakly, and then fainted dead away. Lieutenant Harper tried to catch him, but Colonel Hutchins weighed too much, and it was dead weight. Colonel Hutchins collapsed onto the ground just as a medic arrived on the scene.

The voice of General Hawkins crackled in the radio headset. "What the hell's going on over there!"

Major Cobb snatched the headset away from Colonel Hutchins and identified himself to General Hawkins.

"I said what the hell's going on over there!" General Hawkins demanded.

"Colonel Hutchins just passed out, sir."

"What the hell's the matter with him?"

"He looks like he's lost a lot of blood, sir."

"What happened?"

"He led the charge himself, sir, and he—"

"He led the charge himself!" General Hawkins hollered.

"Yes sir."

"He's too old for that stuff. What the hell's the matter with him?"

Major Cobb didn't know what to say. "I don't know sir."

"Is he hurt badly?"

"I don't know, sir. The medic is looking at him right now."

"Have your troops reached Afua yet?"

"Not yet, sir."

"Let me know when you get there."

"Yes sir."

"Anything else?"

"No sir."

"Tell Colonel Hutchins to call me when he's able. Over and out."

Major Cobb handed the headset to Pfc. Bombasino and knelt beside the medic, Pfc. Allan Tabor from Minneapolis, Minnesota.

"How is he?" Major Cobb asked.

"I don't know."

"Why the hell don't you know?"

Pfc. Tabor bent over, examining Colonel Hutchins' body. "His pulse rate is erratic, but other than that I can't find anything wrong with him. He doesn't have any major wounds that I can see."

"He might've had a heart attack! You'd better take him to the hospital!"

"Me sir?"

"You and Bombasino. *Bombasino!*"

"Yes sir?" said Bombasino, standing nearby with the radio on his back.

"Drive Tabor and Colonel Hutchins to the hospital right away!"

"What'll I do with the radio?"

"Leave it right here."

"Yes sir."

Pfc. Bombasino took off the radio and laid it on the ground. Major Cobb looked at him and Tabor, and decided that an officer ought to go with them.

"Lieutenant Harper!"

"Yes sir."

"You'd better go to the hospital too to make sure the colonel gets the help he needs."

"Yes sir."

Pfc. Tabor and Pfc. Bombasino carried Colonel Hutchins to the jeep. Colonel Hutchins's eyes were closed and his face was pale. He looked like he was dead.

"Private Cruikshank!" shouted Major Cobb.

"Yes sir!"

"Get over here!"

"Yes sir."

Private Cruikshank, one of Major Cobb's clerks in G-3 (Operations), ran toward him. He was a wispy blond youth with big frightened blue eyes, from Sioux City Falls, South Dakota.

"Put that radio on your back, Cruikshank, and stay close."

"Yes sir."

Private Cruikshank picked up the radio and thrust his arms through the straps. He put on the headset, and his blue eyes widened.

"Call for you, sir," he said.

Major Cobb lifted the receiver and held it against his face. "What is it?" he growled.

"This is Lieutenant Jameson," said the voice on the other end. "I'm calling to report that Easy Company has just taken Afua."

"Good work," Major Cobb said. "How are your casualties?"

"Twenty percent, approximately."

"Continue to move south."

"How far should I go?"

"Until you can't go any farther. When that happens, gimme a call."

"Yes sir."

"Over and out."

Major Cobb handed the receiver back to Pfc. Cruikshank. "Get me General Hawkins!"

"Yes sir."

Pfc. Cruikshank spoke into his mouthpiece, while Major Cobb looked down at the map table that had been set up in the jungle. A rock lay on each of the four corners of the map, to prevent the wind from ruffling it. The attack was going well. Evidently the Japs had fewer troops than the Americans. Major Cobb looked at his watch. It was 0600 hours and the sun already was coming on strong.

Pfc. Cruikshank handed Major Cobb the receiver, and Major Cobb held it to his ear.

"Major Cobb speaking sir."

There was no response. Evidently General Hawkins hadn't come on yet. Major Cobb took out a cigarette and lit it up. The cigarette tasted wonderful. It was good to be a winner in war. Victory made everything taste better.

"This is General Hawkins," said the voice on the other end.

"This is Major Cobb. I've just received a report that my Easy Company has taken Afua."

"Excellent," said General Hawkins. "Superior. Who commands Easy Company?"

"Lieutenant Jameson."

"Please convey my personal congratulations to him next time you talk with him."

"Yes sir."

"Anything else?"

"No sir."

"Over and out."

General Adachi's ulcers were acting up again. He sat at his desk in his tent deep in the jungle to the east of the Driniumor River, and burped. His guts felt as if he'd just eaten a handful of red-hot coals. He was in constant pain twenty-four hours a day, but sometimes the pain was extremely intense, while at other times it was only very terrible.

Now it was extremely intense. He lit a cigarette and took a puff, not realizing that cigarettes make ulcers worse by promoting the secretion of corrosive acids in the stomach. He puffed the cigarette and looked down at the map on his desk.

He was the commander of the Eighteenth Army and was General Yokozowa's boss. He'd just received word that the big flank attack had failed, and General Yokozowa was unconscious from his wounds. His southern flank troops were retreating in disarray. The gamble had failed.

General Adachi was so upset his hands were shaking. He was fifty-four years old and wore a Clark Gable—styled mustache. Standing behind his desk, he clasped his hands behind his back and paced back and forth.

He didn't know what to do. His major assault of July 9 had

failed, and this morning his bold strategic maneuver had failed also. He no longer could mount large-scale operations against the Americans. Basically, all he could do now was be a pain in the ass to them.

He wanted to weep for his great Eighteenth Army. It had taken a shellacking ever since forming in November of 1942. Initial battles against the Americans on the Huon Peninsula had taken a heavy toll, and the mortal blow fell on the night of July 9. Now the flank attack had failed after a promising beginning last night. What was left for the Eighteenth Army now?

General Adachi didn't know. He couldn't surrender, because surrender was unthinkable for a Japanese commander. He would have to fight on to the death.

But fight on how, and with what? General Adachi's principal supplies were captured from the Americans during the initial successes of the night of July 9. Those supplies were dwindling. Disease was rampant among his frontline troops. Morale should be nonexistent, but still it was reasonably strong. There had been no mass defections, no faltering of will.

If their will hasn't faltered, neither must mine, General Adachi thought. He reflected upon his men, who'd suffered so much, and he loved them all. They'd fought hard against all the odds, and continued to fight hard now. What could he do for them?

He realized the only thing he could do was give them the opportunity to die honorably, for the Emperor. There could be no surrender. The Eighteenth Army would continue to attack until it could attack no more.

But where will I attack, and how? General Adachi thought. *What can I do?*

A bird sang a song on a branch above his tent, as he returned to his desk and stood behind it, looking down at the map. He felt as if his hands were tied, because there was so little he could do. He simply didn't have sufficient men for a major operation. All he could try were little things to kill and maim as many American soldiers as possible, to irritate them and make them suffer, to make them realize that the Eighteenth Army was dangerous even in defeat.

The only option remaining, General Adachi thought, *is to hit them at their weakest spot. But what is their weakest spot?* He gazed at the map and lit a fresh cigarette. His stomach was on fire, but he tried not to pay attention. He knew the Americans were strongest along the Driniumor River. They were deployed in depth against the river from the Pacific Ocean on the north to the foot of the Torricelli Mountains in the south. General Adachi couldn't hope to breach that line. All he could do was conduct raids against selected portions of it, preferably at night, with suicide units.

He sighed. It disheartened him to think that the Eighteenth Army was reduced to little night raids conducted by suicide units. His only consolation was that he'd been able to provide honorable deaths for most of his men.

He turned his focus to the American left flank near the foothills of the Torricelli Mountains, the scene of that morning's catastrophe. Could something still be accomplished there?

It was difficult to know for sure. Last night General Yokozowa had pushed the Americans back. This morning he tried to achieve a breakthrough, but he'd failed. Would he have succeeded if he'd had more troops at his command?

General Adachi pressed his lips together. *Is this defeat my fault?* he wondered. *Was I too niggardly with my allotment of troops for the operation? If I'd provided more troops, could the breakthrough have been made? If I sent more troops there now, could a breakthrough yet be achieved?*

General Adachi's mind became enlivened by the possibility of a breakthrough that still might be accomplished. It was much more appealing to him than little raiding parties. *What if I transferred substantial numbers of my soldiers to that southern flank? Is it possible that one more strong attack from that direction will crack the American lines?*

He looked at the map and shook his head slowly. *It's no use kidding myself,* he thought. *I can't win anything of significance here now. All I can do is inflict damage and terror. But that would be better than nothing at all.*

General Adachi admitted to himself that he had no hope whatever of capturing the Tadji airfields and the port of Aitape.

There was no point in pipe-dreaming over that. But he could conceivably crack the American lines and inflict heavy casualties. He could wreak havoc and give the Eighteenth Army a victory of sorts before the Americans regrouped and wiped them out for good. But wouldn't it be better to die like a warrior in the aftermath of victory, than be hunted down and killed like a dog in the aftermath of defeat?

General Adachi thought it'd be better to die like a warrior. There was no question about it at all in his mind, and he knew every one of his men would agree. He decided then and there to divert as many of his troops to the south as possible for his last bold suicide attack. He couldn't divert them all, because he needed to maintain a substantial presence on the east side of the Driniumor, so the Americans wouldn't suspect anything.

The troop movements would have to take place in the dead of night. The troops would have to travel in a roundabout manner so that the Americans wouldn't expect anything. Total surprise would be worth five thousand troops, and the attack probably should take place at night to further confuse the Americans. *Besides, everybody knows that the Americans hate to fight at night.*

But who will lead this attack? General Adachi wondered. Ordinarily he would have chosen General Yokozowa, his most ferocious fighting general, but General Yokozowa was unable to lead troops now. Who could take his place? Who was the most daring fanatical officer in the Eighteenth Army?

General Adachi ran the names of his senior commanders through his mind. He wanted a real maniac, a mad dog in human skin. Was there such an officer in his command?

General Adachi remembered a name, and scowled because the name belonged to an officer whom General Adachi considered a disgrace to the Eighteenth Army. The officer had murdered nearly fifty American prisoners of war on the Huon Peninsula, tieing the Americans down and chopping off their heads with his samurai sword. This officer also had been accused of murdering native men and raping native women. No charges had ever been brought against him because most Japanese officers were harsh in their dealings with American sol-

57

diers and natives, and such behavior was fairly common in the Japanese Army, but this officer was particularly atrocious. It was said that he was careless with the lives of his troops, but he usually attained whatever military objectives he was assigned.

General Adachi couldn't remember the officer's name. He'd never met the officer, and believed he was only a captain. However the officer could be promoted to whatever rank was necessary. All that mattered was that he be fierce and unrelenting in the attack.

General Adachi had heard the officer's name mentioned many times, usually with disapproval. Nobody had ever said anything good about the officer in General Adachi's presence. Evidently the officer had no friends. He probably would've been stripped of his rank and shipped back to Japan, if the Eighteenth Army had plenty of men and officers, but the Eighteenth army had been hard-pressed by the Americans ever since it was formed, and it couldn't afford to get rid of anyone who could fire a rifle.

"Lieutenant Ono!" General Adachi shouted.

"Yes sir!" replied a voice in another section of the tent.

"Report to me at once!"

"Yes sir!"

General Adachi heard a rustle of paper and a shuffle of feet. Moments later young beaver-cheeked Lieutenant Ono rushed into his office.

"At ease, Lieutenant Ono."

"Yes sir!"

"Have a seat."

"Thank you sir!"

Lieutenant Ono had a round head and black hair that lay flat on his scalp. His eyes were alert and his nose twitched with excitement.

"Lieutenant Ono," General Adachi said, "I'm trying to remember the name of a certain officer. He's the one who massacred those American prisoners of war on the Huon Peninsula during the winter of 1942. Have you ever heard of him, by any chance?"

"That was Major Sakakibara, sir."

General Adachi nodded. "That's right—I remember now. But I thought he was a captain."

"You promoted him, sir."

"*I* promoted him?"

"Yes sir. On a list with other officers."

"I don't remember."

"There were many names on the list, sir."

"Where is Major Sakakibara now?"

"I don't know, sir. I can get his records."

"Please do."

Lieutenant Ono leapt out of his chair and shot out of the office. General Adachi sipped water from the glass on his desk. Somehow his stomach pain eased during the past few minutes. *Can this be a sign from the gods that I'm on the right track?* he wondered.

Lieutenant Ono burst through the tent flap, carrying a folder. "Here are Major Sakakibara's records, sir." He laid them on General Adachi's desk.

General Adachi opened the folder. A photograph of Major Sakakibara was attached to the top document, and the first thing General Adachi noticed were Major Sakakibara's eyes. The major's eyes were slitted so much that his eyeballs could barely be seen. His mouth was a thin slash across the lower half of his face, and he had outsized ears. His cheeks were concave and the shape of his face was long and thin, almost grotesquely long and thin. The document contained a list of Major Sakakibara's assignments; he currently was commander of the 334th Battalion of the Fifty-ninth Infantry Regiment.

General Adachi thumbed through the folder. Major Sakakibara had been reprimanded numerous times for excessive cruelty to prisoners and natives. He'd been accused of torturing prisoners and burning villages, and had quarreled with many of his senior commanders. Thirty-two years old, he'd joined the Army as a private in 1930 and risen through the ranks.

General Adachi closed the folder. Major Sakakibara was a bad man, there was no question about that. He also was a disgrace to his uniform, but perhaps such a man was needed

59

now that the Eighteenth Army was entering its final hour. Perhaps a mad dog was required to punish the Americans for all they'd done to the once-great Eighteenth Army.

"Lieutenant Ono," General Adachi said, "I want you to prepare a secret directive for my signature."

"Yes sir," replied Lieutenant Ono, preparing his notepad and pen.

"I want to form a new military unit, called the *Southern Strike Force*," General Adachi said. "It will be comprised of units to be specified by me later today, so leave that part blank. The commander of the Southern Strike Force will be Colonel Tomohiro Sakakibara."

"*Colonel* Sakakibara?" Lieutenant Ono asked.

"That is correct. Major Sakakibara is being promoted to Lieutenant Colonel as of today."

"But sir—"

General Adachi held out his hand. "I know what you're going to say. You're going to say that there are many other officers who deserve a promotion more than Major Sakakibara, but these are hard times, and hard times call for extraordinary measures. Major Sakakibara is a foul human being. I know that and so do you. So does everybody else, for that matter. But we need a foul human being now, to punish the Americans for what they've done to this great Army."

Lieutenant Ono bowed his head. "I understand, sir."

"Please prepare the directive."

Lieutenant Ono leapt to his feet and saluted. "Yes sir!"

"And have Major Sakakibara report to me as soon as possible."

"Yes sir!"

"You're dismissed."

Lieutenant Ono performed an about-face and fled from the office. General Adachi lit a cigarette and leaned back in his chair. He felt strangely calm, and his stomach hurt only slightly. He realized that there was nothing for him to be worried about anymore. He couldn't possibly defeat the Americans on New Guinea. There were no more questions or anxieties in his mind.

All he could do was go down fighting, and that would be fine with him. He'd done everything he could.

He placed his polished boots on top of his desk and contemplated the end of his life. How sweet it would be to be transported away from the New Guinea hellhole and delivered into heaven, where he would reside forever with his illustrious ancestors. How wonderful to be relieved of the responsibility for planning gigantic offensives or struggling with insurmountable logistical dilemmas. No longer would he have to look at hungry and wounded Japanese soldiers who broke his heart. General Adachi intended to die in the field or by his own hand in an act of ritual hara-kiri. The end was in sight and he was glad.

He smiled as he puffed his cigarette. *I've done my best,* he said to himself. *A man can't be expected to do more than that.*

The Twenty-third Regiment advanced into the jungle south of the village of Afua. The recon platoon was midway between the center of the line and its left flank. It had become mixed in with Lieutenant Jameson's Easy Company during the melee of the morning, and had participated in the capture of Afua a half hour ago.

The recon platoon moved through the thick pristine jungle, against no resistance. The Japanese had fled after abandoning Afua. They'd been outnumbered severely and evidently chose to run and fight another day.

The recon platoon was organized into a skirmish line, and only eighteen men were still on their feet in the platoon. Bannon was positioned behind the center of his skirmish line, and his men were spaced six feet apart except for Private Worthington, Bannon's runner, who was beside Bannon in case he was needed.

Sweat poured off Bannon's body; it was an unusually hot day even for New Guinea. He glanced at his watch, and it was 0745 hours. Bannon was tired and hungry, and the heat sapped his energy. He felt as though he was advancing through a shimmering green hell. He wondered what had happened to the Japs. He thought he might run into a new Japanese defensive line at any moment, and he didn't want to be taken by surprise.

"Keep your eyes open!" he shouted to his men. "There might be Japs just around the corner!"

"Your mother's around the corner!" Frankie La Barbara replied.

"Shut up, Frankie!"

"There ain't no Japs around here!" Frankie said. "They're all gone!"

"Don't bet on it!" Bannon replied. "Everybody keep your eyes open!"

"Fuck you!" Frankie replied.

It was too hot, and Bannon was too irritable. He swung to the side and walked toward Frankie La Barbara. "What'd you say?" he asked Frankie.

"I said fuck you," Frankie replied, because he was hot and irritable too.

"Everybody stop and take a five-minute break!" Bannon said. "Light 'em up if you got 'em."

"Your mother's got 'em," Frankie La Barbara replied, watching Bannon draw closer.

Bannon threw off his helmet and dropped his rifle and bayonet onto the ground. He dived onto Frankie with both of his arms stretched forward, and grabbed Frankie by the throat.

"You son of a bitch!" Bannon said. "I've had just about enough of you!"

"Your mother's pussy," Frankie snarled, and swung a left hook at Bannon's head.

The blow landed on Bannon's right temple, and Bannon saw a black lagoon. He loosened his grip on Frankie's throat and took a step backwards. Frankie threw a left jab to Bannon's nose and backed him up again. Stepping forward, Frankie punched Bannon in the stomach, and when Bannon bent over, Frankie shot an uppercut to the tip of his jaw. Bannon bent backwards, falling onto his ass.

Frankie looked down at him, his fists balled up and a cruel gleam in his eye. "This fucking cowboy is so fulla shit it's coming out of his ears," Frankie said. "He talks a good game but he don't look so tough now."

Bannon opened his eyes and saw Frankie standing over him. At first Bannon didn't know what happened to him, but a second later he remembered everything. It was a hot day, but it got even hotter under Bannon's collar. He licked his lips and tasted his salty blood.

Frankie laughed as he towered over Bannon. "Hell, I thought you was supposed to be a tough guy, but you ain't tough at all. You ain't showing me much, champ!"

"I'm gonna kill you," Bannon replied, getting up on his elbows.

"I oughtta step on your fucking face," Frankie replied.

Bannon kicked his legs into the air, did a backflip, and wound up on his feet, dancing and punching the air with both his hands.

"C'mon," he said to Frankie. "Let's go."

"Your mother's pussy," Frankie replied, raising his fists.

Bannon moved closer. He gave Frankie some lateral movement and jerked his head around. Frankie tried to measure Bannon for a stiff left jab. He moved to the side to cut Bannon off, and threw the left jab at Bannon's face.

Bannon's face wasn't there because Bannon leaned to the side as the jab whistled by. As Bannon leaned, he hooked Frankie in the face. Frankie was stunned by the punch, but he didn't back up. He raised his fists to cover his face, and Bannon slugged him in the gut. Frankie expelled air through his mouth and wanted to fold up his tent and go home, but he couldn't do that with Bannon coming in for the kill and everybody else watching.

Frankie backed up and Bannon went after him. Bannon faked a jab to Frankie's head, and Frankie raised his fists to block it, but instead Bannon punched Frankie in the breadbasket again. Frankie lowered his guard to prevent the same thing from recurring, and Bannon jabbed him twice in the mouth. When Frankie raised his hands Bannon went downstairs again, hammering Frankie's guts. Frankie threw a wild punch at Bannon's head, and it connected, but it didn't have much on it and Bannon walked right through it. He punched Frankie on the left ear and then the right ear. Their arms got tangled and

63

Bannon pushed Frankie off. Frankie tripped over a rock as he was backing up and he fell on his ass.

"You ain't showin' me much," Bannon said, dancing from side to side over Frankie's body.

"Your mother ain't showin' me much," Frankie snarled. He could barely see Bannon and felt as though he was lying on the deck of a ship in heavy seas.

"Get up," Bannon said.

"I'm trying," Frankie replied.

"Lemme give you a hand," Bannon told him.

Bannon held out his hand. Frankie reached up but Bannon pulled his hand back. Frankie fell down again.

"You dumb fuck," Bannon said. "You ain't shit, Frankie."

"Your mother ain't shit," Frankie replied, defiant till the end.

It really was the end. Bannon reared back his foot and kicked Frankie in the face. Frankie went flat on the ground and didn't move. Bannon took a step backwards and pulled out his canteen. He raised it to his mouth and heard rustling in the bushes.

He turned around and saw Lieutenant Jameson enter the clearing, followed by a few soldiers. Lieutenant Jameson was a brown-haired stringbean with sad eyes and a lantern jaw.

"What the hell's going on here?" Lieutenant Jameson asked.

Nobody said a word. The men from the recon platoon sat around and smoked their cigarettes as if they hadn't heard anything. Frankie lay unconscious on the ground, his face puffy and bruised in spots where Bannon had clobbered him.

"Who's in charge here?" Lieutenant Jameson asked.

"I am," replied Bannon, standing near Frankie.

"What's your name?"

"Bannon, sir."

"What's your rank?"

"Buck Sergeant."

"What happened to that man on the ground?"

"He fainted from the heat, sir."

"He fainted from the heat?" Lieutenant Jameson asked incredulously.

"Yes sir."

64

"How come his face is all bruised?"

"Is his face bruised, sir?" Bannon asked.

"Can't you see the bruises, Sergeant?"

Bannon leaned closer to Frankie. "Oh yeah, I can see 'em now."

"Show me your hands, Sergeant?"

"Whataya wanna look at my hands for, sir?"

"Just show me your hands, Sergeant. I'll ask the questions around here."

Bannon held out his hands and showed them palm up.

"Turn them over," Lieutenant Jameson said.

"What for?"

"Because I said to turn them over."

Bannon turned his hands over. Lieutenant Jameson narrowed his eyes and saw Bannon's knuckles skinned and smeared with faint traces of blood.

"Have you been fighting, Sergeant?" Lieutenant Jameson asked.

"Yes sir, all morning. How do you think I got to where I am now?"

"I mean have you been fighting with this man on the ground?"

"That man on the ground there?"

"What other man would I be talking about?"

"I don't know, sir."

"Don't play dumb with me, Sergeant. I know you've been fighting with that man over there."

At that point Frankie La Barbara opened his eyes. "Where am I?" he asked.

Lieutenant Jameson bent over him. "What's your name, soldier?"

"Who the fuck are you?"

"I'm Lieutenant Jameson from Easy Company."

"What the hell are you doing over here?"

"I'll ask the questions here, soldier. What's your name?"

"Pfc. Frankie La Barbara."

"Have you been fighting with this man here?"

"What man where?"

"Sergeant Bannon here."

65

Frankie La Barbara looked up at Bannon, and pure hatred flowed out of his eyeballs. Frankie pushed himself to his feet and looked at Bannon. Then Frankie smiled.

"Fighting with Sergeant Bannon?" Frankie asked. "Naw, I ain't been fighting with Sergeant Bannon. Sergeant Bannon's my friend—why would I fight with Sergeant Bannon?"

"You sure look like you've been fighting with somebody."

"I've been fighting the Japs, sir."

Lieutenant Jameson put two and two together. He surmised that Bannon and Frankie had been fighting, and since Bannon was a noncommissioned officer, he was automatically in the wrong. On top of all that, Bannon was lying about it. Lieutenant Jameson turned to Bannon and looked him in the eye.

"I'm giving you one last chance to tell the truth, Sergeant. Have you been fighting with that man over there?"

"No sir," Bannon replied, looking straight back into Lieutenant Jameson's eyes.

"You're lying."

"Take those bars off your collar and tell me that."

"Are you threatening me, Sergeant?"

"I don't know, am I, sir?"

"You're being insubordinate."

"I got things to do, sir."

"I'm gonna have you court-martialed."

"I don't much give a shit what you do."

"You're under arrest as of right now," Lieutenant Jameson said. "You're not to leave this platoon area unless so ordered. Is that clear?"

"Where the hell would I go?"

"Stop talking back to me, soldier!"

"Yes sir."

"Have your men dig in right here, and you'd better be here when I come back."

"Yes sir."

"As you were."

Lieutenant Jameson turned around and walked away, followed by his men. Frankie saw his rifle lying on the ground.

66

He moved swiftly toward it, picked it up, and aimed it at the back of Lieutenant Jameson. Bannon ran toward Frankie, tackled him, and brought him down.

"Are you crazy!" Bannon said.

"I was just gonna shoot the son of a bitch," Frankie explained. "We could say a sniper got him. Who'd know?"

"You stupid son of a bitch!"

"Aw shit," Frankie said, watching Lieutenant Jameson disappear into the jungle. "He's gone now."

Bannon looked up to make sure Lieutenant Jameson was out of sight, and he was. He let Frankie go and stood up.

"Okay you guys!" Bannon said. "Dig in right here!"

"When do we eat?" asked McGurk, spattered with dried blood from head to toe.

"After you dig in," Bannon replied.

Frankie stood and aimed his rifle at Bannon. "What're we haveta dig in for?"

"Because Lieutenant Jameson said so."

"I oughta pull this fucking trigger."

"Go ahead."

Frankie smiled and tightened his finger around the trigger. Bannon got tense. Frankie smiled and lowered the barrel of his rifle.

"Don't worry," Frankie said, "I won't shoot you. I only shoot officers."

"You made a lot of trouble for me today, Frankie."

"Fuck you. Who cares?"

"I oughta kick your fucking ass again."

"Go ahead."

"Drop that rifle."

Frankie let it fall to the ground. "C'mon."

Bannon looked at Frankie, and hatred welled up in his heart. "I hate your fucking guts," he said.

"Your mother's pussy."

Bannon took a deep breath and stepped toward Frankie. Then he stopped and sighed. His shoulders sagged. "I'm getting tired of kicking your ass," he said.

"I always said you never had no guts."

Bannon looked around at the others. "I thought I told you guys to dig in!"

Sullenly they took out their entrenching tools and looked around for places to dig holes. Bannon turned to Frankie again.

"I don't give a fuck what you do," he said. "You can dig in, or you can take a walk. It don't matter to me either way."

Frankie laughed. "Fuck you," he said.

FIVE . . .

"You can put on your clothes now," said Dr. Epstein. "Have a seat and I'll be right back."

Dr. Epstein flashed a quick professional smile and walked out of that section of the tent. Colonel Hutchins sat on the examining table and looked around Captain Epstein's office. He saw a desk, a few chairs, and cabinets full of bottles and medical equipment. Draped across one of the chairs was fresh clothing from the Quartermaster, because Colonel Hutchins's clothes had been torn to shreds during the battle.

Colonel Hutchins's personal belongings had been placed on the surface of one of the cabinets. The first thing he did was push himself off the examining table, walk to the cabinet, take out a Lucky Strike, and light it with his trusty old Zippo. He took a deep drag and felt better. Shaking his aluminum hip flask, he frowned as he realized it was empty. Either he'd drunk it all or somebody else had. *Son of a bitch.*

Colonel Hutchins puffed his cigarette as he put on the new green uniform. His body was covered with small bandages that protected the numerous cuts and scrapes he'd acquired in the morning attack. He pinned his insignia to the collars of the shirt and stuffed his arms through the sleeves. Sitting on one of the chairs in front of the desk, he laced on his good old combat boots, covered with muck and blood.

Captain Epstein returned as Colonel Hutchins was lacing the boots. Captain Epstein had kinky black hair and wore thick horn-rimmed glasses. He carried Colonel Hutchins's medical folder and sat behind his desk.

"What's the bad news?" Colonel Hutchins asked, the cigarette dangling out of his mouth as he tied the final knot on his left combat boot.

Captain Epstein had a solemn expression on his face as he perused the documents in Colonel Hutchins's medical folder.

"It's that bad?" Colonel Hutchins asked.

Captain Epstein looked up at Colonel Hutchins. "It certainly isn't good."

"What's wrong with me?"

"Just about everything. You're in bad shape from your neck to your knees. Other than that you're fine."

"There ain't much left, Doc."

"You lead a hard life, Colonel. You've got heart trouble, lung trouble, and liver trouble. You smoke and drink too much and your general physical condition is run down. I'm going to give it to you straight. I don't think you're physically fit for frontline command anymore."

Colonel Hutchins went pale. "You're not gonna write that down anywheres, are you?"

"I sure am."

"But they'll relieve me of command."

"That's exactly what they ought to do."

"But I'm not that bad off."

"Oh yes you are, and on top of everything else you're an alcoholic. You've certainly got the liver of an alcoholic. I'm the one who poured the booze out of your canteen, by the way. If you don't cut down on your drinking, you're going to die."

"Who gives a shit?" Colonel Hutchins said. "Everybody dies."

"Some die later and some die sooner. You're going to die sooner unless you start taking care of yourself."

"Okay, I'll start taking care of myself. Just don't tell anybody that I'm not fit for frontline command."

"I'm afraid that would be dereliction of duty. I have to tell the truth. You're not suggesting that I lie, are you?"

"That's exactly what I'm suggesting!"

Captain Epstein shook his head. "I can't do that."

"Sure you can. Who'll know one way or the other?"

"I will, and that's all that matters to me. Frontline commanders have to be in good physical condition, and you're not. An entire regiment is depending on you, and you might collapse at a crucial moment when they need you the most. In point of fact, you collapsed this morning. It's my responsibility to see that no one is affected by your bad health."

"My health ain't bad. I stood toe to toe with men younger than me this morning, and kicked their fucking asses."

"And then you collapsed, isn't that so?"

"It was loss of blood."

"Coupled with poor health," Captain Epstein added.

Colonel Hutchins leaned forward and made his face mean. "You lily-livered son of a bitch—I ought to shoot you."

"Go ahead," Captain Epstein said. "See if I care."

Colonel Hutchins looked around. "Where's my fucking gun!"

"Over there next to the door."

Colonel Hutchins craned his head around and saw his Thompson submachine gun leaning against the door. He got up from his chair, walked toward it, picked it up, and aimed the barrel at Captain Epstein.

"You're gonna change your recommendation," Colonel Hutchins said.

"No go," replied Captain Epstein.

"Then I'm gonna blow your fucking head off."

"Be my guest," said Captain Epstein, "but do you think they'll let you return to your command afterwards? You know damn well they won't. They'll probably put you in jail, which I suspect is where you belong."

"You son of a bitch!" Colonel Hutchins said.

"Go ahead and shoot," Captain Epstein replied.

Colonel Hutchins saw that elementary intimidation wasn't going to work with Captain Epstein. He lowered his submachine gun and returned to the chair, sitting down and laying the submachine gun on his lap.

"It wasn't loaded anyway," Colonel Hutchins said.

"I know, because I'm the one who unloaded it," Captain Epstein replied.

"You're a real wiseguy," Colonel Hutchins said.

"I didn't get to be a surgeon by being dumb."

Colonel Hutchins leaned forward. "Let's make a deal."

"No deals."

"Hear me out."

"You've got five minutes."

"What if I promise to quit drinking?" Colonel Hutchins asked.

"Don't make me laugh," Captain Epstein said.

"You don't think I can do it?"

"No."

"Why not?"

"It's not so easy."

"I didn't get through this war because it's easy. I didn't kill twenty Japs this morning because it was easy. I can do anything I want."

"You'd have to stop smoking too."

"I'll do it."

"And exercise regularly."

"No problem."

"I don't believe you."

"Why not?"

"Because you're an alcoholic, and alcoholics can't be trusted."

"You son of a bitch," Colonel Hutchins said.

"Everybody knows you're a drunk. It's not exactly a secret."

"They do?"

"You can't drink as much as you do and not smell like a brewery all the time."

Colonel Hutchins leaned back in his chair. He had no idea that everybody knew. Like most alcoholics, he thought he was fooling people. Like most alcoholics, the only person he was fooling was himself.

"You make me sound pretty bad, Doc," he said.

"You are pretty bad. You've got one foot in the grave and the other one on a banana peel."

"You're not gonna retract that recommendation?"

"Absolutely not."

"But I'm a soldier," Colonel Hutchins protested. "This is the only profession I know."

"You can work behind a desk someplace. You can still be of use to the Army that way."

"I'm not a fucking clerk!"

"You're not fit for frontline duty anymore. I'm sorry."

"You're not sorry. You don't give a fuck either way."

Captain Epstein shrugged. "As a matter of fact I don't. I've got four tents full of wounded men out there, and all of them are in worse shape than you. They were cut down by the Japs, but you're cutting yourself down. I've got no sympathy for you." Captain Epstein scrawled something on a piece of paper in front of him. "I have nothing more to say to you. You may leave."

"Just like that."

"Just like that."

"You're a son of a bitch," Colonel Hutchins said.

"And you're a drunk," Captain Epstein replied. "Your men depend on you to tell them what to do, and you're walking around smashed all the time."

"I've never let my men down," Colonel Hutchins declared.

"The hell you haven't. You should be with them right now but instead you're here, because you're an alcoholic."

"Fuck you," Colonel Hutchins said.

"Fuck you too," Captain Epstein replied. "Now if you'll excuse me, I've got wounded men to look after."

"Prick," said Colonel Hutchins.

Captain Epstein ignored him. He picked some papers up off his desk, tucked them under his arm, and walked out of the office. Colonel Hutchins found himself sitting alone with his submachine gun in an atmosphere that smelled like medicine and disinfectant. *What am I gonna do?* he thought. *What if they relieve me of command?*

Colonel Hutchins became demoralized. He felt sick and ill, and he needed a drink. He thought of lighting another cigarette, but something stopped him. *I've got to cut all that stuff out,* he thought. *I've got to get myself back in shape.*

73

He wondered what his next step should be. Captain Epstein would write a report saying he was unfit for frontline command. The report would be delivered to General Hawkins. Could the report be intercepted and destroyed? Yes, but it'd be replaced by another report. Once a copy of the document was put in his records, and another copy forwarded to the Pentagon, that was it.

Except for one possibility. Perhaps he could go to General Hawkins and ask for another chance. He'd promise to stop drinking and smoking, and to exercise regularly. He and General Hawkins had been getting along okay lately. Perhaps it would work.

I'd better get started on that right now, Colonel Hutchins thought. *I should talk to the general before the report reaches his desk. That way I can do some damage control, maybe.*

Colonel Hutchins stood and slung his submachine gun barrel down over his shoulder. He walked out of the office, pushed an orderly out of his way, and headed toward the parking area, where Pfc. Nick Bombasino was waiting with his jeep.

"Take me to General Hawkins's headquarters," Colonel Hutchins said to Pfc. Bombasino, "and make it fast."

It was twelve o'clock noon. Major Tomohiro Sakakibara slept soundly in a cave made of four gigantic boulders tumbled together in the foothills of the Torricelli Mountains. His uniform was filthy, bloody, and torn to shreds, but most of the blood belonged to American soldiers whom he'd slashed with his samurai sword during the dawn attack. American blood still was caked to his samurai sword too. He hadn't shaved for five days, and he smelled as if he'd shit his pants. It was dank and cool inside the cave, and the ground underneath him was tiny rocks. Major Sakakibara was so tired he didn't care.

He'd been asleep for an hour. He'd ordered his battalion to stop and rest in the area, but not much of his battalion was left. Normally a Japanese battalion consisted of four companies, but all he had left was slightly less than the equivalent of one full-strength company stretched out over four companies.

74

The men slept all around him in hollows in the ground, beneath trees, and under bushes. Many were wounded and wore bloody bandages. A fairly substantial number probably wouldn't live another twenty-four hours. Some were still in fighting condition, though. They were his toughest shock troops, and they'd survived because they knew what to do when the shit hit the fan.

A young Japanese lieutenant accompanied by a sergeant and three ordinary soldiers came upon the battalion area. They were challenged by sentries struggling to stay awake, and the young lieutenant, whose name was Arazaki, said that he carried a message for Major Sakakibara from General Adachi himself.

The sentries waved Lieutenant Arazaki and his party through. Lieutenant Arazaki marched into the area, noticing the men sleeping everywhere. The men were bony and ragged, similar to corpses as they lay still and slept with their mouths open. Some snored.

Lieutenant Arazaki didn't relish the task he was assigned to perform. He didn't want to have anything to do with Major Sakakibara, because he knew of the major's dreadful reputation. Major Sakakibara kicked the shit out of his own men and tortured prisoners. He was said to be ruthless, insubordinate, and an ignorant son of a bitch. Lieutenant Arazaki hoped he didn't have any trouble with him.

Lieutenant Arazaki arrived at the front of the cave, stuck his head inside, and was nearly overwhelmed by the stench. In the darkness he could perceive the sleeping figure of Major Sakakibara.

"Sir?" said Lieutenant Arazaki.

The figure didn't stir.

"Sir!" Lieutenant Arazaki said louder.

Again the figure didn't move.

The only thing to do was go into the cave and shake him. Lieutenant Arazaki didn't want to do it because of the smell, but orders were orders. He had to do it. Covering his mouth with his handkerchief, he crawled into the cave. Suddenly Major Sakakibara spun around and pointed a Nambu pistol at Lieutenant Arazaki's head. Major Sakakibara's finger tightened around the trigger, and then he recognized the uniform of an officer in the Imperial Japanese Army. The officer wore the insignia of a lieutenant on his collar, so Major Sakakibara relaxed. He clicked the safety off his Nambu pistol.

"What do you want!" he demanded.

"Sir," said Lieutenant Arazaki, nearly gagging from the stench, "I bring you a message from General Adachi. He wants—"

Major Sakakibara interrupted him. "A message from General Adachi?" he asked, wrinkling his forehead, his tongue protruding a quarter of an inch from the side of his mouth. "For me?"

"Yes sir."

"Do you know who I am?"

"Yes sir. You're Major Sakakibara, the commanding officer of the Three hundred and thirty-fourth Battalion."

"What is the message?" Major Sakakibara asked.

"General Adachi would like to speak with you in person immediately."

"Me?"

"Yes sir."

"Why me?"

"I don't know sir."

Major Sakakibara leaned closer, and Lieutenant Arazaki nearly fainted from the smell. "You must have some idea of what the old bastard wants," Major Sakakibara said.

"I'm afraid I don't sir."

"I wonder what I did wrong this time?" Major Sakakibara mused.

"Are you coming, sir?"

"What's the big hurry?"

"The general would like to speak with you as soon as possible. You are to accompany us."

Major Sakakibara let his tongue protrude out of the left corner of his mouth again and he narrowed his left eye as he tried to figure out what was going on. He didn't think he'd done anything wrong lately, and he was only a major, which wasn't a very high rank relative to the types of officers General

Adachi usually dealt with. *What does he want me for?* Major Sakakibara wondered, licking his upper lip with his tongue.

"Are you coming, sir?"

"You can go back now. I'll be along shortly."

"But the general wants you to return with me."

"There are things I have to do. Tell him I'm busy fighting a war out here, but I'll be at his headquarters in approximately two hours."

Lieutenant Arazaki thought he'd throw up at any moment. "I think you'd better come back with me now, sir."

"I'm not interested in what you think." Major Sakakibara leaned toward Lieutenant Arazaki. "I can't report to General Adachi the way I am now. I stink, don't I? Look at you, you can barely keep yourself from puking. You're getting green around the gills. Get out of here and go tell the great almighty general what I just told you to tell him."

"But—"

"Shut up and do as I say. I don't have any more time to waste on you. Get out of here."

Lieutenant Arazaki looked into Major Sakakibara's eyes, and it was as though a fire was burning behind those narrow slits. Major Sakakibara's mouth was set in a grim line, and a chill ran up Lieutenant Arazaki's back.

"Yes sir," he said.

He turned around and crawled out of the cave, taking a deep draft of fresh jungle air.

"Let's go," he said to his men.

"What about Major Sakakibara?" asked Sergeant Kushikino.

"He'll be along later."

"I thought he was supposed to accompany us."

"Shut up and get going."

"Yes sir."

Lieutenant Arazaki marched out of the area with his men, and Major Sakakibara poked his head out of the cave, blinking at the noonday sun.

The field hospital complex comprised six large tents with their walls rolled up to admit sunlight and fresh air. Mosquito netting kept the bugs out. Wounded officers lay in their own separate tents, segregated from wounded enlisted men. Nurses and orderlies bustled around, administering to all ranks hurt during the night and morning fighting, and the operating tent looked like a butcher shop as doctors sawed off destroyed limbs or removed bullets from the innards of soldiers. Trucks arrived regularly carrying more wounded men from the front.

In one of the hospital tents at the edge of the complex lay Private Victor Yabalonka, the former longshoreman from San Francisco, his chest bandaged and blood seeping through the white swathes of gauze. No cots were available in the enlisted men's tents, and Private Yabalonka lay directly on the hard ground.

He was barely aware of the ground as he opened his eyes in his steamy hospital tent that afternoon. He was awakening from a deep stupor caused by the medication and morphine they'd given him. A terrible pain rose in waves from deep in his chest, but somehow the pain didn't bother him too much. The drugs that befuddled him also made the pain bearable.

At first he didn't know where he was, and he didn't care. His head felt as though it was filled with lead. It was like floating through a sea of sludge. He groaned and tried to move, but he couldn't move. He knew he wasn't dead, but he didn't feel very alive.

He remembered vaguely what had happened to him. A Jap shot him, and his handy pocket Bible hadn't saved him. Getting shot was the last thing he remembered. He realized that the medics must have brought him to the hospital. Other wounded men lay all around him, but he couldn't turn his head to see who they were.

Sunlight streamed through the openings where the tent walls had been rolled up, but somehow everything looked dark and turbid to Private Yabalonka. He knew he was wounded badly and wondered if he was going to die. He'd been in the war long enough to know that wounded men often were shipped back to the hospital, where they died. He knew that chest wounds were serious, and often fatal. *Maybe I'm going to die,* he thought.

He was only twenty-four years old, and thought he was too young to die. Although he was drugged almost to the point of unconsciousness, he still was awake enough to know that he wanted to live. The life force inside him pushed him toward healing while his torn arteries and lungs impeded the flow of blood and oxygen within his body.

He didn't want to die. He thought he had so much to live for. He was young and yesterday he'd been healthy. He'd always taken his good health for granted, but now he realized how precious it was. He couldn't even move. If the Japs attacked the hospital compound, he'd be a sitting duck.

His breathing was shallow and he slipped from consciousness into unconsciousness, and then back again. Sometimes he felt as if he was floating through the air, and other times he thought he had become separated from his body somehow, and looked down at himself lying on the ground inside the tent.

He coughed and sighed, and wondered if he was going to die. He felt desolate and scared. He had no friends or family to succor him, no girlfriend to bend down and kiss his forehead. His buddies were far away and he was among strangers, just another wounded GI, and nobody cared.

This fucking war, he thought, and a tear rolled down his right cheek. A salty taste was in his mouth, and he felt sorry for himself. *I never even had a chance to do anything in my life,* he thought, *and now I'm gonna die.*

He tried to take a deep breath, but his lungs wouldn't fill up with air. It was as though a huge weight sat on his chest. He groaned, and then a figure in a tan uniform appeared above him.

"Are you all right, soldier?" asked Lieutenant Frannie Divers, a red-headed nurse from the state of Washington.

"Ooohhh," was all Yabalonka could say.

"You'll be all right," she said. "Just take it easy."

She dabbed his arm with cotton that had been dipped in alcohol, and then jabbed in a hypodermic needle full of morphine. Yabalonka felt warm waves of comfort pass over him. He closed his eyes and drifted off on those waves.

Lieutenant Frannie Divers looked down at him. She was

exhausted, because there'd been so many wounded men. She hadn't slept last night, and had seen so many bleeding young soldiers that she felt like breaking down and crying.

But she didn't break down and cry, because the men needed her. Followed by an orderly, she moved to the side of the next wounded young soldier, who wore a bloody bandaged stump where his left leg had been.

"How're you feeling?" she asked softly, kneeling beside him.

"What's on your mind, Hutch?" asked General Clyde Hawkins, commanding officer of the Eighty-first Division.

"I've got to talk to you, General," said Colonel Hutchins. "Got a minute?"

"Have a seat," General Hawkins said. "Be right with you."

Colonel Hutchins sat on a chair in front of General Hawkins's desk and wanted to pull out a cigarette, but he'd thrown his pack of Luckies away. He was nervous and jumpy, clicking his teeth and unable to get comfortable in the chair, shifting his ass from one side to the other, crossing and recrossing his legs.

Meanwhile, General Hawkins signed documents on his desk. He had blond hair and a blond mustache, was tall and slim, and had been first captain of cadets when he was at West Point. His father and grandfather had been generals, and he, at fifty years old, was one of the youngest major generals in the United States Army.

Finally General Hawkins laid down his pen and looked up. "What's on your mind, Hutch?"

"I'm in trouble, sir."

"What's the problem?"

"I was with the medics this morning, and Captain Epstein says he's gonna recommend that I be removed from frontline command."

"You look like you've taken a beating," General Hawkins said. "Are you hurt that badly?"

"No sir. Not at all."

"What's the trouble, then?"

"Captain Epstein says I'm in bad physical condition because of my age and things. He says I'm not physically fit for frontline command anymore."

"I'm sorry to hear that," General Hawkins said. "I'm going to miss you. You're the best regimental commander I've got. We've had our differences in the past, but you always got results for me, and that's what matters ultimately in war."

"I don't want to wind up behind a desk," Colonel Hutchins said.

"We all have to do a lot of things that we don't like."

"You don't have to do what Captain Epstein says, do you?"

"If he says you're not fit for frontline command, I'll appear inept if I leave you in frontline command. I'm not General of the Army, you know. My actions are reviewed by my superiors, just as your actions are reviewed by me."

Colonel Hutchins leaned forward in his chair. "But it's not as if I've got a bullet in my brain or anything like that. My problem is that I smoke and drink too much. What if I stopped smoking and drinking, and exercised more? Then I'd be all right, wouldn't I?"

General Hawkins smiled. "I suppose so, but *can* you stop smoking and drinking?"

"I've stopped already."

"For how long?"

"All morning."

"That's not much time."

"It is for me. I threw out my cigarettes and poured my jungle juice out of my canteen. I'll do calisthenics with my troops every morning, push-ups, jumping-jacks, and all that happy horseshit. I can do it. Give me a chance, General."

"I don't know," General Hawkins said. "My ass'll be in a sling if I don't follow Captain Epstein's recommendation."

"Just say you gave me a chance to redeem myself. What's wrong with that? I been in this man's Army for twenty-seven fucking years. Doesn't that entitle me to another chance?"

General Hawkins stuffed a cigarette into his ivory holder and lit the cigarette with his Ronson. He leaned back in his chair and gazed thoughtfully at Colonel Hutchins.

"What the hell do you want to stay at the front for?" he asked. "Haven't you had enough war?"

"War is my job," Colonel Hutchins said, "and I do it better than most people. My place is here, not behind some goddamn desk someplace, putting my signature on requisitions for paper clips and toilet bowls. I'm a professional soldier like you. How'd you like to be sent someplace where you have to be a desk jockey for the rest of your life?"

"I wouldn't want that."

"Neither do I. I'd rather die here than keel over behind a damned desk someplace."

General Hawkins nodded. "I know what you mean."

"Then don't relieve me of command."

"How can I ignore the doctor's recommendation?"

"Just say I've stopped smoking and drinking, and I'm doing calisthenics with my men every morning. Tell 'em you're giving me one more chance, in view of my illustrious service to date."

"And you'll walk out of here and start hitting the bottle again. I'll look like a dope."

"I'm not going to drink again."

"I don't think you can stop."

"I *can* stop. And I can stop smoking too."

"For how long?"

"Until this goddamn war is over."

"That won't be easy."

"I never said it'd be easy, but I said I could do it."

"I don't know," General Hawkins said. "I'd like to give you a chance, but then I'd be taking a chance myself."

"I won't let you down," Colonel Hutchins said. "What do you want me to do—get on my knees and beg?"

General Hawkins puffed his cigarette holder and looked at Colonel Hutchins. He had no idea of who to replace Colonel Hutchins with if he relieved him of command, because he couldn't think of anybody who could fill Colonel Hutchins's shoes.

"All right," General Hawkins said, "I'll give you one chance, but I want to make it clear that it's just *one* chance and no more. If I ever smell alcohol on your breath again, you're out, understand?"

"Yes sir."

"And if I see you with a cigarette in your mouth, you're out too, got it?"

"Yes sir."

"Just remember this, Hutch. Your men need you and I need you. If you take another drink, you'll be letting all of us down. Don't let us down, okay?"

"Okay."

"That's all."

Colonel Hutchins raised himself up and stood at attention in front of General Hawkins's desk. "Thank you, sir."

"Just keep your side of the bargain. That's all I ask."

"Yes sir."

Colonel Hutchins threw a snappy salute, performed a smart about-face, and marched out of the office.

Major Sakakibara emerged from the jungle, a sullen expression on his face and his head tucked into his shoulders. He looked like a hunchback as he made his way to the tent complex that comprised the headquarters of General Hatazo Adachi.

Major Sakakibara wore a clean tattered uniform and he'd taken a bath in a stream using captured American soap to wash his filth-encrusted body. He had no idea why the famous General Adachi wanted to see him, and thought perhaps he was going to be court-martialed for his multifarious frontline atrocities.

"They're all weaklings," he muttered underneath his breath as he approached General Adachi's tent. He was referring to the Japanese high command, not the Americans. Major Sakakibara thought the Japanese high command was too timid and effeminate, lacking the true brutal warrior spirit.

He turned down the corners of his mouth and entered General Adachi's tent. It was full of staff officers, and Major Sakakibara felt ill at ease. He knew that they'd graduated from military academies and possessed all the social graces, whereas he was an uncouth former street peddler who'd risen through the ranks and become an officer due to his courage and ferocity in battle.

He shuffled his feet nervously and looked around, wondering which fancy young staff officer to address. One of them, with smoothly shaven beaver cheeks, looked up at him from behind a desk.

"Major Sakakibara?" he asked.

"Yes," replied Major Sakakibara.

"I'm Lieutenant Ono, the general's aide-de-camp. I'll see if the general can see you now. Why don't you have a seat?"

"That's all right. I'll stand."

"As you wish, sir."

Lieutenant Ono arose and walked away, pushing aside a tent flap and disappearing into the bowels of the tent system. Major Sakakibara sidestepped into a corner and stood with his hands behind his back, feeling conspicuous and out of place, hating the fancy staff officers and clerks working at desks.

There isn't a real soldier here, he thought. *These people wouldn't stand up and fight for the Emperor even if you held a pistol to their heads.*

He narrowed his eyes and wondered anew what General Adachi wanted him for. He didn't think he'd done anything wrong lately, but there was no telling what might bother the higher-ups. They sat in comfortable tents and sipped tea all day, planning grand strategies that failed.

The tent flap was pushed aside, and Lieutenant Ono returned. "Major Sakakibara?" he said.

"Yes."

"Come with me, please."

Major Sakakibara stepped out of the corner and followed Lieutenant Ono through the canvas corridors of the tent complex. They turned left and right, seeing officers and clerks working at desks, and then finally Lieutenant Ono pointed to a tent flap ahead.

"That's General Adachi's office."

Major Sakakibara squared his shoulders and walked forward, pushing aside the tent flap, entering General Adachi's office.

General Adachi sat behind his desk, smoking a cigarette and drinking tea out of a small white cup. Major Sakakibara basically was a street peddler at heart, and went weak in his knees before such a famous and distinguished general. Somehow he forced himself to march toward General Adachi's desk and deliver a proper salute.

"Have a seat," General Adachi said in a friendly manner, a slight smile on his face.

Major Sakakibra sat, but kept his back erect as if on parade.

"Care for a cup of tea?" General Adachi asked.

"No sir."

"Don't you like tea?"

Major Sakakibara was flustered. His face turned red. He felt awkward and out of place, and wished he could be someplace else.

"I like tea, sir," he stuttered.

"Then have a cup."

"Yes sir."

General Adachi poured tea from a pot into another small white cup, moving his chin to indicate that Major Sakakibara should take the cup. Major Sakakibara leaned forward and picked it up. General Adachi raised his cup in the air.

"To the Emperor's health," he said.

"To the Emperor's health," Major Sakakibara repeated.

Both officers sipped their tea. Major Sakakibara was so nervous his hand trembled. He felt like a shithouse rat. *What does the general want from me?* Major Sakakibara wondered.

"How are you today?" General Adachi asked genially.

"Very well, sir."

"And your men?"

"I don't have very many men left, sir, and my supplies are running low."

"Yes," General Adachi said, "casualties have been heavy lately. The Americans outnumber us and it's difficult to overcome their numerical superiority. In fact, it would be accurate

85

to say at this point that the Eighteenth Army has been defeated on New Guinea."

Major Sakakibara wanted to say that Japanese soldiers weren't defeated until they were dead, but he didn't have the courage. "Yes sir," was all he could reply.

"However," General Adachi said, "we can still inflict punishment on the Amercians, and by so doing, we can win honor for ourselves and the entire Eighteenth Army, don't you agree?"

"Yes sir."

"They should pay dearly for what they've done to our great army, shouldn't they?"

"Yes sir."

"I'm glad you think so, because that's why I've asked you to come here this afternoon."

Major Sakakibara wondered if he was having a dream, because the situation he was in didn't make sense to him.

"You appear uncomfortable, Major Sakakibara," General Adachi said.

Major Sakakibara didn't know how to reply. He managed a mumbled: "Yes sir."

"You are uncomfortable?"

"Yes sir," Major Sakakibara said.

"Why?"

"Because you are such a distinguished general, sir, and I am only a lowly soldier."

"We are all lowly soldiers here on New Guinea," General Adachi said, "and our situation is most perilous right now, but at least we can die like soldiers, is that not so?"

"Yes sir."

General Adachi leaned forward, and his eyes burned into Major Sakakibara's face. "I have decided that you will lead our last attack against the Americans."

Major Sakakibara was so stunned he could barely speak. "I sir?"

"Yes you."

Major Sakakibara was flabbergasted. He'd thought he was going to be court-martialed or reprimanded for his foul deeds, but instead he had been chosen to lead the Eighteenth Army's last attack! "But sir," he said, "you have so many officers with higher rank and a more noble background than mine. Why me?"

General Adachi looked him straight in the eye. "Because you are a mad dog, Major Sakakibara, and that's what I need right now."

Now suddenly the conversation made sense to Major Sakakibara, because it was easy for him to see himself as a mad dog. For a long time he had thought deep in his heart that he was made for high command, because he was a fighter, and now General Adachi realized that too.

Major Sakakibara bowed his head. "I am honored, sir."

"I am promoting you to lieutenant colonel herewith, Major Sakakibara, and you will be an acting full colonel when you lead the attack. Now come to the map table with me, and I will show you what I want you to do."

Colonel Hutchins swung his legs out of the front seat of his jeep and planted them on the ground. He pushed his weight onto his legs and nearly fell onto his face, his legs trembled so much.

His alcohol and nicotine withdrawal were coming on strong. Pfc. Nick Bombasino looked at him from behind the wheel of the jeep.

"Are you all right, sir?"

"I'm fine."

"You don't look so fine."

"Who the fuck asked you?"

Colonel Hutchins hobbled toward his command post tent. It was set up in a thick dark part of the jungle north of Afua, and camouflage netting was hung in the trees overhead just in case a stray Japanese bomber might fly by. He entered his orderly room, and his face was drained of color. Master Sergeant Koch, the sergeant major of the Twenty-third Regiment, sat behind his desk and looked up at Colonel Hutchins.

"Are you all right, sir?"

Colonel Hutchins turned toward him. "Why're you asking me if I'm all right? Who do you think you are: one of those

87

goddamned pill rollers up at division?"

"You look a little peaked, sir."

"Your ass is a little peaked. Anything happen while I was gone?"

"Lieutenant Jameson was here. He said he had to speak with you about something important, and he'd be back later. Major Cobb also wants to have a talk."

"Tell him I'm back."

"Yes sir."

Colonel Hutchins shuffled past Pfc. Levinson, the regimental clerk, who sat at his typewriter and pounded away at the keys. Pfc. Levinson didn't look up from the document he was typing, and Colonel Hutchins entered his office. He hung his steel pot and submachine gun on a peg and dropped down in his chair behind his desk.

I can't go on like this, he thought. *I need a smoke and I need a drink.*

He opened the top drawer of his desk, and lying in front of him were five packs of Chesterfield cigarettes. His mouth watered at the thought of smoking them, but he couldn't smoke them. He'd given General Hawkins his word and a man's word was supposed to mean something.

He opened another desk drawer and saw three canteens full of white lightning. He knew if he kissed the mouth of one of those canteens his jitters would go away and he'd feel wonderful, but he couldn't do it. He had to break his drinking habit. *I'm a colonel in the American Army and I can do anything,* he tried to tell himself.

The phone on his desk rang, and he jumped six inches in the air. He picked up the phone. "What is it?"

He heard Sergeant Koch's voice. "Lieutenant Jameson is back, sir."

"Send him in."

"Yes sir."

Colonel Hutchins leaned back in his chair and ran his tongue over his teeth. His heart was racing and his lungs felt as though they were balloons with holes in them.

Lieutenant Jameson entered his office, marched to his desk,

and saluted. Colonel Hutchins returned the salute haphazardly and told the lantern-jawed officer to sit down.

"What's on your mind, Jameson?"

"I saw something very disturbing today, sir. A sergeant in this regiment evidently had been fighting with an enlisted man, and evidently he beat him up."

"So what?" Colonel Hutchins asked grumpily.

"That's a violation of the Uniform Code of Military Justice, sir. It's a court-martial offense. Moreover, the noncom behaved in a surly manner to me when I questioned him about the incident."

"Who is this noncom?"

"Sergeant Bannon, of your recon platoon."

"Leave him alone," Colonel Hutchins said.

"Leave him alone?"

"You heard me. Leave him alone."

"But he was fighting."

"That's what soldiers are supposed to do."

"Not among themselves!"

"Sometimes that's necessary too."

"But the Army's still the Army, sir. Basic discipline has to be maintained."

Colonel Hutchins pointed his finger at Lieutenant Jameson. "The main thing is to win battles, and the recon platoon has come through for me more times than I can count. I know what they are. They're the scum of the earth, but so what. Leave them alone."

"I'm afraid it's a little too late for that, sir."

"What do you mean?"

"I spoke with Sergeant Bannon and placed him under arrest. Now I have to follow through."

Colonel Hutchins groaned. "Jameson, why are you making all this trouble for me?"

"I'm not making any trouble, sir. It's Sergeant Bannon who made all the trouble, and we can't let him get away with it."

Colonel Hutchins's guts twitched inside his stomach. His heart pounded like Gene Krupa's drums. He didn't feel like arguing with Lieutenant Jameson over Sergeant Bannon. All he wanted was a drink and a smoke.

"Levinson!" he hollered.

"Yes sir!" replied a voice in the other section of the tent.

"Get your ass in here!"

A moment later Pfc. Levinson burst into the office. He was skinny, nineteen years old, with black hair and a big hooked nose. "Yes sir?"

Colonel Hutchins opened his top drawer and took out his three packs of cigarettes. "Get rid of these for me."

"Yes sir."

Pfc. Levinson scooped up the cigarettes. "Can I have them, sir?"

"Just don't smoke them in front of me." Colonel Hutchins opened his bottom drawer and pulled out his three canteens full of white lightning. "Pour this shit out in the latrine."

"Yes sir."

"Get going!"

"Yes sir."

Pfc. Levinson stuffed the cigarette packs into his pockets, and then picked up the canteens. Colonel Hutchins resumed his conversation with Lieutenant Jameson.

"So you want to court-martial Bannon," he said.

"That's right sir."

Colonel Hutchins wondered what to do, as Pfc. Levinson fled from the office. Colonel Hutchins realized he was in no position to buck the military justice system just then, because he was in trouble himself over his excessive drinking. If he said no to Lieutenant Jameson, Lieutenant Jameson would initiate court-martial proceedings without him, and Colonel Hutchins would appear to be obstructing justice. That would be bad timing, because it would coincide with Dr. Epstein's recommendation that Colonel Hutchins be relieved of command. Colonel Hutchins realized he was in the soup again, and this time it was serious. It wouldn't be a good idea to attract too much attention to himself just then. He'd better keep his head down and his mouth shut.

"All right," he said to Lieutenant Jameson, "you do whatever you think you have to do. If you want to have Bannon court-martialed, I won't stand in your way, but I'm telling you right now: I like Bannon because he's a good soldier and a natural-born leader of men. If you have him court-martialed, I'll appear as a character witness for him. Do we understand each other?"

"Yes sir," Lieutenant Jameson replied.

"Anything else you want to bring up with me?"

"Yes sir. Just one thing. I and many like me can't understand your devotion to the criminals, goons, and roughnecks in your recon platoon. We consider them a menace to the regiment."

"Is that so?" Colonel Hutchins asked. "Well let me tell you something, young Lieutenant. Those criminals, goons, and roughnecks have saved the asses of people in this regiment many times, and that includes your ass too."

"Not my ass," Lieutenant Jameson said. "I've had very little to do with your recon platoon, thank God."

"You don't know what they've done for you, but I do," Colonel Hutchins told him. "Just because you haven't had much to do with them personally, that doesn't mean they haven't saved your ass at long range, without your knowledge. But if you want to court-martial Bannon, go right ahead. It's your privilege. Do what you have to do, but get the fuck out of this office right now. I'm tired of talking with you about this."

"Yes sir," said Lieutenant Jameson.

Lieutenant Jameson stood, gathered up his papers, saluted, and walked out of the office. In the outer tent area he saw Sergeant Koch sitting behind his desk and Pfc. Levinson standing in a corner, shuffling papers. The packages of cigarettes and canteens full of white lightning lay on top of his desk.

Lieutenant Jameson departed, and Pfc. Levinson told Sergeant Koch he had to run some errands for Colonel Hutchins. Sergeant Koch told him to hurry back.

Pfc. Levinson put the canteens and cigarettes into his light field pack and carried them out of the tent. He ran across the regimental headquarters area to the radio tent and ducked inside.

"Can I use one of these radios for a minute?" Pfc. Levinson said to Sergeant Rowse, in charge of the communications center. "I've got to transmit a quick message for the colonel."

"Go right ahead," Sergeant Rowse said. He lounged behind his desk, reading a copy of the *Army Times,* and didn't even look up.

Pfc. Levinson sat beside one of the radio operators and asked him to initiate a radio transmission to the front.

Bannon sat in his foxhole, thinking about the events of the day. He and his men had just finished lunch, and they were dug into their positions. He smoked a cigarette and blew smoke out the corner of his mouth. He was exhausted, but couldn't fall asleep. His nerve endings tingled with anxiety as he wondered what the Japs were doing in front of him.

No Japs had had been seen all morning, and Bannon thought they might be massing for a sneak attack farther back in the jungle or on the plateaus of the Torricelli Mountains. It wasn't like them to run away and stay gone. Bannon didn't realize that the Japs were beaten too badly to attack again so soon. He knew them to be savage fighters even in defeat. They'd retreated before, but never stayed away for long.

Pfc. Worthington, his runner, lay in the foxhole with him, his walkie-talkie glued to his ear in case a message came through. Suddenly his eyes opened wider and he spoke his code identification into the mouthpiece of the walkie-talkie. Then he turned to Bannon.

"It's for you," he said.

"Who is it?"

"Somebody at regiment."

Oh-oh, Bannon thought. He took the walkie-talkie from Worthington's hand and held it against his face.

"Sergeant Bannon speaking, sir."

A voice came to him over the hills and through the jungle via the miracle of shortwave radio. "This is Pfc. Levinson at regiment," it said.

"Oh hi," replied Bannon, who knew Levinson somewhat because they'd both been with the regiment since the first landings at Guadalcanal. "What's going on?"

"I just thought I oughtta tip you off to something I just heard about. You're gonna get court-martialed."

"I been expecting it," Bannon said. "Are you sure it's gonna go through?"

"I think so," Pfc. Levinson replied. "Lieutenant Jameson just had a meeting with the old man about you. The old man tried to talk Lieutenant Jameson out of the court-martial but he couldn't."

"What's Lieutenant Jameson gonna court-martial me for?"

"He said you beat up one of your men, and then you were insubordinate when he questioned you about it."

"Shit!"

"Just thought I'd call to let you know about it."

"When'll the court-martial take place?"

"A week or two, maybe more."

"Fuck!"

"That's all I got to say. I gotta get back to work. See ya later, Bannon. Good luck. Over and out."

The shortwave connection went dead in Bannon's ear. Bannon handed the walkie-talkie back to Private Worthington.

"What's going on?" Worthington asked.

"I'm gonna get court-martialed," Bannon replied, taking a long deep drag on his cigarette, "for kicking Frankie's ass."

"He deserved it."

"Maybe you should be a witness for me."

"Why me?" Worthington asked.

"You saw everything, didn't you?"

"Yeah, but I don't want any trouble."

"Forget it," Bannon said. He turned away from Worthington and puffed his cigarette, feeling morbid and depressed. *If the Japs don't get me, the court-martial will*, he thought. *Son of a bitch*.

He wished Sergeant Butsko was there to take all the heat, instead of him. Bannon wondered where Butsko was just then and what he was doing. He wished Butsko would come back soon and take charge of what was left of the recon platoon, because Bannon didn't think he could handle it much longer. *I hate these fucking guys*, Bannon thought. *The whole bunch of them aren't worth the powder to blow them to hell*.

SIX . . .

In other parts of the world, people didn't worry about imminent Japanese attacks or possible courts-martial. The baseball season was in full swing back in the States, and President Roosevelt ran for re-election against Thomas A. Dewey, the former governor of New York. Men went to sleep at night in most of the world without worrying about Japanese soldiers crawling next to them and slitting their throats.

Young men and women danced in ballrooms to the music of Benny Goodman and Artie Shaw, and children played in meadows carpeted with clover. Artur Rodzinski conducted the Philharmonic Symphony Orchestra of New York, and the hit movie of the summer was *The White Cliffs of Dover*, a romantic drama starring Irene Dunne and Alan Marshal. *Life* magazine featured a full-page photograph of an Arizona woman writing her Navy boyfriend a thank-you note for the Jap skull he'd sent her, and the skull was shown sitting on her writing table.

The sun shone bright and hot over the Hawaiian Islands. The Schofield Barracks were on the island of Oahu, not far from Honolulu, and as Bannon lay worrying in his foxhole, Master Sergeant John R. Butsko, walking with a slight limp, approached the building that housed the records of all soldiers stationed at the military installation.

Butsko's face was bruised due to a barroom brawl in which he'd been an instigator two nights before. The bandages underneath his uniform covered wounds sustained in battle on the island of New Guinea. Butsko was six feet tall, built like a brick shithouse, and had a face that some considered quite gruesome, while others considered it merely ugly. It was scarred and his nose was bent out of shape. His eyes resembled the slits in the turret of a tank.

At his side was Lieutenant Lou Norton, from the Public Information Office. Lieutenant Norton's assignment was to keep Butsko out of trouble, because Butsko had been in that barroom brawl two nights ago. It had been an embarrassment to the Army, because Butsko was supposed to receive the Congressional Medal of Honor in a week or so. Heroes who received the Congressional Medal of Honor weren't supposed to get into barroom brawls.

Norton was taller than Butsko and quite brawny, because the previous officer who'd been assigned to look after Butsko had been too small to handle him. Lieutenant Norton won the Congressional Medal of Honor himself at Saipan, so he was no stranger to violence. He was twenty-three years old and from Tucson, Arizona.

Together they walked up the steps of the building and entered its lobby. A sergeant sat behind a desk and Butsko sauntered toward him.

"I'm looking for my records," Butsko said. "Where the fuck are they?"

"What outfit are you with?"

"I'm not in any outfit."

Lieutenant Norton leaned over the desk. "He's in transit."

"Room two-twenty-three," the sergeant said.

Butsko and Lieutenant Norton climbed the stairs at the right side of the lobby. Butsko wanted to see his records because he wanted to find out where his wife, Dolly, was living.

He'd thought she was living in a suburb of Honolulu, but when he went there to see her, he'd found out that she'd moved away. He knew she was receiving his pay allotment, so her current address should be in his records.

They reached the second floor and walked down a long cool corridor. Soldiers and other officers got out of their way because they were two rather large men. Butsko wore his Combat Infantryman's Badge over the left pocket on his khaki shirt, which meant he was a combat veteran, and Lieutenant Norton wore one solitary ribbon over his shirt pocket. It showed white stars against a blue field, and indicated that he had won the Congressional Medal of Honor, the highest medal the United States of America awarded for heroism in battle.

They came to Room 223 and went inside. The first thing they saw was a counter behind which male and female military clerks worked. Butsko leaned against the counter and waited, but nobody asked him what he wanted. He shifted his weight from foot to foot and wondered where in hell Dolly was. Her whereabouts had become a nagging mystery to him.

He and Dolly had never got along well. They were the kind of married couple that caused neighbors to call the police, because they fought so much. Butsko was convinced she married him so that she could get his allotment and not have to work. She was a lazy bitch and all she wanted to do was drink, dance, and fuck.

"Hey!" Butsko said. "Anybody working in this office here!"

A WAC with tired eyes stood behind her desk and walked toward him. She was a brunette and her big tits reminded him of Dolly.

"What's your problem?" she asked.

"I wanna look at my records."

"Name and rank?"

Butsko told her, and she wrote the information on a piece of paper.

"Be right back," she said, walking away, her ass swaying from side to side.

"Shake it but don't break it," Butsko said. "Wrap it up and I'll take it."

The WAC didn't acknowledge hearing what he said. She walked into the next room and Butsko turned to Lieutenant Norton.

"I hope they're in here," he said.

"You hope what's in here?"

"My fucking records."

"Where else would they be?"

"How in the fuck am I supposed to know?"

Lieutenant Norton looked into Butsko's eyes. "Listen," he

said, "I keep telling you to cut out the filthy language when you're in public. It looks bad."

"I know, I know," Butsko replied. "I'm supposed to be a hero and I'm not supposed to act like a scumbag anymore."

"That's right."

"Well I can't help myself. Once a scumbag, always a scumbag. You know how it is."

"No, I don't know how it is. People can change, and you'd better shape up."

"Oh yeah," replied Butsko, glaring at Lieutenant Norton. "Yeah."

"I'm gonna kick your ass one of these days," Butsko said.

"The hell you will, and I just told you to watch your language, soldier."

"Yes sir," Butsko said without conviction.

"Lemme tell you something," Lieutenant Norton said. "We're getting tired of your baloney. If you keep it up we're gonna ship you back to the front, and you can forget about that medal. You're getting to be more trouble than you're worth."

"Yes sir," Butsko said.

Butsko and Lieutenant Norton glowered at each other, then looked in other directions. Butsko saw a butt can on the counter and took out a package of cigarettes, lighting one up. He and Lieutenant Norton hadn't been getting along very well ever since Lieutenant Norton had been assigned to keep an eye on him. *I'll probably have to punch this son of a bitch out before long,* Butsko thought, but whenever he got ready to do it, he saw the ribbon on Lieutenant Norton's shirt and couldn't bring himself to follow through. Lieutenant Norton was a combat soldier just as Butsko was. They'd both done enough fighting.

The WAC returned with a brown cardboard folder. "Here they are," she said. "Are you gonna look at them here, or are you gonna take them someplace?"

"I'm gonna look at them here," Butsko said.

She walked away. Butsko looked at her ass and it reminded him of Dolly because Dolly had a big wide ass like that. The only place where Butsko and Dolly ever got along was in the sack. She always told him he was the best lover she'd ever had, although that never stopped her from screwing other guys. One night he beat the shit out of her and they'd thrown him in the stockade. When he got out he put in for a transfer to the Philippines. The Japs bombed Pearl Harbor a few weeks after he arrived in Manila, and he hadn't seen Dolly again until approximately a year ago, when he beat the piss out of her then-current boyfriend and put him in the hospital.

Butsko opened his folder and searched for his pay records. He saw notations of his various courts-martial and demotions, plus his promotions. He saw the list of decorations he'd won already and the commendation he'd received after escaping from a Japanese POW camp in northern Luzon, following the Bataan Death March. He saw the date of his enlistment, the twentieth of May in 1935, and he saw the roster of posts on which he'd served.

Finally he found his financial records. He glanced through them rapidly, with mounting excitement, and then, flicking a page, he saw his pay records, and the addresses where the allotment checks had been mailed.

The address of the bungalow in Honolulu had been crossed out, and the new address was in Santa Monica, California. Butsko took out his notepad and wrote it down. *What's the bitch doing in Santa Monica?* he wondered. *She's probably got a new boyfriend who lives there.*

"I got what I was looking for," Butsko said.

"Good deal," replied Lieutenant Norton.

Butsko held his records up. "Hey you!"

The WAC looked up at him. "Are you calling me?"

"Yeah. I'm finished with my records. I'm gonna leave 'em right here. Take care of them."

"I'll put them away right now," she said, standing behind her desk.

"I'd appreciate it."

The WAC took the records from his hand and walked away. Butsko looked at her ass again.

"I shoulda got her name," Butsko said.

"What for?" Norton asked.

"I'd like to take her out for a drink and maybe put it to her in some dark corner someplace."

"Forget about it. You're not going anywhere without me."

"You mean I can't even get laid without you?"

"You can get laid without me *after* you get your decoration."

"How long's that gonna be?"

"A few more weeks."

"I gotta go a few more weeks without pussy?"

"Unless you don't mind me being there."

"Shit," Butsko said. "To hell with that."

"Let's get out of here," Norton said.

The lieutenant and the sergeant walked out of the office and strolled down the corridor, rolling their massive shoulders, and everybody got out of their way.

General Hall's headquarters was a conglomeration of Quonset huts built by the Corps of Engineers near the Tadji airstrips. General Hawkins climbed the steps to the hut where General Hall's office was located, and stepped inside.

A circular fan on the ceiling moved the humid air around, and Master Sergeant Seymour Bunberry, the Persecution Task Force's sergeant major, sat behind the front desk. Sergeant Bunberry was built on the porky side, wore glasses, and puffed a curved Sherlock Holmes–styled pipe.

"General Hall wants to see me," General Hawkins said.

"Have a seat, General."

General Hawkins sat on a folding wooden chair nearby, wondering what General Hall wanted to see him about. It had been a few days since they'd talked last, and there'd been little Japanese activity on the southern flank of the American lines. General Hawkins had been told previously by one of General Hall's aides that a major offensive was being planned to clear out the remaining Japs on the east side of the Driniumor River. General Hawkins surmised that his division might have to play a part in the operation.

He looked up and watched other officers come and go. He nodded to them and they nodded back at him. They all knew each other well, sometimes too well.

General Hawkins glanced at his watch. It was 1500 hours on the button, the time of his appointment, and yet he had to wait. Officers had to wait to see him at his headquarters, and now he had to wait at General Hall's headquarters. No matter how high up you were in the Army, there was always somebody higher. Sitting on top of them all was the President of the United States, and he had to go to Congress or directly to the people when he wanted to get something done. Even the President had to eat shit once in a while.

Finally Sergeant Bunberry called his name. "You can go in now," he said.

General Hawkins stood and walked through the maze of canvas-lined corridors until he came to General Hall's office. He went inside and reported, saluting and standing at attention.

"Have a seat, Clyde," General Hall said.

"Thank you sir."

General Hall had been reading documents, and laid a handful on his desk. He had salt-and-pepper gray hair shorn short and a salt-and-pepper mustache. His face was tanned and rugged, and he looked like a tough guy who didn't take any shit from anybody.

"Hear the news about Tojo?" General Hall asked.

"No sir."

"He resigned two days ago. I just found out about it this morning."

General Hall was shocked. General Hideki Tojo had been prime minister of Japan since 1940, heading a government that was essentially a military dictatorship, with Emperor Hirohito as the figurehead. Tojo had always been The Enemy to General Hawkins. It was hard to believe that he would suddenly resign.

"I wonder why he left office," General Hawkins said.

"He's losing the war, why else? Results are all that matter in war, isn't that so?"

"Who's in charge now?"

"General Koiso and Admiral Yonai. They're sharing power for the time being."

"Never heard of them."

"Neither did I until this morning. Koiso was governor general of Korea, and he's a past commander of the Kwangtung Army. Admiral Yonai was the Naval Minister and he served on the Jap Supreme War Council."

"Do you think the Japs are ready to give up?"

"Not according to a speech Yonai made after accepting office. He said he was going to carry forward the policies of the Tojo administration."

"Damn," said General Hawkins. "I wish something'd happen to ease our situation here."

"The only thing that'll ease our situation here is if we beat the Nazis in Europe, and that's a long way off. When we beat the Nazis we'll get more men and equipment here, and that's all we need. Anyway, let's get down to the reason I asked you to come here. Patrols have reported Jap troop movements toward your area. The Japs might be massing for another attack, so stay on your toes. You might want to set ambushes on the main trails to discourage the bastards, understand?"

"Yes sir. Could you tell me how many Japs are involved in the shift?"

"Maybe a few hundred, possibly up to a thousand, but I don't think the Japs can field more men than that in any concerted operation. They've taken a beating here during the past few weeks."

"So have we."

"Not as much as them. I'd like you to prepare for an attack as soon as you leave here, and formulate plans to interdict those Jap troop movements. The official order will come to you in writing later today, but I thought I'd tell you myself to get you started, and there's something else I'd like to speak with you about too." General Hall leaned back in his chair. "You may smoke if you like."

"Thank you, sir."

General Hall took out a Pall Mall and stuck it between his lips. General Hawkins stuffed an Old Gold into his ivory cigarette holder. Both men lit up. The office filled with blue clouds of tobacco smoke.

"I understand," said General Hall, "that you're going to

relieve one of your regimental commanders."

"I don't know what you're talking about," General Hawkins replied, although he knew very well what General Hall was talking about. *Oh oh, here it comes,* General Hawkins thought.

General Hall shuffled some papers on his desk and raised one of them. "His name's Hutchins," General Hall said, "and he's an alcoholic, according to the doctor's report. Do you mean to say you haven't received this report? It's addressed to you with copies to me and various other headquarters."

"Oh *that* report," General Hawkins said. "Yes, I received it of course."

"When are you going to relieve him of command?"

"I'm not going to relieve him of command."

"No?"

"No."

"Why not?"

"Because he's the best regimental commander I've got."

"But he's a drunk!"

"Not anymore. He's stopped drinking and smoking. The man has a will of steel, and he's a great frontline commander who's tested and proven, as far as I'm concerned. You don't throw men like that away just because they have a little drinking problem."

"Little drinking problem?" General Hall asked. "The doctor says he's an alcoholic."

"Officers like Colonel Hutchins will win this war, not doctors like the one who wrote that report."

General Hall looked at the piece of paper in front of him. "The doctor's name is Epstein, *Captain* Epstein. Do you know him?"

"Of course I know him. He's in charge of my division medical headquarters."

"Is he a qualified physician?"

"I assume he is."

"Then he must know what he's talking about."

"But he doesn't know anything about war. That's my department, and I've decided to leave Colonel Hutchins in charge of the regiment that he's led successfully for so long. The only reason he wound up in the hospital was because he directed the spearhead of my dawn attack a few days ago in person on foot, and he's a little too old for that. If he led his attacks the way you lead yours, he would've never gone to the hospital and everything'd be all right."

"But he's a drunk."

"Not anymore."

"Are you sure?"

"The man gave me his word, and that's enough for me."

General Hall snorted. "How can you accept the word of an alcoholic?"

"I trust this man. He's a fine frontline commander, and besides, who am I supposed to replace him with?"

"That's what I wanted to speak with you about," General Hall said calmly. "I was going to recommend Colonel MacKenzie, my intelligence officer. He's a brilliant officer and he needs some time commanding troops if he wants to get his star."

General Hawkins puffed his cigarette. He was starting to get the picture. Colonel MacKenzie was one of General Hall's protégés, and General Hall wanted to help him get ahead.

"My division isn't a training ground for staff officers who want to get stars," General Hawkins said. "We're face-to-face with the enemy out there and I need every experienced frontline commander that I can get."

"Even if they're drunks?"

"I told you he doesn't drink anymore, but even when he did he was better in tough situations than most officers who don't drink."

General Hall wrinkled his forehead. "Do *you* drink?" he asked.

"What kind of question is that, sir?"

"Answer it."

"I drink socially, and that's all."

"Ever been drunk?"

"Who hasn't ever been drunk?"

"Ever get drunk with Colonel Hutchins?"

"Once."

"You don't have a drinking problem, do you Clyde?"

"No sir."

"That's good, because I wouldn't want any of my frontline commanders to have drinking problems. Frankly, I'm surprised that you'd tolerate such a situation yourself. Don't you think the men deserve sober leaders?"

"Colonel Hutchins leads a crack regiment," General Hawkins said. "His men love him and would follow him anywhere. Colonel Hutchins is the one who should be getting a star."

"Even though he's a drunk?"

"Results are what counts in war. You just said so yourself."

"I could relieve him of command over your head, you know."

"If you do, I'll resign."

General Hall leaned back in his chair. He knew General Hawkins had friends in high places. General Hawkins was the son of a general and grandson of a general. If General Hawkins resigned, there'd be a big stink. The time had come to back off.

"Very well, Clyde," General Hall said. "I'll rely on your judgment in this matter, but if I ever find out that Colonel Hutchins is fucking up, his ass will be grass and I'll have the lawnmower."

"That'll never happen," General Hawkins said.

"You certainly have a lot of faith in this alcoholic colonel."

"Yes sir, I do," General Hawkins replied.

Major General Shunsake Yokozawa rocked from side to side on the stretcher as he was carried along the trail. He raised his head feebly and saw the jungle dancing below. Two of his aides carried him up the side of one of the mountains in the Torricelli chain. His intention was to commit ritual hara-kiri on a plateau near the summit.

General Yokozawa was weak from fever and loss of blood. He suffered intense pain in his stomach where he'd been shot. Medics had removed the bullet and sewn him up, without the benefit of morphine. General Yokozawa was nearly insane from the terrible throbbing pain. He couldn't wait to kill himself and get it over with once and for all.

His aides carried him higher up the mountain. The trail wasn't too steep, and that's why General Yokozowa had selected this particular area. He didn't want to kill himself in a smelly tent in a gloomy section of the jungle. He wanted to die in the sunshine and fresh air, with a decent view of the heavens before him.

The sun was bright, and sweat plastered General Yokozowa's clothes to his body. The pain in his gut was almost unbearable. Sometimes it increased and caused him to pass out for a few moments. His aides grunted as they carried him along, aware that they were participating in a solemn ceremony. It was their duty to make sure General Yokozowa's suicide went smoothly.

Finally they came to the small plateau not far from a cave where General Yokozowa had once maintained a headquarters. They lay the stretcher on the ground and took off their packs. Lieutenant Higashi bent over General Yokozowa.

"Are you all right sir?"

"A bit of water, please?"

"Yes sir."

Lieutenant Higashi took out his canteen and held it to General Yokozowa's trembling lips. General Yokozowa sucked the mouth of the canteen as if he were a baby sucking a bottle. Nearby, Lieutenant Gedo spread out the tatami mat upon which General Yokozowa would sit. He laid down a length of red silk in front of the mat, and on the silk he placed the ritual hara-kiri knife in its sheath.

Lieutenant Higashi gazed compassionately at his commander. General Yokozowa was pale and gaunt, appearing to be ninety years old. Deep lines of suffering were etched into his face. His lips were pressed together resolutely, so that he wouldn't cry out in pain.

Lieutenant Gedo walked toward Lieutenant Higashi, bent low, and whispered in his ear: "All is ready."

"Excellent," said Lieutenant Higashi.

General Yokozowa opened his eyes. "What was that?"

"Lieutenant Gedo just told me all is ready."

"Then let's get on with it."

"Yes sir."

Lieutenants Higashi and Gedo lifted General Yokozowa up by his armpits and carried him to the tatami mat. They lowered him gently, and General Yokozowa crossed his legs underneath him. General Yokozowa wore a full-dress uniform with all his insignia, decorations, and medals. He even had his boots on.

The two lieutenants let General Yokozowa go, and he sagged first to one side, and then to the other. He leaned forward, and then backwards.

"Are you all right sir?" Lieutenant Higashi asked.

"Unbutton my shirt," General Yokozowa croaked.

"Yes sir."

Lieutenant Higashi kneeled before the general and unbuttoned his shirt, baring the bandages on his stomach. He also loosened the general's belt and unbuttoned his fly.

"Is that all right, sir?"

"Remove the bandages," General Yokozowa said.

"Yes sir."

Lieutenant Higashi swallowed hard and dug his fingernails into a corner of the bandage. He hoped he wouldn't tear General Yokozowa's guts out when he pulled the bandage. Taking a deep breath, he tugged the bandage.

"Do it quickly!" barked General Yokozowa.

Lieutenant Higashi set his teeth on edge and yanked strenuously. He heard a tearing sound as the bandage peeled away from General Yokozowa's skin, revealing the stitched edges of his wound.

General Yokozowa nearly fainted from the pain. He closed his eyes and heard air rushing in his ears.

"Are you all right sir?" Lieutenant Higashi asked.

"Leave me alone."

"Yes sir."

General Yokozowa heard the footsteps of his aides recede into the distance. He opened his eyes and saw the jungle gleam like an emerald in the sunlight. The breeze kept away the insects. Blinking his eyes, he focused on the knife before him. The time had come to commit hara-kiri.

He lifted the knife and removed it from its sheath. Sunlight caught the blade and made it shine like diamonds. General Yokozowa held the knife up to the sun and prayed that his ancestors would forgive him for failing to succeed in the attack. He expressed gratitude for the opportunity to expunge himself of the vile American blood polluting his veins.

Sucking in air between his clenched teeth, he turned the blade toward him and held the hilt in both his hands. Looking down, he saw his stitched belly. He was in terrible pain, and knew it would worsen considerably as soon as he plunged in the knife. It was best to get everything over with as soon as possible.

He drew himself erect, looked down, and touched the blade against the skin on the left side of his stomach. His task would be to cut his stomach open from the left side to the right side, so that his soul could escape and fly to heaven.

I apologize for all the wrong I've done, and for all the good that I haven't done, he thought. *I apologize for my stupidity and weakness.*

He plunged the knife into his stomach, and was overcome by an ocean of pain. It was so fierce that he blacked out for a few seconds, his back bending forward and his head hanging in his lap. Blood poured out of the wound and onto his pants.

He opened his eyes, realizing that the pain was greater than he'd thought. He hadn't believed it was possible for a human being to endure such fierce pain. *I've got to get this over with quickly,* he thought, *otherwise I might bungle the job.*

He took a deep breath and summoned together his strength. Holding the hilt of the knife with both hands, he pulled it across his stomach, slicing through skin, stitches, and guts, but his strength ran out as the blade cut into his navel.

General Yokozowa was engulfed by the most terrifying pain of his life. His vision became blurred, but he could see his intestines spilling out onto his lap, along with pints of blood. It was a horrible ghoulish sight, and he couldn't handle it. The loss of blood was too great. The knife fell out of his hands and he groaned as he fell to the side.

Meanwhile, Lieutenant Higashi and Gedo watched him from behind a scraggly mountain bush nearby.

"I think he did it," Lieutenant Gedo said.

"I'll take a look," Lieutenant Higashi replied.

He tiptoed out from behind the bush and advanced cautiously toward General Yokozowa, who lay on his side, his legs still crossed and his right knee sticking straight up in the air. The breeze sent him a whiff of General Yokozowa's guts, and it smelled dreadful, like rotting feces. Drawing closer, the young lieutenant saw General Yokozowa lying in a pool of blood. Guts hung out of General Yokozowa's stomach. Lieutenant Higashi kneeled and saw that the general had only cut halfway across his stomach, and the general still was alive, moaning softly.

Lieutenant Higashi saw the knife lying near General Yokozowa's hand. He picked it up, held it in his fist, and stabbed the point into General Yokozowa's throat, where his jugular vein was located. Warm blood gushed out onto Lieutenant Higashi's hand. General Yokozowa sighed and went limp on the ground. He was dead. Lieutenant Higashi wiped the blood off the knife with his handkerchief, and stood up.

"He's dead!" he called back to Lieutenant Gedo.

Lieutenant Gedo crawled out from behind the bush and advanced toward Lieutenant Higashi. He'd seen General Yokozowa during his heyday, and now he was just another bloody corpse.

The young lieutenants laid General Yokozowa's body on the stretcher and lifted it up. They carried the stretcher down the mountain trail, heading toward the steaming jungle below.

The sun sank toward the horizon. Colonel Hutchins was in the throes of alcohol and nicotine withdrawal. He paced back and forth behind his desk, his hands clasped behind his back. He tried to think of war, peace, naked women, and even his childhood, but his lungs cried out for a cigarette and his mind begged for booze.

Sweat ran in rivulets down his body, and he clicked his teeth nervously. It was tormenting to know that he could have a cigarette just by walking into his outer office and asking for one. He could have a drink if he went to the mess hall and ordered Corporal Dunphy to brew up some white lightning. Relief was available, but Colonel Hutchins didn't want to be relieved. He had to beat his addictions somehow.

He chewed his lower lip and snorted like a bull. He wished he could sit down, but he couldn't be still. He had to keep moving because motion somehow kept his longing under control. He wondered how much longer he'd suffer. They said the first few days were the hardest. He was in his fifth day now and it was still tough going.

His mind became weak. He wondered why he was making himself suffer. What was he trying to be a hero for? Why was he so persistent? Just so he could command a regiment in war? What was so great about that? What was so terrible about going to Washington, D.C.?

I've fought in enough wars, he thought. *Why do I want to keep fighting? What's wrong with me? Why don't I just go back to the States and take it easy in my old age? I'm getting too old for this shit. To hell with the war.*

He clenched his fists and let them loose again. He licked his teeth with his tongue. He wanted desperately to smoke a cigarette, and then get roaring drunk. His knees felt weak and his toes tingled. *I can't go on like this*, he thought. *I'm gonna crack up any moment now.*

He was tempted to walk out to where Sergeant Koch was sitting and bum a cigarette, but he couldn't do it. He'd given his word to General Hawkins that he'd stop smoking and drinking, and a man wasn't worth anything if he wasn't worth his word.

I'm gonna beat this stuff, he said to himself. *I don't know how I'm gonna do it, but I'm gonna do it.*

He flared his nostrils and sucked in air. Lifting the cup on his desk, he swallowed down the tepid coffee in it.

"Levinson!" he shouted.

"Yes sir!" replied Pfc. Levinson in the outer office.

"Get me some more coffee!"

"Yes sir!"

He heard a rustle in the other office, and assumed that was Pfc. Levinson running toward the mess hall. Colonel Hutchins thought his head would explode. He felt like screaming and jumping up and down. He wanted to strangle somebody. Maybe he should see the pharmacist and get a sedative, but no, he didn't want to be groggy and then have the Japs attack. He wanted to stay on his toes just in case. He almost wished the Japs *would* attack, so he could be distracted from cigarettes and booze.

He pushed aside the tent flap and walked toward the desk of Master Sergeant Koch, who looked up at him in alarm.

"Are you all right sir?"

"You got any chewing gum, Koch?"

"Yes sir."

"Lemme have some."

"Yes sir."

Sergeant Koch took a pack of Wrigley's spearmint gum out of his shirt pocket and handed it to Colonel Hutchins.

"Mind if I take two sticks?"

"Help yourself, sir."

Colonel Hutchins pulled two sticks out of the pack and returned to his office. He unwrapped the gum and folded it into his mouth, chewing ferociously. *I don't know how I'm gonna get through this,* he thought, *but somehow I'll do it.*

SEVEN . . .

General Hall sat behind his desk, drafting a letter to General Krueger at Hollandia, describing progress in the campaign at Aitape. There was a knock on his door.

"Come in!"

The door opened, and Colonel MacKenzie entered the office. Colonel MacKenzie had freckles, red hair, and a complexion that was perpetually peeling because his skin couldn't hold a tan.

"Have you heard the news about Hitler, sir!" Colonel MacKenzie asked.

"What news!"

"An attempt on his life was made this morning!"

"Is he dead?"

"No."

"Is he incapacitated at least?"

"No."

"Damn!"

Colonel MacKenzie sat on a chair in front of General Hall's desk. "Some of his top-ranking Army officers did it, sir. There's speculation that Rommel was in on it."

"Where'd it happen?"

"At Hitler's headquarters in Rastenburg. They put a bomb underneath his map table. Evidently Hitler moved before the bomb went off, and it killed some other Nazis. But it only wounded Hitler. He gave a speech that said he was all right."

"Too bad they missed him," General Hall said. "But even if they got him, I don't suppose it'd make much difference.

Tojo resigned a few days ago, and the war's still going on. There are always plenty of fanatics to take over when one fanatic dies or resigns."

"Yes sir, but it looks as though the Axis powers are starting to crack, sir."

"Not fast enough for me." General Hall leaned back in his chair. "Have a seat."

"Thank you, sir."

"I wonder," said General Hall, "if there's a widespread dissatisfaction with Hitler in Germany, or if this attempt on his life was made by a small group of conspirators?"

"We don't know that, sir. We'll probably never know all the facts about the Nazi regime until the war is over."

"I suppose you're right. Oh, by the way, it doesn't look as though I'll be able to give you that regiment in the Eighty-first Division, as we'd discussed. General Hawkins wants to keep his drunken colonel in command. Claims he's irreplaceable."

Colonel MacKenzie smiled indulgently. "Well, General Hawkins certainly is an unusual officer."

"Something else'll open up for you before long, so don't worry about it. Perhaps that colonel of his will really screw up, and he'll have to let him go."

"I'm perfectly willing to wait, sir," Colonel MacKenzie lied. "I'm in no hurry."

"Good. Patience is a virtue in war, as it is in every other field of endeavor."

It took a few days, but Acting Colonel Sakakibara had finally assembled the approximation of a staff for his Southern Strike Force.

The officers were lined up in front of him, standing at attention in a jungle clearing. Few of them had ever held staff positions before, but that didn't mean anything to Colonel Sakakibara. He had deliberately selected the most aggressive officers in the Eighteenth Army for his new Southern Strike Force command, even though many of them had records nearly as bad as his.

Colonel Sakakibara walked back and forth in front of them,

gazing into their eyes, examining their faces for cowardice or weakness. They kept their eyes front, not daring to move their eyeballs, because they were terrified of Colonel Sakakibara. His reputation had spread far and wide in the Eighteenth Army ever since receiving command of the Southern Strike Force. Everyone knew how cruel he was, both to American prisoners and his own officers and men who had the misfortune to displease him.

Colonel Sakakibara inspected the last officer in the rank, and then performed an about-face, marching back to a point facing the center of the rank. Everyone expected him to let them stand at ease while he gave his speech, but he made them remain at attention.

He squared his shoulders and stood at attention also, his arms stiffly down his sides and his fists balled up. He leaned forward slightly, and some officers were certain he'd fall on his face, but somehow, miraculously, he managed to defy the laws of gravity and remain on his feet.

"Gentlemen, I will be frank with you!" Colonel Sakakibara declared. "This war is being lost because of cowardice at all levels of command! There are too many fancypants generals walking around with their maps and their bottles of sake! I want you to know that there will be none of that foolishness in the Southern Strike Force! Our duty is to attack and kill, and that is what we shall do! We need no special maps, because we know where the enemy is! We need no long staff meetings, because we know what we must do! Our task is quite simple, and we don't need to make it complicated! Our task is to annihilate Americans, and we must not give any thought to our own lives! We must resolve here and now to consecrate our lives to the Emperor, and then we must go out and fight as if we are no longer in possession of our lives! There must be no hesitancy when we attack the Americans! There must be no thought whatever about saving our skins! We must think only of killing as many Americans as possible, regardless of the risk of our own lives, because our own lives are not our own anymore, they now belong to our mighty and holy Emperor! Do you have any questions?"

Nobody dared to say anything. Everybody gazed straight ahead, not moving a muscle.

"I hate stupid questions!" Colonel Sakakibara said. "I'm pleased that you're not asking any! I consider that a good omen! When I dismiss you I want you to take command of your units and speak to your men as I'm speaking to you! Make certain they understand that you expect them to die for the Emperor when we attack! In this attack we hold nothing back! We have no reserves and there will be no retreat! We go into battle to win or die for the glory of our Emperor! Is that clear?"

Again, no one said anything. Colonel Sakakibara drew his sword from his scabbard and held it high in the air. *"Banzai!"* he shouted. *"Tenno heika banzai!"*

"Banzai!" they replied. *"Tenno heika banzai!"*

It was evening, and the sun sank toward the horizon. The recon platoon had just finished chow. Bannon sat in his foxhole and felt awful. He had a headache, and his broken nose hurt him. The men in his platoon gave him an argument every time he asked them to do something. Bannon was getting angrier and angrier at them. He wanted to shoot a few of them, especially Frankie La Barbara. *I never wanted to be a platoon sergeant,* he thought. *Why does all the shit have to fall on me?*

"Message for you," said Private Worthington lying next to him, listening to the walkie-talkie.

Bannon took the walkie-talkie and held it to his ear. "Sergeant Bannon speaking, sir."

"This is Captain Mason," said the voice on the other end. "I want you to take a patrol out tonight to grid thirty-four on your map. You know where grid thirty-four is?"

Bannon whipped his map out of his pocket and found the grid. "I've got it, sir."

"Do you see the trail that intersects the grid?"

"Yes sir."

"That's a major trail and we want to know if anything's happening on it after the sun goes down. You're to leave at nightfall and return at dawn. Got it?"

"How many men should I take, sir?"

114

"As many as you think you need. Any other questions?"

"No sir."

"Over and out."

Bannon groaned as he handed the walkie-talkie back to Worthington.

"What's the matter?" Worthington asked.

"We gotta go out on patrol."

"Do I have to go?"

"Yes."

"How come I always have to go?"

"Because you're my runner, and where I go, you go."

"Why can't somebody else be your runner?"

"Because I want you."

"Why?"

"Because that's what I said."

Bannon climbed out of the foxhole and looked around. His men were sprawled out in their foxholes, anticipating a night of quiet sleep. They wouldn't want to go out on patrol. Bannon knew who he wanted. First of all, he'd need McGurk to take the point.

"McGurk!" he said.

"Whataya want?" asked McGurk, raising his head above the rim of his foxhole.

"You're going out on patrol tonight."

"I don't feel so good," McGurk complained.

"Neither do I, but we've got to go."

"Maybe they can get some other platoon to go."

"You know better than that. We're going, and there's no way out of it. Be ready to move out when the sun goes down."

"I'm tired of these patrols," McGurk said.

"So'm I," Bannon replied, "but we gotta do what we gotta do."

Bannon walked past McGurk's foxhole and headed toward the foxhole occupied by the Reverend Billie Jones, hearing a snore as he approached. He looked into the foxhole and saw the Reverend Billie Jones sound asleep.

"Jones!" Bannon said.

Jones didn't move. Bannon picked up a pebble and dropped

it on Jones's steel pot. The pebble landed with a *ping* and Jones jumped six inches into the air.

"Whatsa matter!" Jones hollered.

"You're going out on patrol with me at sundown."

"Can't you get somebody else?"

"No."

"But I'm dog tired, Bannon. I need to get me some sleep."

"Tough shit. Go see the chaplain and get your ticket punched, but make sure you're back by sundown."

"Why me?" the Reverend Billie Jones asked.

"Why not you?" Bannon replied.

Bannon walked away, and he was getting mad. No one would dare talk back to Butsko if he was the one organizing the patrol, because Butsko would beat the shit out of them. The men were afraid of Butsko, but they weren't afraid of him. *They don't respect me,* Bannon thought. *And I hate their fucking guts.*

Bannon approached Frankie La Barbara's foxhole. Frankie La Barbara sat inside, smoking a cigarette and writing a letter to his wife Francesca back in New York City.

"Hey Frankie," Bannon said.

"Whataya want?" Frankie asked.

"We're going out on patrol tonight."

"Maybe you are, cowboy, but I'm not."

"Oh yes you are."

"Oh no I'm not."

"I just gave you a direct order."

"Shove your direct order up your ass."

Bannon took a deep breath. He knew that the only way to make Frankie go out on the patrol was to beat the shit out of him, and Bannon was tired of fighting with Frankie. A great wet blanket of fatigue fell over Bannon. He didn't feel like dealing with the men in the recon platoon anymore. He was no Butsko and no Lieutenant Breckenridge. All he wanted to do was go back to Texas and ride the range. He was fed up with the war and fed up with being acting platoon sergeant.

"Fuck you," Bannon said. "I quit."

He turned around and walked back to his foxhole. Jumping inside, he opened his pack and checked out the contents. He had two boxes of C rations inside, enough for two days. He hoisted the pack to his back and thrust his arms through the straps.

"See you later," Bannon said to Worthington.

"Where you going?"

"That's for me to know and for you to find out."

Bannon slung his M 1 rifle over his shoulder and walked off toward the jungle. He found a trail and moved along it. In seconds he was out of sight. Worthington scratched his head and wrinkled his nose. *I think our acting platoon sergeant just went AWOL,* he said to himself.

It was four o'clock in the afternoon on the island of Oahu. Butsko lay on his cot in the Bachelor Officers Quarters, smoking a cigarette. The bright late-afternoon sun shone through the window, making the room glow orange. His shoes were off and he wore a tan class A uniform with his Combat Infantryman's Badge above his left shirt pocket. He puffed the cigarette and thought about Dolly, wondering what the hell she was doing in Santa Monica, California. There was a knock on the door.

"Come in!"

The door opened and big Lieutenant Norton walked in the room. "Hiya," he said.

"Hiya," Butsko replied.

"I came to get you for chow."

"You're early."

"I can wait."

"Why don't you wait downstairs?"

"Because I don't feel like it."

"You're a real ball-buster, you know that?"

Norton straddled the wooden chair in front of the small wooden desk. "You sound like you're in a bad mood."

"I'm like a prisoner in jail, and I'm supposed to be in a good mood?"

"You're not a prisoner. You can go anywhere you want."

"Provided you're with me."

"Right."

"That's what I'm saying—I'm a prisoner."

"Don't worry about it. Tomorrow you'll be in Los Angeles. You can look up your wife."

"You gonna stay with me when I fuck her?"

"I'll be in the next room."

"What kind of deal is that supposed to be?"

"I'm just doing my job."

"What a job."

Norton looked at his watch. He took out a cigarette and lit it up. He had a prominent nose and jaw, and tanned features. "You wanna go to the mess hall early?"

"What for?"

"Beat the rush."

"Fuck the rush. This is our last night here. We should go to town and have a decent meal."

"Last time you went to town you started a fucking riot."

"Some jarhead marine attacked me. It wasn't my fault."

"And it wasn't your fault you were found drunk in that bed there with a woman, right?"

"I don't remember anything."

"We can't let that happen again."

"How could it happen again? You'll be with me, won't you?"

"You're damned right I will."

"How'd you like to get laid?" Butsko asked.

"Forget about it."

"You don't like to get laid?"

"You and I aren't leaving this base, so forget about it."

"I know this fancy whorehouse in town. The girls are real pretty and it won't cost you anything."

"Why wouldn't it cost me anything?"

"Because I got my back pay today, remember?"

"You'll pick up the tab?"

"That's right."

Lieutenant Norton thought about it for a few moments, then

shook his head. "I think we'd better stay on the base."

Butsko made an expression of disgust. "What are you, a fairy or something?"

"Don't gimme any shit, Butsko."

"Are you afraid of a little pussy, Norton?"

"My job is to keep you out of trouble, and that's what I'm gonna do."

"The best way to keep me out of trouble is to put me in the sack with a broad."

"You'll get drunk and you'll start a fight."

"I'd rather fuck than fight, but I'll tell you something: if I have to spend another night on this base, I'm liable to blow my cork. I might punch somebody in the mouth when I go to that mess hall. I'm liable to throw a table through a fucking window."

"If you do, we'll toss you right in the stockade."

"I can see the headlines in the paper now. *Medal of Honor winner gets tossed into the shitcan.* That'll go over real big on the home front."

"Maybe we'll have to shoot you," Lieutenant Norton said ominously.

"There's an easier way out of this," Butsko said. "Just get a car and drive me to the whorehouse. I'll get laid and you'll get laid. Nobody has to know anything. Whataya say?"

"No."

"Asshole."

"Scumbag."

"Fuck you," Butsko said. "I hate your guts and I'm not cooperating with you anymore. I'm gonna fuck up real bad and make you look bad. You won't like what I'm gonna do to you."

"We'll see about that."

"We sure will."

The sun sank toward the horizon as Private Worthington approached the command post of Headquarters Company. He heard soldiers doing calisthenics and saw them through the trees, jumping up and down, clapping their hands over their heads and against their thighs.

Worthington proceeded along the trail and came to the clearing where the calisthenics were taking place. A sergeant stood in front of four ranks of men, jumping up and down and exhorting them on, and to the left of the sergeant was Colonel Hutchins, jumping with the rest of the men.

Private Worthington stopped cold. It looked as though the colonel was going to have a heart attack at any moment. His face was red and his uniform was soaked with sweat. His jaw hung open and his tongue hung out of his mouth.

The sergeant stopped jumping. "All right, gentlemen!" he said. "The next exercise will be *squat-jumps!* Readeep . . . one— two—threep . . . "

The soldiers placed their hands behind their heads and placed their left feet forward, dropping to a squatting position. Then they jumped up and dropped down again, moving their right feet forwards and their left feet backwards, ending up in another squatting position. They performed this exercise again and again, by the numbers. Private Worthington knew this was the most difficult and painful of all the calisthenics. Men often collapsed after they finished the routine. He watched Colonel Hutchins jumping up and down, his face turning purple, and thought: *They'd better get a medic out here pretty damn soon.*

Private Worthington entered the orderly room of the Headquarters Company command post, and saw Sergeant Maxwell seated behind the desk.

"I gotta see Captain Mason," he said. "It's important."

"What's important?"

"What I got to tell him."

"Whataya got to tell him?"

"I came here to tell him, not you."

"You don't tell me, you don't get in."

"If I tell you, you gotta keep it quiet."

"I'll keep it the way I wanna keep it."

"You drive a hard bargain, Sergeant."

"What's on your mind, scumbag?"

"Somebody in the platoon is AWOL."

120

"Who?"

"Bannon."

"Bannon?"

"Yeah."

"I always thought he was the most sensible person in the platoon."

"I thought so too, but he's gone over the hill."

"Over the hill where?"

"I don't know. He just walked off into the jungle."

"The Japs'll probably get him, and if they don't, we will."

"Can I talk to Captain Mason about it?"

"Whataya wanna talk to Captain Mason for?"

"To tell him."

"Whataya wanna tell him for?"

"Because Bannon was supposed to take a patrol out tonight."

"Oh," Sergeant Maxwell said. "I see. Well, I'll talk to him about it."

"Do you think there's any way you can keep this quiet for a while, because maybe Bannon'll come back. In fact, maybe he's back already."

"I'll talk to the old man about that one too."

"Thanks, Sergeant."

"Get the fuck out of here."

"Oh, by the way, Sergeant, there's one more thing. I think you'd better call the medics, because Colonel Hutchins is out there doing PT, and it looks like he's gonna collapse at any moment."

Sergeant Maxwell looked up at Worthington. "Mind your own business, young Private, and I thought I told you to get the fuck out of here."

"Hup Sarge."

Private Worthington performed an about-face and walked out of the orderly room. He emerged into the great humid outdoors again and saw the Headquarters Company soldiers still engaged in their PT (physical training). They were performing push-ups now, touching their chins to the muck and then raising themselves up again, as the sergeant counted the numbers.

Private Worthington saw Colonel Hutchins keeping up with the rest of them, but he didn't appear as though he could keep up the pace much longer. *That poor son of a bitch,* Private Worthington thought, *I wonder what he's trying to prove.*

Meanwhile, back at the recon platoon bivouac, Private McGurk was sharpening the sword he'd picked up on the battlefield the previous night. It was a beautiful old sword with gold inlaid into the hilt, and carvings of crysanthemums on the blade. He ran his Arkansas Washita stone back and forth over the blade that gleamed in the light of the setting sun.

Frankie La Barbara walked by on his way to the latrine. "Whatcha doing in there?" he asked.

"Sharpening this sword."

"Looks like a good one."

"I never seen one like it before," McGurk said.

"Mind if I take a look?"

"Be my guest."

Frankie jumped into the foxhole, and McGurk handed it over. Frankie squinted as he examined it, and could see that it was very old. The metalwork was exquisite. Frankie had never seen one like it before either.

"You wanna sell it?" Frankie asked.

"What'll you gimme?"

Frankie figured he could sell it to a sailor or a rear-echelon officer for maybe fifty bucks. "Ten bucks," he said.

"No deal," replied McGurk.

"Fifteen?"

"C'mon."

"It's not worth more than fifteen."

"I wouldn't sell this sword for less than fifty dollars," McGurk said, because he knew what swords were worth too.

"You're fucking crazy!" Frankie replied. "You'll never get fifty dollars for that sword!"

"Then I'm not selling it."

"If you change your mind, lemme know."

"I ain't changing my mind."

Frankie crawled out of the foxhole and walked away. McGurk

continued to sharpen the sword. He paused after a few more strokes and touched his thumb to the edge. It was sharp as a razor. *Damn good steel in this sword,* he thought. *I wonder who it belonged to?*

EIGHT . . .

It was eleven o'clock at night. Bannon lay underneath a bush with his head on his knapsack, and tried to sleep. Birds squawked in the trees and a wild dog barked in the distance. An occasional rifle shot or machine-gun burst could be heard far away.

I've done it, Bannon thought. *I'm free.* He had no qualms whatever about going AWOL. He simply didn't give a fuck anymore. *Let those guys see what it's like to get along on their own. I hope they get their asses shot off.*

Bannon figured he'd been reported as AWOL by now, but no one would come to look for him. His plan was to climb the Torricelli Mountains and hide in the valley on the other side, where no Japs or American troops were, and live off the land until the war was over. Then he'd come out of hiding and say he'd been taken prisoner by the Japs, and he'd escaped. Nobody'd be around to say he'd lied. They'd probably give him a fucking medal.

He thought he was a real smart fellow, and wondered why he hadn't done this long ago. *To hell with this war,* he thought. *Let somebody else do the fighting for a change.*

Colonel Hutchins paced the floor of his tent in the darkness. Back and forth he went, his arms clasped behind his back as he chewed a great gob of gum.

All he wanted was a good stiff shot of white lightning and a cigarette. He would've sold his grandmother down the river for one or the other if she was still alive. Every pore in his body was crying out for nicotine and alcohol. He was tempted to give in. Every second was a struggle, and he even questioned the validity of the struggle. *Why am I doing this to myself?* he wondered. *What the hell's in it for me?*

It was a question he couldn't answer, but he was determined to continue his abstinence. He'd given his word and there could be no backing out now. He wondered how many more days it'd take before the longing would diminish. *I can't take this shit much longer,* he said to himself.

He clasped and unclasped his hands as he marched back and forth in the darkness. On his desk was a pile of work that needed to be done, but he couldn't concentrate on it. All he could do was suffer. He wished he could fall asleep, but his nerves were jangled. He wanted to get sleeping pills from Lieutenant Rabinowitz, his pharmacist, but what if the Japs attacked while he was knocked out? Who'd lead the regiment?

Colonel Hutchins walked out of his tent and looked up at the sky. A half moon shone above, but patches of stars were covered by clouds. *Looks like rain,* he thought. *Son of a bitch.*

The patrol from the recon platoon lay alongside the big trail in grid thirty-four. They were commanded by Lieutenant Edward Sears, whom Captain Mason had sent to take over the platoon when he found out that Bannon had gone over the hill.

Lieutenant Sears was twenty-two years old, tall and wiry, and he'd been warned about the men in the recon platoon. He knew they were ornery sons of bitches who didn't like to take orders, and he'd have to earn their respect. He'd been assigned to the recon platoon because he was an experienced combat officer, leading infantry platoons on New Georgia and Bougainville before coming to New Guinea.

He lay in the bushes and watched the trail. Sometimes clouds would pass over the moon and the jungle became dark. You couldn't see three feet in front of you, but then the breeze would blow the clouds away and the jungle would lighten up, permitting distant objects to be seen.

Lieutenant Sears looked at his watch. He wore a soft fatigue cap high up on the back of his head and low over his eyes. His light brown hair was shorn practically down to his scalp and he had a long neck with a big bulging Adam's apple. It was 2330 hours, and the sun would come up around 0500 hours. That's when he could leave.

So far nothing had passed by on the trail. Evidently the Japs weren't moving into the Afua area as Headquarters had believed.

The narrow street was paved with cobblestones. It was near the Honolulu waterfront and the air smelled like salt and oil mixed together. Two drunken marines staggered in the light of a street lamp. Butsko and Lieutenant Norton passed them by, rolling their shoulders, walking along confidently, wearing their cunt caps low over their eyes.

"There it is right there," Butsko said. "It's even got a red light on the porch."

Lieutenant Norton looked at the building. It was a two-story house painted white and its front steps connected it with the sidewalk. "You say they know you here?" he asked.

"They sure as hell do. The madam is a friend of mine."

The door to the house opened and a sailor appeared. Tottering from side to side, he squared away his white cap on his head and descended the stairs. At the bottom he saw Butsko and Lieutenant Norton steaming toward him, and he got out of the way.

Butsko and Lieutenant Norton climbed the steps. A window was cut into the door, covered with a shade on the inside. Butsko reached toward the doorbell. Lieutenant Norton grabbed his arm.

"Remember what you said," Lieutenant Norton told him. "I don't want any trouble."

"Neither do I," Butsko said.

Lieutenant Norton loosened his grip. Butsko pressed the doorbell. The shade opened and two slanted eyes peered out at them. The door opened, revealing a vestibule bathed in a red glow, with beaded curtains hanging down.

A gigantic Chinese man stepped out from behind the door. He wore a white short-sleeved shirt and dark pants held up by suspenders. A big smile was spread over his face.

"Sergeant Butsko!" he said. "I not see you for long time! I thought maybe you got dead!"

"Only the good die young," Butsko replied, shaking his hand. "Lemme introduce my friend, Lieutenant Norton."

The Chinese man saluted Lieutenant Norton. "Welcome, sir! Good to have you aboard!"

Lieutenant Norton shook his hand.

"His name's Sing," Butsko said, "Mister Sing."

"How do you do, Mister Sing," Lieutenant Norton said.

A cloud of perfume hit the soldiers in their nostrils, and a few seconds later a woman in a low-cut red cocktail dress appeared in the vestibule. She took one look at Butsko and her eyes lit up.

"Well look what the cat just dragged in!" she said, wrapping her arms around Butsko and kissing him on the lips. "I thought they killed you long ago!"

"I'm still around," Butsko replied, "and I'm still looking for pussy."

"You came to the right place."

"This is Rita," Butsko said, making introductions, "and this is Lieutenant Norton."

"He's cute," Rita said.

"How do you do," Lieutenant Norton replied, blushing slightly.

"Let's have a drink," Rita said.

"That's okay by me," Butsko replied.

"Right this way," Rita said, leading them through a smoky dark corridor. "When'd you get in town?"

"About a week ago."

"How come you're limping?"

"Jap shot me in the leg."

"That son of a bitch!"

They came to a parlor, and Rita clapped her hands. A Chinese maid appeared. "Drinks for my friends," Rita said.

"What you want?" the Chinese maid asked.

"Whisky straight," Butsko said.

"The same for me," Lieutenant Norton added.

The Chinese maid walked away, and a moment later young

127

women filed into the room. They wrapped their arms around Butsko, licked his ears, and grabbed his dick. More women entered the room and did the same to Lieutenant Norton. Lieutenant Norton lost his balance and fell on top of a sofa. Four young women fell on top of him.

"Help!" Lieutenant Norton said weakly.

Rita walked up to Butsko and pinched his cheek. "It's good to see you again, you old son of a bitch," she said. "Everything's on the house. Help yourself to anything you want."

"Anything?" Butsko asked, his face covered with lipstick.

"Anything," she replied.

"How about you?"

"Me?"

"Yes you."

"I don't do that stuff anymore."

"You said anything." Butsko looked at the nearest girl. "Didn't she say *anything*."

"She damn sure did," the girl replied.

Butsko looked at Rita. "You said *anything*."

Rita smiled and shrugged her shoulders. "Well," she replied, "maybe just tonight, for an old friend."

Bannon lay sound asleep underneath a bush in the New Guinea jungle. He dreamed about west Texas, the rolling desert hills and mountains. He was riding a horse, bouncing up and down in the saddle, his big cowboy hat knifing through the wind. His legs bounced against the saddle, making a slapping sound that became progressively louder. Finally the sound became so loud and irregular that Bannon was forced to open his eyes.

He sat bolt upright in the jungle and looked around, a scowl on his face. He heard sounds like machetes whacking against trees not far away. The machetes were headed in his direction. It sounded as if there were four of them. *What the hell's going on here?* he wondered.

At first he thought the sound came from American soldiers looking for him, but then he realized that was unlikely. No one would send American soldiers into no-man's-land to hunt an

AWOL. Who in the hell was chopping up the jungle? *It's got to be the goddamned fucking Japs!*

Wait a minute, he thought. It occurred to him that Japs might be moving through the thick of the jungle, staying away from main trails so they wouldn't be observed. Also, the sound could be *American* soldiers moving stealthily into position for a surprise attack.

Bannon wondered what to do. If he moved perpendicular to the path of the advancing machete-bearers, he could get out of their way and continue his journey to the Torricelli Mountains. But if they were Japs, their presence in the area should be reported.

He decided that his first step should be to find out whether they were Japs or Americans. The best way to accomplish that would be to climb a tree and observe them as they passed by. He looked around for a tree that would be easy to climb, and saw one with low-hanging branches. Kneeling down, he mussed up the ground where he'd been, obscuring his footprints with damp leaves. He backed up, continuing to cover his tracks, and then jumped into the air, grabbing the branch. He pulled himself onto it and proceeded to climb the tree until he was fifteen yards high. He figured that'd be close enough to the ground to see the Japs, if in fact they were Japs, but far enough away so that they couldn't see him.

He sat on a branch, rested his back against the trunk of the tree, and slapped a mosquito that landed on his jaw. A moment of panic struck him when he thought he'd left a can of C rations on the ground below, but then remembered that he'd buried it underneath a bush. Everything was okay. The Japs wouldn't know he'd been there, if indeed Japs were coming.

The soldiers came closer. Bannon heard them hacking through the jungle, and then somebody shouted an order in Japanese! Now Bannon knew who he was dealing with. Japs were in fact moving through the jungle, evidently staying off the main trails because they didn't want to be observed. *The bastards are up to something,* Bannon realized. *They're probably gonna launch one of their sneak attacks on the regiment again.*

Bannon had no difficulty making up his mind about what to do about it. As soon as the Japs passed through the area, he'd climb down the tree and return to the regiment, to report what he'd seen. He sat motionless on the branch and hoped no Jap would look up and see him.

The sounds of the machetes came closer. Bannon narrowed his eyes and perceived four columns advancing through the jungle. A machete-bearer was at the head of each column, hacking through the vegetation. The Japanese moved quickly. One of the columns passed through the clearing underneath the tree where Bannon sat, and Bannon held his breath. He hoped nothing would fall out of his pockets, or that the moonlight wouldn't glint off any of his equipment. The column advanced across the clearing and plunged into the jungle on Bannon's left. Bannon counted the helmets underneath him, and the total was fifty-six.

The sound of machetes receded into the distance. Bannon waited until he couldn't hear them anymore, then he shinnied down the tree, pulled himself together, and headed back to the American lines, to report what he'd seen.

NINE . . .

The Southern Strike Force arrived in the jungle south of Afua at just before dawn. The Japanese soldiers were exhausted, hungry, and mangy. They were ordered *not* to dig in, because the sounds of their shovels could be heard by the Americans, who weren't far away. The fatigued Japanese soldiers lay on the ground and fell asleep immediately.

Colonel Sakakibara didn't fall asleep immediately. He called a meeting of his staff officers and spread out his map on the ground. Narrowing his eyes to slits, he examined the map in the dim light. He estimated where he was and gauged the distance between him and the Americans. He figured the Americans couldn't be more than a thousand yards away. He wished all his troops were with him so that he could attack that very day, before the Americans knew they were in the area, but at least half of his striking force would arrive the next night, so the earliest he'd be able to attack would be tomorrow. *But maybe I should give myself more time*. He stood up over his map and looked at his staff officers. A frown was on his face and his eyes gleamed with determination.

"We can attack on the morning of the day after tomorrow," he said to his officers, "but the Americans have come to expect night and dawn attacks. Therefore we will attack exactly at noon on the day after tomorrow, in broad daylight, and perhaps take the Americans by surprise. Pass this information on to your men. Make sure they get plenty of rest, but I don't want any sound whatever to come out of this bivouac. Anyone who makes such a sound will die by my sword. Is that clear?"

131

The assembled officers nodded.

"Send out listening posts and guards," Colonel Sakakibara said. "The officers of the day will remain awake. Everyone else may get some sleep. Meeting dismissed."

Some officers disappeared into the jungle, to carry out orders. Others had no orders to carry out, and lay on the ground near Colonel Sakakibara, falling asleep instantly. Colonel Sakakibara glanced at his map one last time, then rolled it up. He sat on the ground and thought about his attack. He knew he would fall in battle, because his small force couldn't hope to overwhelm all the Americans facing him. His life would be over soon, and he would die gloriously for the Emperor, killing as many Americans as possible before he himself was killed.

He saw himself like a crysanthemum blossom, falling to the ground at the peak of perfection. He wouldn't have to become old, sick, and feeble. He wouldn't have to become a beggar in his old age, or rely on charity. He would have the great privilege of dying for the Emperor while still a vigorous young man, and he'd go to heaven as a vigorous young man, not an old fart.

He closed his eyes and fell asleep, thinking of the glories of an honorable death at an early age.

The recon platoon returned to its bivouac shortly before dawn. Lieutenant Sears made his way to Headquarters Company and found Lieutenant Mike Bell in the command post. Lieutenant Bell was from Ohio, and he was the officer of the day.

"Where's Captain Mason?" Lieutenant Sears asked.

"Guess he's still asleep," Lieutenant Bell replied. "How was the patrol?"

"It was a good one," Lieutenant Sears said. "Not a fucking thing happened."

Lieutenant Sears made his way to Captain Mason's pup tent, but Captain Mason wasn't inside. *Where in the hell can he be?* Lieutenant Sears decided that Captain Mason was either in the latrine or the mess tent, getting his morning cup of coffee. He headed toward the latrine, and as he drew closer he saw Captain Mason emerge from it.

Captain Mason had short black hair and rugged features that always seemed on the verge of a sardonic smile. "You're back!" he said to Lieutenant Sears.

"Yes sir."

"Any problems?"

"No sir."

"See anything interesting?"

"No sir."

"Nothing at all?"

"No sir."

"I guess the Japs are quiet tonight," Captain Mason said. "I'll relay the information to Colonel Hutchins right now. You write out your report and have it on my desk no later than"— Captain Mason glanced at his watch—"oh-six hundred hours."

"Yes sir."

Lieutenant Sears headed back to the command post tent, to write out his report, and Captain Mason walked toward Colonel Hutchins's headquarters, to relay this new intelligence information.

Colonel Hutchins sat at his desk, his eyes bleary and bloodshot, his jaw hanging slack. He hadn't slept all night and felt as though he was going to die at any moment.

No longer did he crave booze or cigarettes. He was too sick to crave anything except basic health and well-being. He had a headache and a stomach ache. Every muscle and joint in his body hurt. The thought of food made him nauseous. He was constipated and his lower abdomen felt as though it was filled with cement.

He wondered if he was fit to command his regiment. He deliberated whether to go to the hospital and collapse, letting someone else take over. He felt as though he was going to die at any moment, but maybe a cup of coffee would help.

"Officer of the day!" he said hoarsely.

"Yes sir!" said a voice in the other part of the tent.

"Get me a cup of black coffee right away!"

"Yes sir."

Colonel Hutchins wiped his forehead with the back of his

133

hand. He was covered with cold sweat, and then he farted noisily. He saw silver streaks spinning around inside the tent. He never realized, when he'd sworn to stop drinking and smoking, that it'd get this bad.

He held his hand out in front of him, and it shook uncontrollably. *I'm falling apart,* he thought. *Maybe I ought to tell General Hawkins that I'm unfit for command.*

"Sir?" said a voice on the other side of the tent flap.

"Bring that coffee in here!" Colonel Hutchins demanded.

"I don't have any coffee, sir."

"I thought I told you to get me some goddamned coffee!"

"You never told me to get you any coffee. I just got here. This is Captain Mason speaking."

"Oh, Phil—I didn't realize it was you. Come on in. Whataya want?"

Captain Mason pushed aside the tent flap and entered Colonel Hutchins's office. "The patrol from the recon platoon is back," he said. "They didn't see anything at all on the trail that crosses through grid thirty-four."

"Good," Colonel Hutchins replied. "At least we won't have to worry about Japs for a while."

"Are you all right, sir?" Captain Mason asked.

"Yes, I'm all right."

"You look terrible."

"I feel terrible, but I'm all right."

"Maybe you should go to the hospital."

"I'm not going to any hospital. All I need is a cup of coffee."

"I'll get one for you, sir."

"That's okay. Somebody's already doing that." Colonel Hutchins went limp in his chair. His face became quite pale.

"Perhaps I should get a medic in here," Captain Mason said.

"No," replied Colonel Hutchins.

"You look awfully sick, sir."

"I'm not sick. I'm just a drunk who's gone off the bottle."

"Maybe you'd better go back on it."

"I'm not going to drink another drop in my life, even if it kills me."

"Looks like it might, sir."

"Then let it."

They heard the approach of footsteps in the other section of the tent. A few moments later the officer of the day appeared, carrying a pot of coffee and a cup, which he placed on the desk. With trembling hands, Colonel Hutchins poured coffee into the cup and raised it to his lips. The coffee burned his tongue as he gulped it down.

Captain Mason took a package of Chesterfields out of his shirt pocket. "Cigarette, sir?"

"Get them goddamn cigarettes out of here!" Colonel Hutchins looked at the officer of the day. "What the hell are you doing standing there looking at me like I'm a geek!"

"I'm sorry sir, I—"

"Get the hell out of this office!"

"Yes sir."

The officer of the day turned and fled. Colonel Hutchins looked at Captain Mason. "You may leave also."

"Yes sir."

"Thanks for the information."

Captain Mason marched out of the office. Colonel Hutchins gulped down the remaining coffee in the cup and then poured another cup. His heart beat faster and his forehead felt warm. He tried to forget his physical symptoms and concentrate on what Captain Mason had told him. No Jap activity had been reported on that main trail. If no Japs were observed on the other trails, it could mean that the Japs were finished with their attacks on the southern flank of the American line. That would indicate that the Japs were conducting a general withdrawal, and the battle for Central New Guinea would be over.

It'd been a helluva battle, Colonel Hutchins reflected, trying not to think of his shaking hands and pounding heart. He'd lost more than half of his regiment since arriving on New Guinea on June 28, less than a month ago. But it seemed like a year. It certainly had been a nightmare. Colonel Hutchins hoped the fight was over so he and his men could be pulled off the line and sent back to Honolulu for Rest and Recuperation.

The phone on his desk rang, and Colonel Hutchins's nerves were so jangled he jumped into the air. His hands trembled wildly as he picked up the receiver. "What is it!" he demanded.

He heard the voice of the officer of the day. "Sergeant Bannon says he has to speak with you immediately, sir."

"What the hell for?"

"He says it's very important, sir."

"It'd better be. Send him in."

Colonel Hutchins hung up the phone. He wondered why Sergeant Bannon was coming to see him so early in the morning, but Colonel Hutchins always made special allowances for his good old recon platoon.

Bannon entered the office, advanced to Colonel Hutchins's desk, and saluted. "Sergeant Bannon reporting sir!"

"What the hell do you want?"

"I saw approximately two hundred Japs moving through the jungle last night!"

"What!"

"I saw—"

"I heard you the first time. I thought there weren't any Japs in grid thirty-four last night."

"I wasn't in grid thirty-four last night."

"Where the hell were you?"

"I was in the vicinity of grid eighty-nine."

Colonel Hutchins looked at Bannon and scowled. Bannon was filthy and unshaven, and his eyes were at half-mast. "Why the hell weren't you in grid thirty-four?"

"Because I was AWOL."

Colonel Hutchins raised his eyebrows. "You were AWOL?"

"Yes sir."

"Why were you AWOL?"

"Because I couldn't stand the bullshit in my platoon anymore."

"What kind of bullshit was that?"

"The men talk back to me all the time."

"Punch 'em in their fucking mouths!"

"I do, but they still talk back to me. I'm tired of punching them in their mouths. I have at least five fights a day with the sons of bitches, and I'm tired of it."

"I heard about that," Colonel Hutchins said. "Lieutenant

136

Jameson wants to court-martial you for fighting with your men, you know."

"I know," Bannon replied.

"You've put me on the spot. I don't know what the hell to do about that court-martial."

"Sorry, sir."

"You should've talked to somebody about this problem a long time ago."

"I guess I shoulda but something snapped in my mind, I guess. I just walked into the jungle."

"Just like that?"

"Just like that."

"Then what happened?"

"I kept walking until I got tired, and then I sacked out. Sometime later I heard troops headed my way. I climbed a tree to see who they were, and it was four columns of Japs, each about fifty men strong."

"Which way were they headed?"

"Southwest."

"Let's take a look at the map."

Colonel Hutchins stood and walked falteringly toward his map table.

"Are you all right sir?" asked Bannon.

"Yeah."

"You don't look all right."

"Neither do you."

Colonel Hutchins bent over the map table and looked down at grid eighty-nine. If the Japs were traveling in a southwesterly direction, that meant they were headed to the south of Afua. Evidently they were going to attack the southern flank of the American line again, where the Twenty-third Regiment was located. They were moving through the thick of the jungle so they couldn't be observed on the trails.

"Them sneaky sons of bitches," Colonel Hutchins said.

"Looks like they're up to something, sir."

"I'd better put the regiment on alert as of right now."

Colonel Hutchins hobbled back to his desk and collapsed on the chair. He picked up the receiver of his telephone and hit the button. The voice of the officer of the day came through.

"Yes sir?" he said.

"Notify all commands to go on alert as of right now! Tell them that a Japanese attack is imminent."

"Yes sir!"

Colonel Hutchins hung up the telephone. "That's taken care of. Have a seat, Bannon."

"Yes sir. Mind if I smoke?"

"You're goddamn right I mind. Keep your cigarettes where they are. I don't even wanna see them."

"You're trying to stop smoking, sir?"

"I'm trying to stop smoking and drinking at the same time."

"Maybe you should just taper off, sir. Stopping all at once might be more than your system can handle."

"Are you a doctor, Bannon?"

"No sir."

"Then keep your fucking medical opinions to yourself."

"Yes sir."

Bannon was uneasy in the colonel's office. He wished he could get the hell out of there, but he couldn't leave until the colonel dismissed him. Meanwhile, Colonel Hutchins gazed at Bannon and recalled when he was a young soldier too, in the battle for Mont Blanc Ridge. Once he'd been vigorous and healthy, with a flat stomach and a sparkle in his eyes even when they were at half-mast, like Bannon's. Now he was an old physical wreck. Time had taken its toll.

"Have you been reported AWOL?" Colonel Hutchins asked.

"I don't know, sir."

"I'll have to find out about that and get it changed around, because you were on a special patrol last night, weren't you?"

"I was?"

"Yes you were. It was so special and secret that only I knew about it. That's why you were reported AWOL, right?"

"If you say so, sir."

"I say so. Now tell me about the problems you're having running the recon platoon."

"Well sir," Bannon said, leaning back in the chair, "I guess it all boils down to the fact that I'm not Lieutenant Breckenridge

138

or Sergeant Butsko. The men respected them, but they don't respect me even if I kick their asses five times a day."

"Maybe you'll have to kick their asses ten times a day."

"I don't think I got the energy."

"What's your alternative?"

Bannon thought for a few moments. "Maybe you can transfer me to another company."

"Forget about it."

"How come?"

"Because I need you where you are. You're the only one who can lead that platoon."

"I can't lead them at all. They never do anything I say."

"At least you know them inside and out. You'll have to get tougher with them."

"I'm tired of getting tough with them."

"You got no choice. You're in the Army and there's a war on. You've got to keep trying just the way I keep trying and everybody else keeps trying. What do you think Butsko would say if he knew you were shirking your responsibilities?"

"He'd kick my ass, sir."

"He'd probably shoot you and then spit on your dead body. If he ever returns to this war zone you'd better run when you see him coming."

Bannon gulped. He'd never considered that Butsko might return someday and find out he deserted the recon platoon. Butsko really would fuck him up if that ever happened. Bannon was terrified of Butsko, and so was everybody else except Colonel Hutchins.

"I'll go back," Bannon said.

"Now you're talking," Colonel Hutchins replied.

"I'll kick the shit out of those bastards all day long if that's what I've got to do."

"Just don't get caught."

"Yes sir . . . I mean no sir, I won't get caught."

"I'm promoting you to staff sergeant as of right now," Colonel Hutchins said.

Bannon's eyes goggled. "Huh?"

"You heard me. You now got a rocker underneath your

stripes. Go back to that recon platoon and start kicking ass. That's an order. But if you ever get caught again, I don't know a fucking thing about it."

Bannon jutted out his lower jaw. "Yes sir!" He stood, saluted, performed a snappy about-face, and marched out of the office. Colonel Hutchins picked up his telephone.

"Put me through to Captain Mason."

"Yes sir," said the officer of the day.

Colonel Hutchins thought about cigarettes and whisky for a few moments, and then he heard the voice he wanted.

"Captain Mason speaking sir."

"This is Colonel Hutchins. Are you carrying Sergeant Bannon as an AWOL?"

There was silence on the other end for a few moments. "Well no sir, I'm not," Captain Mason said.

"Why the hell not?"

"I wanted to give him a chance to come back."

"That's good, because he just came back, and I just promoted him to staff sergeant. Make sure you include that on your morning report. Got it?"

"Yes sir."

"Sergeant Bannon was out last night on a special personal reconnaisance for me," Colonel Hutchins continued, "and he found out that Japs are moving through the jungle on new trails they're cutting, and they're heading toward the area south of us. That's why I promoted him. Get the picture?"

"What should I do about Lieutenant Sears?"

"What's the story with him?"

"I assigned him to the recon platoon."

"Unassign him. He's in over his head down there. Bannon's going to handle the recon platoon."

"Think he can do it?"

"He'd fucking better."

"We'll be approaching Los Angeles Airport in approximately forty-five minutes," said the voice of the pilot over the loudspeaker system.

Butsko turned to Lieutenant Norton. "We're almost there," he said, becoming a shade paler.

"You'd better behave yourself—that's all I've got to say."

"Don't worry about a thing," Butsko said, a quaver in his voice.

Butsko had attacked enemy tanks barehanded, but he was afraid of what would happen when the transport plane landed in Los Angeles. A big Army public relations event had been planned, with photographers and reporters and movie stars, and Butsko would be one of the centers of attention. He felt nervous, because he was sure he'd make a fool of himself in front of all those cameras. He might laugh at the wrong moment, or forget where he was and scratch his balls. A million things could go wrong, and he was sure they all would at the same time.

The plane roared across the blue skies near the California coast. Butsko looked around at the other soldiers sitting on benches that lined the fuselage. Several of them were scheduled to receive medals also, and they too were accompanied by officers assigned to look after them, the way Lieutenant Norton was assigned to look after him.

Butsko looked at the other men who'd receive medals. They were soldiers, marines, and sailors, and he could see that some didn't need escorts because they appeared to be ordinary nice guys who did what they were told, and somehow had performed heroic feats when the shit hit the fan. A few of the others were similar to Butsko. They were ugly, mean sons of bitches who didn't like to take orders or knuckle under to authority, and they too had performed heroically when the shit hit the fan, more out of being ornery than any great altruistic impulses. They definitely needed escorts, as Butsko did.

The interior of the fuselage buzzed and the windows were small. Butsko craned his head and looked outside. He couldn't see anything except the beautiful blue water of the Pacific Ocean merging with the paler blue of the sky. Land wasn't in sight yet, but soon it should appear on the horizon.

Butsko wanted to smoke a cigarette. He also needed a drink.

Somehow he didn't feel worthy of the honors he soon would receive. All he'd done was what he'd always done: kill Japs and fight like a motherfucker. He wished he could be back with his good old recon platoon, and wondered how they were doing without him. He assumed they'd get along okay as long as Lieutenant Breckenridge was there to command them, but if anything happened to Lieutenant Breckenridge the platoon probably would fall apart. Butsko didn't think anybody except Lieutenant Breckenridge or he could handle the good old recon platoon.

His thoughts turned to Dolly, who was supposed to be living straight ahead in Santa Monica. What the hell was she doing? Who was she living with? Butsko was certain she was shacked up with somebody. He knew Dolly had hot pants and wouldn't stay alone for long. She needed regular fucking, otherwise she tended to get nuttier than she was ordinarily.

"How're you feeling?" Lieutenant Norton asked.

"Scared shitless."

"There's nothing to be afraid of."

"Maybe not for you."

"All you have to do is behave yourself, and you'll be all right. Keep your hands off the women."

"I'm all fucked out. I don't give a shit about women right now."

Lieutenant Norton grinned. "That was some night we had, huh?"

"I toldja you'd like the place. I also toldja I wouldn't get in any trouble, and I didn't."

"Now I trust you a little more than I did."

"Big fucking deal."

The plane hit a gust of wind and was swept upwards suddenly. Butsko felt his stomach ride up into his throat. The voice of the pilot came over the loudspeaker system.

"We're going down," he said.

Butsko looked out the window. He saw the beaches and forests of California. It was the first time he'd seen the good old U.S. of A. since the summer of 1942. He didn't know whether to laugh or cry.

"You said they'd be movie stars down there?" Butsko asked.

"That's right, and keep your hands off them."

"Who are they?"

"I don't know yet. We'll find out when we land."

"I hope Lana Turner's there. Boy, would I love to stick my dick into her."

"You behave yourself around those movie stars, Butsko. The whole country's gonna be watching you, and you don't want people to think America's heroes are a bunch of sex maniacs, do you?"

"I don't give a fuck what they think."

Lieutenant Norton was aghast. "You don't care what the people on the home front think?"

Butsko thought that over. "Yeah, I guess I do."

"If you start any shit, you'll give the whole Army a bad name."

"I suppose you're right," Butsko said, "but if Lana Turner brings her little ass within reach, I'm gonna grab it."

"You'd better not."

Butsko laughed. "Don't worry about it. I'll behave myself."

"You'd better."

"Whataya mean, I'd better?"

"Because I'll kick your ass, Butsko, and don't think I can't do it."

"Yeah?"

"Yeah."

"Well I'm gonna behave myself," Butsko said, "but not because I'm afraid of you. I'm gonna behave myself because I don't wanna hurt the feelings of all the nice folks on the home front, and also because I'm afraid of the fucking stockade. I been in enough stockades, and they're almost as bad as Jap POW camps."

"I'm glad you realize that. If you're smart, you'll always keep that in your so-called mind once we land."

"Fuck you," Butsko said.

"Fuck you too," Lieutenant Norton replied.

The voice of the pilot came over the loudspeaker system. "We're going down," he said.

The nose of the plane tilted toward the earth, and the plane lost altitude. Butsko looked out the window and saw the great state of California coming closer.

This is it, he thought. *California here I come.*

"Have a seat, Bob," said General Hawkins.

Colonel Hutchins dropped to a chair in front of General Hawkins's desk. Colonel Hutchins had a stomach ache and a headache, but he'd managed to move his bowels after drinking all that coffee, so now his constipation was gone. He felt nervous and twitchy due to all the caffeine.

"How're you feeling?" Colonel Hutchins asked.

"Better."

"Still off the bottle?"

"Yes sir."

"No smoking?"

"That's right."

"Good for you, Bob. I'm glad to hear it."

"I think the worst is over," Colonel Hutchins said. "They say the first few days are the hardest."

"Do you think you're fit to command your regiment?" General Hawkins asked. "Tell me the truth, Bob. It's important that I have a good clear head in command of the Twenty-third, because trouble's ahead."

"I'm as good as ever," Colonel Hutchins said, and then he coughed. "Well, maybe not as good as ever, but almost as good as ever. What's the trouble that's ahead?"

"Japs are moving into the area south of your regiment as you know," General Hawkins replied, "and they're not there for a Boy Scout jamboree. They're going to attack, and it'll probably be an all-out suicide charge, so you'd better be ready and you'd better stop them. I don't want the Japs to have any breakthroughs."

"They won't get through the Twenty-third unless it's over my dead body," Colonel Hutchins said.

"I can rely on you, Bob?"

"Yes you can, sir."

144

"Even now, when you're having certain . . . ah . . . physical problems."

"Now more than ever, sir, because what you call my physical problems are making me mad."

"Okay Bob," General Hawkins said. "I'm going to hold you to your word. And by the way, if the Japs do get through the Twenty-third, General Hall will probably say you're not fit for command. He'll make me relieve you."

"If the Japs get through the Twenty-third," Colonel Hutchins replied, "nobody'll have to relieve me because I just told you I'll be dead before that happens, and I mean it."

One wheel of the transport plane touched down on the runway, and then another wheel. The plane rocked from side to side as it hunkered down and sped over the tarmac. Butsko looked out the window and saw trees and buildings whizzing by. He was on American soil at last. The war seemed far away, almost like a nightmare from which he'd awakened. A week ago he was on the front lines, and now he was in Los Angeles.

The plane slowed down. Butsko turned around. The other soldiers grinned nervously, their faces flushed with color. They wiggled around in their seats and didn't know what to do with their hands.

"We're here," Lieutenant Norton said, a note of relief in his voice.

Butsko looked out the window again. The plane turned around and he saw the airport's main terminal. A huge crowd of people stood in front of the terminal, and sunlight glinted off the tubas and trombones of the band. A big lump formed in Butsko's throat.

"Jesus," he said.

"Whatsa matter?"

"Lookit all them fucking people."

"Don't worry about it. They won't bite you."

The plane came to a stop, and Butsko saw the people move in a giant disorderly wave toward the plane. He turned around and saw the soldiers, sailors, and marines fidgeting in their

145

seats, removing their safety belts. He loosened his safety belt and ran his fingers through his thick black hair. He knew his face was lumpy and scarred, and hoped he wouldn't scare any civilians when he got off the plane.

A stairway on wheels was pushed to the door of the fuselage, and the door was opened. The bright California sunshine glowed like gold. The soldiers lined up in front of the door. A captain stood in front of the door. His name was Lynden Farr and he was in charge of the PR operation.

"All right men," he said, "this is it! This'll be your first encounter with the press, and I want you to relax. There's nothing to be afraid of. You've all faced much more terrifying things than reporters with pencils in their hands. Just talk slowly and answer questions honestly. Smile a lot for the cameras. Make America proud of you. Let's go!"

Captain Farr turned around and stepped out onto the staircase. The band began to play John Phillip Sousa's "Stars and Stripes Forever," and Butsko felt a chill run up his spine. The soldiers moved toward the staircase. Lieutenant Norton pushed Butsko.

"Move it out, soldier," he said.

Butsko placed one foot in front of the other. He joined the long line of servicemen and advanced toward the door. It drew closer and he stepped out into sunshine so bright he had to squinch up his eyes. The band played spiritedly, and a crowd of people were spread over the runway. Bulbs flashed on cameras and the newsreels rolled. Microphones were set up and announcers babbled away. Butsko noticed a bunch of attractive women near the microphones, and a number of them were blondes. He hoped Lana Turner was one of them.

Lieutenant Norton nudged Butsko and Butsko descended the staircase. The crowd cheered and balloons were released into the air. Flags flew from tall poles held up by the hands and leather belts of the color guard. Butsko blinked in amazement as he walked down the stairs. He could see soldiers being kissed by women, and other soldiers interviewed by men carrying microphones. It was like watching a movie, but it was real and he was part of it.

146

Butsko was a nasty son of a bitch, but the patriotic mood of the occasion overwhelmed him. His foot touched down on the tarmac and he felt glad to be back in the good old U.S. of A. Overcome with emotion, he got down on his hands and knees and kissed the ground. The photographers snapped pictures of him and the newsreels whirred.

Butsko got to his feet and a man in civilian clothes thrust a microphone in front of his face.

"How does it feel to be back in the States, soldier?" the man asked.

"Great," Butsko replied, and the newsreel cameras recorded his gnarled battle-scarred face in a variety of close-ups, medium shots, and long shots.

"What's your name, soldier?"

"John Butsko, sir."

"Where you from?"

"McKeesport, Pennsylvania."

"When's the last time you were home?"

"I can't even remember."

Lieutenant Norton pushed Butsko forward. A beautiful woman took Butsko's hand and led him toward other servicemen lined up to the rear of several civilians wearing business suits. The civilians shook the hands of the servicemen, pumping Butsko's arm so hard he thought it would break off at his elbow. One of the civilians stepped up to a podium that sprouted eight microphones. The civilian gave a speech full of oratorical flourishes, welcoming Butsko and the others to the great city of Los Angeles.

A flashbulb popped in front of Butsko's face, and he was blind for a few moments. When he could see again he was standing behind the microphones with other GIs and numerous beautiful women. Butsko looked at the one next to him, and his eyes bugged out of his head because she looked just like Lana Turner.

"Hey," Butsko said to her, "are you really Lana Turner?"

"I sure am," she replied with a big smile. "What's your name?"

Butsko's mind was blown. He opened his mouth but no

147

sound came out. He coughed and managed to say in a hoarse whisper: "I'm Butsko."

"How do you do, Sergeant Butsko," she said, shaking his hand as the flashbulbs burst and the movie cameras caught Butsko's every twitch. "Let me introduce a friend of mine, Rita Hayworth."

Butsko's jaw hung open. Rita Hayworth and her beautiful auburn hair advanced toward him, holding out her hand. Butsko didn't know whether to shit or go blind. She took his hand in hers.

"Welcome home, soldier," she said.

"Thanks," Butsko replied weakly.

With a smile she bent forward and pursed her wonderful curvaceous lips. Butsko went weak in his knees. Her lips touched his cheek lightly, and Butsko thought he'd faint.

"We're all grateful for everything you've done," Rita Hayworth said, and Lana Turner bent toward Butsko, kissing his other cheek, knocking his cunt cap askew on his head.

Butsko smiled stupidly, as the cameras rolled and flashbulbs popped in the air.

McGurk smoked a cigarette, sitting with his back against a tree. A figure approached on a jungle trail, and McGurk sat up straighter.

"It's Bannon!" he said.

Everybody turned around and watched Bannon walk into the clearing. "Hey," Frankie La Barbara said, "the fucking AWOL's back!"

Bannon veered toward Frankie's foxhole and trudged on resolutely. He stopped at the edge of the foxhole and looked down at Frankie. "What'd you call me?" he said.

Frankie looked up and snarled. "I called you a fucking AWOL."

Bannon unslung his M 1 rifle and gripped it by its barrel, like a baseball bat. "Say it again."

"You're a fucking AWOL."

Bannon swung the butt of his rifle at Frankie's head, and

Frankie tried to get out of the way, but he wasn't fast enough. The rifle butt whacked Frankie, and Frankie went down for the count.

"Who's next?" Bannon asked.

Nobody said anything. Bannon held his rifle in his right hand and walked toward Private Joshua McGurk from Skunk Hollow, Maine, who now stood in front of the tree he previously had been sitting against.

"Hi," said Bannon.

"Hi," replied McGurk.

"Remember yesterday when I told you to go out on the patrol?"

"Yep."

"Remember all the shit you gave me?"

"Who me?"

Bannon aimed his rifle at McGurk's left thigh and pulled the trigger.

Blam!

Smoke billowed out of the barrel of the rifle, and a red dot appeared on McGurk's thigh. McGurk hollered in pain and collapsed onto the ground. Blood oozed out of the hole in his leg.

"From now on," Bannon said, "anybody who talks back to me is gonna get shot, only next time I'll aim higher. Any questions?"

Nobody said anything.

Bannon slung his rifle and headed back to his foxhole. As he drew closer he saw Worthington standing inside, looking at him with eyes wide as saucers.

"What the fuck are you looking at?" Bannon asked.

"Nothing," Worthington replied.

"Nothing *what!*"

"Nothing *Sergeant!*"

"That's better."

Bannon jumped into the foxhole and pushed Worthington to the side. Worthington's back hit the wall of the foxhole with a *thump.*

"Get the fuck out of my way," Bannon growled, "and call a medic for that idiot out there who just got shot by a Jap sniper."

Worthington hesitated, and Bannon gave him a backhander across the mouth.

"What're you waiting for, young soldier!" Bannon shouted. "You wanna get shot by a Jap sniper too?"

"No Sergeant!"

"Then get on that walkie-talkie right now and call the medics, you fuck-up!"

"Yes Sergeant!"

His lip bleeding, Worthington raised the walkie-talkie to his face and called Headquarters Company. Bannon sat in the bottom of the foxhole, stood his rifle up against the dirt wall, and snarled.

TEN . . .

Colonel Hutchins spent the rest of the next day near his telephone communications, and whenever he left his headquarters he brought Pfc. Nick Bombasino with him, Pfc. Bombasino carrying a backpack radio.

Colonel Hutchins expected the Japs to attack at any moment, but they didn't attack that day. He slept fitfully during the night, on a cot near his desk, but the Japs didn't attack at night either. The next morning was quiet also. Colonel Hutchins wondered when the Japs would attack. He knew they weren't having a picnic south of his regiment's position. They were going to attack sooner or later, and the anxiety was driving him nuts.

Alcohol and nicotine withdrawal were driving him nuts too, but he thought the worst was over. The pains in his guts and his headaches weren't quite as severe as they'd been, but during the brief periods when he slept during the night he dreamed of chainsmoking cigarettes and guzzling bottles full of fine bourbon whisky. It all tasted wonderful, but he awoke in the morning with the jitters.

The morning was dark and brooding. Clouds covered the sky and it appeared as though it would rain. Colonel Hutchins knew it was just the kind of weather that the Japs liked to use as a cover for their attacks.

Chewing gum like a maniac, he decided that the Japs probably would attack that day. He passed down the order that all listening posts be moved forward fifty additional yards, to spot the Japs before they got too close.

Then he sat at his desk and waited, drumming his fingers

151

on the top of his inkpad, glancing at maps and hoping the Japs would attack so he could wipe them out for once and for all. At mid-morning he decided to go out and inspect his front lines.

Colonel Sakakibara stood with his fists on his hips and looked down at the map spread before him on a collapsible table. He saw where the American positions were and where his position was. His men were deployed across a broad front in a long skirmish line. They weren't dug in and they'd made no noise. Some had no bullets for their rifles, and some carried American M 1s. A few had hand grenades. Every soldier's bayonet was affixed to the end of his rifle.

Colonel Sakakibara checked his watch. It was eleven-thirty in the morning. His attack was scheduled to begin at noon, and dark oleaginous clouds covered the sun.

Colonel Sakakibara stepped back from the map table and lit a cigarette, which he knew might be his last cigarette. He intended to lead the attack himself, in front of all his men. He was resolved to kill as many Americans as possible, and he wanted to go down fighting.

"I don't need the maps anymore," he said to his aides. "Fold up the table and put it away."

A patrol from the recon platoon set up a listening post in no-man's-land, far in advance of the Twenty-third Regiment's main positions. The patrol consisted of Bannon, Frankie La Barbara, Worthington, and the Reverend Billie Jones. Bannon and Worthington were side by side, lying on the ground, and Worthington held the walkie-talkie against his ear, listening for news.

Bannon looked at the sword that McGurk had left behind when he was carried off by the medics. Bannon had seen many Japanese swords since his first days of fighting on Guadalcanal, but this one was by far the oldest and most beautiful. He admired the inlaid gold and carvings of crysanthemums, wondering who'd made the sword and who'd owned the sword and how many Americans it had killed.

He perked up his ears, hearing the hush of rain against the

treetops. The storm that everybody expected had finally arrived. A jagged streak of lightning shot across the heavens, but Bannon couldn't see it through the thick foliage over his head. A few seconds later he heard a peel of thunder, and knew that heavy rain was on the way.

He didn't mind the rain itself, but the sound of the storm would make it difficult for him to hear the approach of the Japs. The jungle was so thick he wouldn't be able to see the Japs until they were right on top of him. He didn't like that idea so much. He wished McGurk was there to help out, because McGurk was a woodsman from Maine and he was much better at locating Japs in the jungle.

Bannon regretted shooting McGurk, but it had to be done. If he didn't establish authority in the platoon, the platoon wouldn't be worth a shit. The men would have contempt for him, and Butsko probably would shoot him when he returned.

Bannon didn't want the Japs to take his men by surprise. He wondered if it might be a good idea to send one man ten or fifteen yards in advance of the others. That way the man could warn the others. Who should he send? He looked at Worthington, who'd hunted big game in Africa before the war.

"Worthington," Bannon said.

Worthington turned toward him. "Yes Sergeant?"

"Think you can handle a special little job for me?"

"What kind of special little job, Sergeant?"

"I'd like you to move ahead ten or fifteen yards and look out for Japs."

"All by myself?"

"That's right."

Worthington shrugged. "I don't know."

"What don't you know?"

"I've never done anything like this by myself before."

"There's got to be a first time for everything. You're not afraid, are you?"

"You're fucking right I'm afraid."

"I thought you were the guy who hunted lions and tigers before the war."

"There aren't any tigers in Africa. The tigers are in India."

"Well whatever it was that you hunted."

"Yeah, I used to hunt big game."

"Then you should know your way around a jungle, right?"

"I wasn't in many jungles. I did my hunting mostly on the veldt."

"What the fuck is the veldt?"

"Sort of like plains."

"Oh. So in other words you're not worth a fuck?"

"What do you mean—I'm not worth a fuck?"

"If you can't be my point man, you ain't worth a fuck."

"Why don't you be the point man?"

Bannon grabbed Worthington by the front of his shirt. "Who do you think you're talking to, young soldier?"

Worthington recalled McGurk getting shot by Bannon earlier in the day. "Sorry Sergeant."

"Get the fuck going and watch out for Japs."

"What'll I do with the walkie-talkie?"

"Give it to me."

Worthington handed the walkie-talkie to Bannon. "Should I go now?"

"Yeah, and if you see any Japs, crawl back here and let us know. Any questions?"

"What if the Japs see me first?"

"You'd better not let them see you first."

"But if I try to crawl back here to report them, they might see me moving through the underbrush."

"They'd better not fucking see you moving through the underbrush. Any other questions?"

"No Sergeant."

"Get going."

Another bolt of lightning streaked across the heavens, followed by a terrific thunderclap. Rain poured down onto the jungle and dripped through the trees onto the advancing skirmish line of Japanese soldiers.

Colonel Sakakibara was in the center of the line, slightly ahead of everyone else. He marched resolutely through the jungle, not flinching as branches scratched his face and arms, and vines scraped across the top of his helmet. He knew he was going to die, and was happy about it. At last the grim ordeal of the war would be over for him. He would meet his honorable ancestors in heaven, after chopping up as many American soldiers as he could with his samurai sword.

The long wave of Japanese soldiers swept through the jungle, rain soaking their uniforms and dripping off the ends of their noses. The ground was mushy and rapidly becoming mud. Monkeys chattered in the trees as they raced for shelter across branches high in the air. It was ten minutes before high noon.

Worthington crawled through the underbrush, trying to estimate whether he was ten yards ahead of the others yet. It scared him to think that he was all by himself in no-man's-land. He didn't want to get too far away, but he didn't want to be too close either. If he was too close Bannon might notice and shoot him in the leg the way he'd shot McGurk in the leg.

Worthington, along with the other members of the recon platoon, was amazed at the change that had come over Bannon during the past forty-eight hours. Bannon had been unsure of himself before and actually had tried to *reason* with the men. Now he was as rotten and nasty as Butsko. He talked to the men as though they were nincompoops, which was the way Butsko had talked to them. It was almost like having Butsko back in the recon platoon, and Worthington wasn't sure whether he preferred the old Bannon to the new Bannon.

Torrents of rain fell on him as he crawled through the muck. The jungle was gray-green and misty in front of him, and visibility was poor. Worthington decided he was far enough in the jungle, and slithered underneath a bush. He picked a few leaves out of the way so that his vision would be unobscured, and settled down to wait for the onslaught of the Japs.

He had no idea whether or not Japs would assault the regiment that day, so he wasn't especially primed for his job. High winds whistled through the jungle and thrashed leaves and ferns. Worthington knew it would be difficult to discern between the effects of the wind and the movement of Japanese soldiers. *Me and my big mouth,* he thought. *I should've never told anybody I used to hunt big game in Africa.*

Mosquitoes buzzed around his bare arms and face and sucked out his blood. He slapped them but they wouldn't go away. The rain washed the citronella off his body. He was miserable and moderately frightened. Removing his helmet so that he could see better, he glanced to his right and left to make sure no Japs were sneaking up on him.

Rain poured onto the jungle and thunder reverberated across the sky. Worthington thought it'd be a bloody horrible mess if the Japs attacked. The fight would be hand-to-hand sooner or later, and it was difficult fighting hand-to-hand if you couldn't get your footing on the slippery mud.

This fucking war, Worthington thought. *This fucking Army.* That morning he'd spoken to Captain Mason and put in for Officers Training School. Captain Mason told him it might take a few months before the orders came down, *if* they came down. There was no guarantee that Worthington would be accepted to OCS, but Captain Mason had said that Worthington had a good chance. The road to Tokyo was paved with young lieutenants, and the Army always needed a steady stream of replacements.

Private Worthington relaxed underneath the bush. He knew he was well camouflaged and no Jap coming through the jungle would see him before he saw the Jap. Everything was okay. Maybe being point man might not be such a bad idea. It was an important job, and he was tired of being just another dope in the recon platoon.

He yawned and let his mind drift back to Greenwich, Connecticut, where his family maintained a large home with its own tennis court, not far from the Atlantic Ocean. He recalled how he used to play tennis on that court, dressed in white shorts and shirts, with his male and female friends. He remembered sailing on the family yawl on Long Island Sound, and how comfortable and gracious his life had been before the war.

Now he was wet, smelly, and unshaven, wearing a tattered uniform, taking orders from Bannon, an ex-cowboy who was a little too quick on the trigger for Worthington's liking. Worthington hoped Lieutenant Breckenridge would be released from the hospital and returned to the recon platoon soon, because Lieutenant Breckenridge was a gentleman at least, with a college education and a decent social background. Private Worthington could tolerate taking orders from Lieutenant Breckenridge, but he wasn't too happy about taking orders from Sergeant Bannon.

Leaves and branches were twisted and yanked by the wind in the jungle in front of him. Peals of thunder filled his ears along with the roar of the steady downpour. It was like lying underneath a waterfall. He wiped raindrops off his nose with the back of his hand, and then noticed a Japanese soldier suddenly step into view through the churning jungle ahead of him.

Worthington froze, the back of his hand against his nose. The Japanese soldier kicked the tangled branches at his feet and moved forward. Worthington saw another Japanese soldier appear to the left of the first one, and then a third advance to his right. *They're coming,* Worthington thought. *This is it.*

He had to warn the others, but he couldn't crawl faster than the Japs could walk. That meant he'd have to get up and run like a motherfucker. The best thing to do would be to fire a warning shot.

The Japanese soldiers stepped closer, and they hadn't seen him yet. Worthington raised his M 1 rifle to his shoulder and looked through the peepsight. He zeroed in on the middle Jap, squeezed the trigger, and *blam!*—the Japanese soldier stopped suddenly, an expression of surprise on his face, and then he sagged to his knees.

Japanese soldiers jabbered noisily. Worthington got to his feet, turned around, and ran away.

"The Japs are coming!" he hollered. *"Get ready!"*

He should've crawled away silently like a sniper instead of running like a maniac, but he was too excited. Bullets whizzed around his head and one hit him squarely in the back. Its force hurled him face first against a tree, and he lay there for a few moments, blood trickling down his back. Then he slid down the tree and fell in a clump to the ground.

The Japanese soldiers knew they'd been spotted, and the time had come to charge. Their officers raised their samurai swords in the air and screamed: *"Banzai!"*

"Banzai!" replied the men. *"Banzai!"*

They pushed through the thick foliage, kicking ferns and branches out of their way as they rampaged forward. Torrents of rain fell on them as they rushed through the jungle on their suicide charge.

"Get ready!" Bannon said. "They're coming!"

His men got behind their weapons and flicked off the safety switches. They held their fingers on the triggers and waited for the Japs to appear. Bannon picked up his walkie-talkie and called Captain Mason. He saw Japs spill out of the jungle in front of him, baring their teeth and shaking their rifles and bayonets. Machine guns and rifles opened fire, cutting the Japs down, and finally Captain Mason got on the radio.

"We're under attack!" Bannon said. "Japs're coming at us across a broad front. I ain't got time to talk anymore. Over and out."

He dropped the walkie-talkie and picked up his M 1 rifle, lining up the sights and aiming at a Jap jumping like a wild horse through the jungle. He squeezed the trigger and *blam!*— the Jap tumbled asshole over teakettle to the ground.

A furious hail of fire erupted across the front of the recon platoon, but more Japs charged out of the jungle, jumping over their fallen comrades, and they were only thirty yards away. Their officers and sergeants urged them on and every Japanese soldier wanted to kill at least one American before he was killed himself.

Distance narrowed between the GIs and the Japanese soldiers. The GIs didn't have much shooting room, and now the Japanese soldiers were almost on top of them, howling and screaming, snorting and farting. The hand-to-hand combat was only seconds away.

"Hit 'em!" Bannon shouted. *"Let's fucking go!"*

Bannon grabbed his captured samurai sword and jumped out of his foxhole. A Japanese soldier ran toward him and Bannon swung wildly at him, the blade of the samurai sword striking the barrel of the Japanese soldier's rifle, deflecting it out of the way.

Bannon stepped inside the Japanese soldier's guard and kicked him in the balls. The Japanese soldier hollered as he dropped to his knees, and Bannon kicked him in the face, jumped over him, and swung the samurai sword downwards, connecting with the top of a Japanese soldier's head, slicing it in two like a cantaloupe, and Bannon yanked the sword loose, swung from the side, and whacked a Japanese soldier on his right biceps muscle, busting through muscle and bone, and the Japanese soldier's arm fell to the ground.

The Japanese soldier blinked in amazement as blood gushed out of the stump where his arm had been. He dropped his rifle and reached for his knife with his left hand, but he was losing too much blood, and the jungle undulated in front of his eyes as if the trees were made of elastic bands. The Japanese soldier blacked out and Bannon rushed past him, swinging his samurai sword sideways and chopping off a Japanese soldier's head. The head went flying into the air like a baseball off the bat of Ted Williams, and on the backswing Bannon smashed another Japanese soldier in the ribs.

The sword went in deep and Bannon couldn't pull it out. The Japanese soldier fell to the ground and Bannon's sword went down with him. Bannon placed his foot on the Japanese soldier's chest and tugged the sword loose, as violent hand-to-hand mayhem erupted all around him.

"Banzai!"

Bannon looked up and saw a Japanese officer running toward him, swinging his samurai sword in the air. He swung the samurai sword toward Bannon's head, and Bannon leapt at him, grabbing the Japanese officer's wrist in his hands, spinning around and throwing him over his shoulders.

The Japanese officer landed on his back with a loud *thud,* and was knocked senseless momentarily. Bannon dived on top of him and punched him in the mouth. The officer flailed the air wildly with his hands, and Bannon punched him again. The officer's lights went out and his arms fell to the side.

"Banzai!"

Bannon looked up and saw two Japanese soldiers running toward him, aiming their rifles and bayonets downwards toward his heart. He saw a Nambu pistol in a holster on the belt of the Japanese officer underneath him, and he drew the pistol out, got to his feet, took aim, and pulled the trigger.

Nothing happened, because the safety was on. The two Japanese soldiers rumbled closer. Bannon flicked the safety off and opened fire. The Nambu pistol barked angrily and kicked in his hand. He fired five quick panic shots, and four of them landed. The Japanese soldiers collapsed at Bannon's feet.

"Banzai!"

Bannon saw another Japanese soldier running toward him, pointing his rifle and bayonet toward Bannon's heart. Bannon aimed his Nambu pistol at him and *blam!*— the bullet smacked the Jap between the eyes, blowing his head apart.

Bannon looked around. He saw Frankie La Barbara jam the bayonet on the end of his rifle into the stomach of a Japanese soldier, and the Japanese soldier shrieked horribly. The Reverend Billie Jones clobbered a Jap on top of his head with his Browning Automatic Rifle (BAR), caving in the top of the Japanese soldier's head. Other soldiers from the recon platoon and Headquarters Company were locked in close hand-to-hand combat all across that part of the jungle, as the rain poured down on them and made the ground slick as rat shit.

Bannon threw away the Nambu pistol and picked up the old samurai sword out of a puddle of rainwater stained a murky red by the blood of a dead Japanese soldier lying nearby. He heard footsteps sloshing through the muck, and looked up to see three Japanese soldiers running toward him, screaming at the tops of their lungs.

Bannon had lost his helmet somewhere along the way, and rain pelted the plastered down sand-colored hair on top of his head. He raised the samurai sword and waited for the Japanese soldiers to come closer. *"Banzai!"* they cried as they closed the distance between Bannon and them.

They lunged forward with their rifles and bayonets, and Bannon dodged to the side. He swung down diagonally with the samurai sword, striking a Japanese soldier on his shoulder, the momentum of the blow pushing the blade of the samurai sword into the Japanese soldier's chest, slicing his esophagus.

The Japanese soldier belched great gobs of blood and fell to the ground. Bannon pulled his samurai sword loose and swung it sideways at the next Japanese soldier, but the Japanese soldier caught the blow on the stock of his rifle, and banged Bannon in the mouth with his rifle butt.

Bannon was knocked senseless, and he fell to the ground. He lay still and the Japanese soldier moved quickly into position over him, preparing to deliver the death stab, when suddenly, out of the wind and rain, the Reverend Billie Jones appeared.

"Jap bastard!" the Reverend Billie Jones hollered, swinging his big twenty-pound BAR from the side.

The Japanese soldier raised his rifle and bayonet to block the blow, but his strength couldn't match the power of big Billie Jones. The BAR crashed against the Japanese soldier's rifle and bayonet and then hit the Japanese soldier on the head. The Japanese soldier's skull crunched under the impact of the blow, and he closed his eyes as his knees wobbled from side to side.

The Reverend Billie Jones looked ahead into the roaring thunderstorm and hunched over, waiting for more Japs to attack, but none came at him immediately. He prodded one of his combat boots into Bannon's kidney.

"C'mon, get up!" he said.

Bannon groaned, and the Reverend Billie Jones prodded him again. Bannon opened his eyes. "Where am I?" he asked.

"You'd better get up!" the Reverend Billie Jones said.

"Banzai!"

The Reverend Billie Jones looked to his side and saw Japanese soldiers burst through the rain, heading straight for him. A shadow appeared in the corner of his eye and rushed toward the Japs. This shadow was Pfc. Frankie La Barbara from New York City, and his shirt had been torn off his body in a previous fracas with a Japanese soldier. His dogtags dangled from his neck as he charged toward the new contingent of Japanese soldiers rushing out of the jungle.

"You fucking cocksuckers!" Frankie La Barbara screamed, thrusting his upper body forward, plunging his rifle and bayonet into the stomach of a Japanese soldier. He pulled his rifle and bayonet out, bashed the next Japanese soldier in the chops, kicked the next Japanese soldier in the balls, smashed the next Japanese soldier in the mouth with his rifle butt, and slashed the last Japanese soldier diagonally from throat to hip, ripping him wide open. The Japanese soldier's guts spilled out of his stomach as he fell in a heap onto the ground.

Frankie La Barbara looked to his right and left, and couldn't see any more Japanese soldiers coming at him. He turned around and saw Bannon picking himself up off the ground next to the Reverend Billie Jones. Frankie snarled and spit at the ground. He reached into his shirt pocket for his package of cigarettes, but his fingernails scraped against the hair of his chest because he didn't have his shirt anymore.

He shrugged and walked back toward Bannon and the Reverend Billie Jones. "Either of youse guys got a smoke?" he asked.

Colonel Hutchins was inspecting the Headquarters Company mess tent when the fight broke out. Japanese soldiers poured out of the jungle nearby, and Colonel Hutchins unslung his .45 caliber Thompson submachine gun. His first thought was that he shouldn't have been caught so close to the front, since he wasn't a kid anymore, and his second thought was *go get them fucking Japs.*

The old war dog in him responded, and he ran toward the mess tent's exit. *"Follow me!"* he shouted to the cooks and bakers. *"Get the fuckers!"*

Colonel Hutchins emerged from the tent and saw Japanese and American soldiers locked in hand-to-hand combat all around him. He wanted to charge into the thick of the fray, but a little voice inside his head told him to take it easy because he wasn't a kid anymore. *I'll just lay back and lead the fight,* he said to himself. *I'm not the man I used to be.*

He stood beside the entrance to the tent, as the cooks and

bakers came out, armed with rifles and bayonets, butcher knives, and meat cleavers.

Colonel Hutchins pointed toward the Japs. *"Go get 'em!"* he hollered.

The cooks and bakers looked at him curiously. They didn't seem particularly anxious to attack the Japs. Some looked toward their rear, as if planning avenues of escape.

Colonel Hutchins realized that the men expected him to lead them forward, and if he wasn't going to charge, why should they? He remembered at that moment the one main principle about war that he'd learned in his nearly twenty-seven years in uniform. If you wanted men to obey you, you had to get out front and lead them.

He knew he wasn't in particularly good physical condition, but duty was calling. He knew what he had to do and he knew how to do it. Raising his submachine gun in the air, he threw his left foot forward and ran toward the melee at the edge of the jungle.

"Let's go!" he shouted. *"Follow me!"*

He rushed toward the fighting, holding the butt of his submachine gun tucked in between his elbow and his waist. The cooks and bakers followed him, brandishing their weapons, because they couldn't lay back and let Colonel Hutchins charge all by his lonesome.

The Japanese soldiers saw the silver bird on Colonel Hutchins's lapel, and knew he was a high-ranking American officer. Shouting gleefully, they lunged toward him with smiles on their faces, anxious to win glory for themselves by killing him.

Colonel Hutchins saw them coming and squeezed the trigger of his submachine gun. Fat hot bullets spat out the barrel and mowed the Japanese soldiers down. More Japanese soldiers arose behind them, and Colonel Hutchins shot them in their faces, chests, and stomachs. He shot a few of them in their balls, and put bullets in a substantial number of Japanese legs.

The Japanese soldiers fell like wheat before a scythe, but more poured out of the jungle behind them. They advanced steadily through the clerks, truckdrivers, cooks, and bakers, and Colonel Hutchins stuffed a fresh clip of ammunition into his Thompson submachine gun.

He ran forward and fired point-blank at the head of a Japanese soldier, blowing it to smithereens. Pivoting, he leveled a stream of bullets at the chest of another Japanese soldier, and mangled his heart, lungs, and aorta. Spinning around, he shot another soldier in the face, fired a burst into a Japanese soldier's belly, parried the bayonet thrust from the next Japanese soldier, and bashed that Japanese soldier in the face with the butt of his submachine gun.

More Japanese soldiers charged out of the jungle. One came at him with bloodlust in his eyes, and Colonel Hutchins aimed his submachine gun at him, pulling the trigger.

Click!

The gun was empty, and the click sounded like a tank being dropped onto a rocky road from the height of five hundred yards. Colonel Hutchins let go the submachine gun and dived onto the rifle and bayonet streaking toward his heart. His hands closed around it and the tip of the blade came to a halt a half inch in front of his stomach.

Colonel Hutchins snarled and pulled the rifle and bayonet, but the Japanese soldier wouldn't let go. The Japanese soldier tugged with all his strength, and Colonel Hutchins purposefully turned it loose. The Japanese soldier fell onto his ass, and something gleamed in the corner of Colonel Hutchins's eye. It was a meat cleaver near the hand of a butcher who'd been bayoneted by a Japanese soldier, and Colonel Hutchins bent over, picking up the meat cleaver.

Blood stained its blade; the cleaver had drunk Japanese blood already that afternoon. The Japanese soldier who'd fallen to the ground struggled to get up, and Colonel Hutchins attacked him, swinging the meat cleaver sideways, connecting with the Japanese soldier's right temple, chopping off the top of the Japanese soldier's head, and it flew into the air like an upside-down saucer, with blood and bits of brains scattering in all directions.

The Japanese soldier dropped at Colonel Hutchins's feet,

and Colonel Hutchins looked up to see two Japanese soldiers running toward him. He threw the meat cleaver and hit one Japanese soldier in the face, the blade cracking open the Japanese soldier's skull, but the other Japanese soldier maintained his forward momentum.

Colonel Hutchins was weaponless again, and didn't have time to pick anything up from the ground. All he could do was whip out his Ka-bar knife and look for an opening. The Japanese soldier pushed his rifle and bayonet forward, and Colonel Hutchins banged it to the side with a sweep of his forearm. He stepped inside the Japanese soldier's guard and punched up with the Ka-bar knife, burying it to the hilt in the Japanese soldier's stomach.

The Japanese soldier sighed and fell to the ground. Colonel Hutchins pulled the knife out, and his hand was soaked with blood. He looked around and saw his cooks, bakers, truck-drivers, and clerks standing toe to toe with the Japs and cutting them down. Colonel Hutchins could see that not many Japs had participated in the attack, but they weren't retreating. Evidently they were going to stand their ground and die fighting.

Colonel Hutchins thought he'd oblige them. He saw his Thompson submachine gun lying on the ground nearby, and picked it up. He loaded in a fresh clip of .45 caliber bullets and stood up, looking around for a Jap to shoot.

Meanwhile the recon platoon and Headquarters Company fell back to the village of Afua, which had been ravaged badly during the past weeks of fighting. Every hut in the village was damaged, and debris lay all over the ground. Soldiers tried to kill each other among the huts as rain poured on the village and filled firepits with water.

Bannon was fighting with a Japanese soldier, and tripped over a firepit, falling on his face. The Japanese soldier reared back his rifle and bayonet and plunged it down toward Bannon's back, but Bannon spun out in the nick of time, and the Japanese bayonet drank only the muddy water that had collected in the firepit.

Bannon bounded to his feet with his captured samurai sword in his right hand. The Japanese soldier raised his rifle and bayonet and feinted a lunge at Bannon's gut. Bannon jumped backwards, swinging down his sword to block the blow that didn't come, and he was wide open. The Japanese soldier grinned fiendishly as he propelled his rifle and bayonet toward Bannon's stomach, and Bannon sucked in his gut and dodged toward the side. The bayonet ripped his shirt, and he swung upwards with his sword, but his blow didn't have much steam on it. The blade of his sword hit the Japanese soldier on his wrist, and blood flowed out.

The Japanese soldier was so hyped he barely felt the pain. He stepped back to measure Bannon for another stab, and Bannon stalked after him, because he wanted to kill the son of a bitch.

The Japanese soldier feinted again, but this time Bannon didn't fall for it. He swung down with the samurai sword, and chopped off the Japanese soldier's left arm.

The Japanese soldier watched his arm drop to the ground, and blood poured out after it. The Japanese soldier suddenly felt dizzy, but he still was game. *"Banzai!"* he cried, shoving the rifle and bayonet forward with his right hand, and *bam!*— Bannon hit him on the head with a downward sweep of the samurai sword.

The blade split the Japanese soldier's skull wide open, and for an instant Bannon saw a perfect view of the inner workings of the human head, but then the Japanese soldier's brains tumbled out of their casings, and blood splattered in the rain. The Japanese soldier was thrown to the ground by the force of the blow, and a rat crawled out of a hole to take a bite of the Japanese soldier's brains.

Bannon breathed deeply as he looked around. Soldiers were everywhere in the little village, in and out of the huts, trying to stab, strangle, and bash each other, even trying to drown each other in the puddles being formed by the torrential rain.

Bannon caught his breath. Not many Japanese soldiers still were on their feet. The Japanese attack had run out of steam

166

evidently but the last remaining Japanese soldiers weren't going to retreat or surrender. They appeared willing to fight to the death in Afua.

What a fucking place to die, Bannon thought. He didn't see any Japs nearby, and didn't feel like looking for trouble. He stood in the middle of a bunch of huts and stared at dead Japanese soldiers littering the ground. A few American soldiers lay on the ground too, and Bannon recognized a few familiar faces from Headquarters Company.

One of the American soldiers groaned, and Bannon turned toward him. The American soldier lay on his back, and had a thick black mustache. Bannon didn't know his name, but had seen him around before. The soldier's shirt was soaked with blood and his lap was full of guts.

The soldier turned his head and looked at Bannon through glazed eyes. Bannon dragged his feet toward the soldier and dropped to one knee in front of him.

"I'm dying," the soldier said.

"No you're not," Bannon replied. "I'll get a medic." Bannon cupped his hands around his mouth and hollered: *"Medic!"* Glancing to his left and right, he couldn't see any medics answering his call. *"Let's have a medic over here!"* he shouted again.

"Lemme have a drink of water," the soldier whispered.

"Sure thing."

Bannon pulled out his canteen and unscrewed the top, holding the mouth to the soldier's lips. The soldier let the water flow into his mouth, gurgling it down with great effort.

"Not too much, now," Bannon said, pulling the canteen back.

"It hurts," the soldier said.

Bannon wished he had a syrette of morphine on him, but he didn't. He called again for a medic, but none came forth. Bannon looked around and saw American soldiers staggering among the huts. A few still were fighting Japs, and others dropped to the ground to get some rest and drink water out of their canteens.

"Let's have a medic over here!" Bannon yelled.

But no soldier with a red cross on his arm stepped forward to help out.

"Got a cigarette?" the soldier asked, his voice little more than a series of gasps.

"Sure," replied Bannon.

Bannon took two cigarettes from his pack. He placed one between the lips of the wounded soldier, and the other between his own lips. He lit both cigarettes with his trusty old Zippo and the wounded soldier puffed faintly.

"I'm gonna die," the soldier mumbled, the cigarette dangling out of his mouth.

"No you're not," Bannon replied. "Just hang on. A medic'll be here in a little while."

"Bullshit. You're just saying that."

"No I'm not. There's got to be a medic around here."

"There don't have to be no medic around here," the soldier whispered. "I'm dying and you fucking well know it. Look at me."

Bannon looked at the soldier's sweat-streaked face.

"I want you to do something for me," the soldier said.

"Name it," Bannon replied.

"I wantcha to write to my wife and tell her I died like a man."

"If you die, I promise I'll do it."

"Her address is in my wallet."

"Right."

"Take my wallet now."

"I don't wanna take your fucking wallet, because you're gonna live."

"I ain't gonna live and you know it."

"Don't give up, soldier. Your wife wouldn't want you to give up."

The soldier looked over Bannon's shoulder, and his eyes widened. "Watch out!"

Bannon jumped up and turned around. A Japanese officer wearing shabby boots tiptoed toward him, his samurai sword in his hand. This Japanese officer was none other than Acting

Colonel Sakakibara, his uniform torn and bloody, blood oozing out of a bayonet cut on his left pectoral muscle.

"You sneaky son of a bitch," Bannon said, raising his captured samurai sword.

Colonel Sakakibara's eyes narrowed to slits. The battle was lost, and he knew he didn't have long to live. Americans were everywhere and sooner or later one of them would kill him, but he wanted to take as many of them as possible with him into the land of the dead.

Colonel Sakakibara looked at the tall lanky American soldier with sand-colored hair. The American soldier was bloody and ragged too. He looked tired, just as Colonel Sakakibara was tired.

"I'm going to kill you," Colonel Sakakibara muttered in Japanese.

Bannon couldn't speak Japanese, but he caught his drift. "You're as good as dead," he replied.

Both men advanced toward each other. Bannon had greater reach but Colonel Sakakibara was the more experienced swordsman. Colonel Sakakibara held the handle of his sword in both his hands and raised the sword over his head. Bannon also held his sword in both hands, but laid it back for a side-swing, like a batter at the plate in Wrigley Field.

They stopped in front of each other and looked at each other's eyes. Colonel Sakakibara's eyes were so slitted they appeared to be closed, while Bannon had a mean determined expression on his face. Bannon thought about the wounded American soldier lying behind him. He remembered all his friends and buddies who'd been killed by Japanese soldiers, and he wanted to make the one in front of him pay for every drop of American blood that had ever been spilled in the southwest Pacific.

Bannon and Colonel Sakakibara glowered at each other, and electricity crackled in the air between them. Both took a deep breath, and suddenly both of them swung at the same time. Their samurai swords whistled through the air and clanged against each other with such force that sparks flew and the sound could be heard all across the village of Afua.

169

Bannon's hands stung from the violent clash, and he took a step backwards. So did Colonel Sakakibara. They stared at each other again, and Colonel Sakakibara pawed the ground with his left foot as he raised his samurai sword over his head again. Bannon held his sword over his shoulder like a baseball player at bat and circled to his right. Colonel Sakakibara followed him with his slitted eyes, pivoting on the balls of his feet. Other American soldiers in the area came closer to see what was going on, and one of them was Pfc. Frankie La Barbara.

"Step back," Frankie said to Bannon. "I'll shoot the son of a bitch."

"I can handle him," Bannon said. "He's mine."

Bannon felt personally challenged by the defiance and hatred in Colonel Sakakibara's eyes, and he wanted to show him who was boss. Colonel Sakakibara knew that his number had come up, and if the American soldier in front of him didn't kill him, the others in the gathering circle would. All he could do now was kill the lanky American soldier with the strange hair, and then Colonel Sakakibara would be off to heaven to drink tea with his ancestors.

"Yyyaaaaaahhhhhh!" screamed Colonel Sakakibara as he charged Bannon and swung his samurai sword down. Bannon leaned to the side and the sword whistled past his left shoulder. He swung sideways with all his strength, and his sword slammed into Colonel Sakakibara's rib cage, busting through bones and cartilage.

Colonel Sakakibara felt as if an airplane had flown into him. The force of the blow threw him to the ground, blood bubbling out of his mouth. He smiled and looked into the sky, seeing his ancestors beckoning to him. Bannon raised his sword straight into the air and brought it down hard, chopping off Colonel Sakakibara's head.

Colonel Sakakibara's head rolled away from his body and lay on its side. Bannon took a step backwards and let his hands fall to his sides. Frankie La Barbara swooped down toward Colonel Sakakibara's body and grabbed his sword.

"Lemme have this one," Frankie said to Bannon. "You already got one of your own."

"Take it," Bannon said. "I don't give a fuck."

Bannon looked at the headless Japanese officer for a few moments, then turned around and trudged toward the soldier to whom he'd given a cigarette. He saw the wounded soldier sprawled out on his back, his mouth hanging open and his eyes glazed over. His chest wasn't moving and Bannon was sure he was dead. He kneeled wearily beside the soldier and felt his pulse, but there was nothing. A few flies buzzed around inside the soldier's mouth. Bannon pulled open the soldier's shirt and pressed his ear against his heart, but heard nothing. The soldier was dead, and Bannon had promised to write a letter to his wife, whoever she was.

Bannon rolled the soldier over and pulled out his wallet. Opening it up, he looked through the soldier's i.d. and found the address of his wife; she lived in Fort Wayne, Indiana.

Bannon dropped the wallet into his shirt pocket, turned around, and walked away.

ELEVEN . . .

Colonel Hutchins spoke into the mouthpiece of the backpack radio carried by Pfc. Nick Bombasino from South Philly. "We stopped 'em!" he shouted.

"Good work," replied General Hawkins on the other end of the radio transmission. "How were your casualties?"

"Could've been worse. It was a banzai attack and the Japs went all out, but there weren't that many of them. I figger I've got maybe a hundred casualties."

"Where'd you stop them?"

"The lines are pretty jagged. Their deepest penetration was to Afua. Their commanding officer was killed there."

"Well," said General Hawkins, "I think the Japs are pretty well finished on New Guinea now. It'll be mainly a mopping-up operation from now on."

"My men need a rest, sir."

"I'll pull them off the line tomorrow and put them in reserve. They've done a great job, and I intend to come out there myself and tell them so."

"That'd be a fine idea, sir."

"How'd *you* make out, Hutch?"

"I managed to kill a few Japs of my own, sir."

"Good work. That's all for now. Carry on. Over and out."

Colonel Hutchins returned the mouthpiece to the waiting hand of Pfc. Bombasino. Colonel Hutchins turned around and looked at his staff officers. "Let's get back to headquarters," he said. "There's nothing more for us to do out here."

• • •

General Hawkins called General Hall on the telephone. It took a while for the call to go through, but finally General Hall's voice came through the long wire strung out through the sodden jungle.

"What's on your mind, Hawkins?" General Hall asked.

"Just thought I'd tell you, sir, that my Twenty-third Regiment just stopped a major Jap banzai attack on your south flank."

"How many Japs were involved in the attack?"

"A few hundred."

"I didn't hear any artillery activity down there, but I don't suppose the Japs have any artillery anymore."

"They don't have much of anything left, sir. It was just a straight-on banzai attack and it posed no great threat to anything, but it took its toll in casualties. Colonel Hutchins reported approximately one hundred casualties, sir."

"Colonel Hutchins? That name rings a bell."

"He's the one you wanted to relieve of command a week ago, sir."

"Oh yes, the alcoholic."

"He's not an alcoholic anymore, sir, and he's the one who stopped the Japs."

General Hall snorted. "Well I'm sure he didn't do it alone."

"He led the defense, and he won."

"Well, as you pointed out, the Japs didn't have much left."

"A breakthrough could've occurred under a less experienced commander. I can't help wondering how your Colonel MacKenzie would have fared."

"I guess we'll never know that, will we?"

"Guess not, sir."

"Anything else?"

"No sir."

"Please convey my congratulations to Colonel Hutchins."

"Yes sir."

"Over and out."

The deuce-and-a-half truck took the corner on two wheels and screeched to a halt in front of the Eighty-first Division Medical

Headquarters. Orderlies rushed forward to let down the tailgate, and then the unloading of wounded began.

The rain had tapered off to a drizzle, and Lieutenant Breckenridge watched from underneath a tree. He saw orderlies carrying wounded men on stretchers into the tents, the more seriously wounded going directly into the operating tent.

News had traveled along the grapevine back to the rear that a fierce battle had broken out in the segment of the line held by the Twenty-third Regiment. Lieutenant Breckenridge wondered how his platoon was faring. Word had not been received yet that the battle had been won, and for all Lieutenant Breckenridge knew, the Japs might break through and get back as far as the hospital. They'd done it before and Lieutenant Breckenridge had no reason to believe that they couldn't do it again.

Lieutenant Beverly McCaffrey, a nurse at the hospital, stepped out of a tent and looked around, finally spotting Lieutenant Breckenridge underneath the tree. Lieutenant McCaffrey was a blonde and she wore baggy army fatigues that disguised her voluptuous figure. She and Lieutenant Breckenridge had been conducting a part-time romance ever since they'd met approximately six weeks ago during an earlier Japanese attack.

"Dale!" she said, running toward him.

He turned to her and watched her boobies flop up and down underneath her fatigue shirt. "What's going on?" he asked.

She stopped in front of him and looked up into his eyes. "I just found out that one of your men has been here for a few days!"

"Which one?"

"Private Victor Yabalonka."

Lieutenant Breckenridge was surprised. "He's been here for a few days?"

"You haven't seen him around because he's flat on his back. He's been shot in the chest and he might not pull through."

"My God," said Lieutenant Breckenridge. "Which tent is he in?"

"That one there."

"Wouldja take me to him?"

"Sure."

Lieutenant McCaffrey walked toward a tent, as the rain fell lightly on her hair and made it stringy. Lieutenant Breckenridge followed, dragging his feet slightly because he still wasn't completely cured from his own wounds.

They entered the tent and the walls were rolled up to let the light and breeze come through, but not much breeze was evident and the interior of the tent was like a steambath. Lieutenant McCaffrey made her way among the wounded soldiers lying on the ground, and finally stopped next to Private Victor Yabalonka.

Lieutenant McCaffrey kneeled down, and Lieutenant Breckenridge kneeled next to her. Yabalonka lay on his back and with his eyes closed and his face ashen. The bandages on his stomach showed dots of blood.

"I've got to go," Lieutenant McCaffrey said. "I've got work to do."

"Can't you get somebody to change his bandage?"

"Everybody's busy right now, but I'll try. See you later."

"Yo."

Lieutenant McCaffrey stood and walked away. Lieutenant Breckenridge stared down at Yabalonka's pale sweaty face. Yabalonka had been strong and sturdy before, but now he looked as though he was ready to croak. Lieutenant Breckenridge wondered what had happened to him.

Lieutenant Breckenridge knew that his old recon platoon was gradually being whittled away. Only five or six of the old bunch were still fit for duty, and even he and Butsko, who'd commanded the platoon for so long, were out of action.

This fucking war, Lieutenant Breckenridge thought. He hated the war and thought it stupid, but it had to be fought. The Japanese, Germans, and Italians were trying to take over the world, and someone had to stop them. It was a big mess, with young men dying every day in Europe and the South Pacific, and still there was no end in sight.

At least it's over for me now, he thought. The wound in his shoulder was his fourth, and he'd been told that he'd be shipped back to the States. He'd probably spend the rest of the war training troops on some peaceful post somewhere back in the

States. Lieutenant Breckenridge had done that before and hadn't liked it, but he thought he could handle it now. *I've had enough of this war,* he thought. *Let somebody else do the fighting for a change.*

He looked down at Yabalonka. *But what about this poor son of a bitch here?* Yabalonka looked like he wouldn't last long. Lieutenant Breckenridge knew vaguely that Yabalonka had been a longshoreman in San Francisco before the war, but that was all he knew about Yabalonka's past. He knew much about Yabalonka's present, though. Yabalonka was a good soldier who followed orders and did his best. He was the kind of man you could rely on to give one hundred percent all the time. Now he looked like he was going to die. Lieutenant Breckenridge felt almost like crying. *He's just a kid,* Lieutenant Breckenridge thought. *What a fucking shame.*

"Hi Lieutenant Breckenridge," said a voice behind him.

Lieutenant Breckenridge turned around and saw Private McGurk limping toward him, a bandage wrapped around his left thigh.

"You're here too?" Lieutenant Breckenridge asked.

"Well I ain't someplace else." Private McGurk gritted his teeth in pain as he knelt down on the other side of Yabalonka.

"What happened to you?" Lieutenant Breckenridge asked.

"Bannon shot me."

"What!"

"I said Bannon shot me."

"He did!"

"He damn sure did."

"What the hell'd he shoot you for?"

"I gave him some shit, I guess."

"And he *shot* you?"

"Yep."

Good God, thought Lieutenant Breckenridge, *what in the hell is going on back there in the recon platoon?*

McGurk leaned over Yabalonka and looked at his pallid features. "How's Yabalonka doing?"

"He don't look so good to me," Lieutenant Breckenridge said.

"Yesterday the doctor told me he had a fifty-fifty chance of pulling through."

"At least that's even odds."

"He looks worse today," McGurk said. "Yesterday he talked a little, but he didn't make much sense."

"Poor son of a bitch must be delirious." Lieutenant Breckenridge looked up at McGurk. "How's everything back in the platoon?"

"A fucking mess, sir."

"Whataya mean?"

"Sergeant Bannon's gone a little loco. He's getting real mean."

"That's the only way to handle you guys. Do you think it's easy to handle you guys?"

"Guess not," McGurk said. "The doctor said I'd be fit for duty again in about a week. I sure hate to go back to that platoon."

"I don't know," Lieutenant Breckenridge said. "Sometimes I miss the old gang."

"The old gang's just about all gone now," McGurk said. "Ain't much to go back to anymore."

The jeep stopped and Colonel Hutchins jumped out of the passenger seat. He walked toward his command post tent with his chest puffed out and his gut sucked in, his Thompson submachine gun slung barrel down over his shoulder.

He felt terrific. His regiment had beaten back a Jap attack and he'd stood toe to toe with Japs in the thick of the battle without feeling any fatigue. *If I'd known I'd feel this good I woulda stopped smoking and drinking years ago.*

He entered his tent and looked at Sergeant Koch. "Anything happen while I was gone?"

"I piled some correspondence on your desk, sir."

"That all?"

"Yes sir."

Colonel Hutchins entered his office and hung his helmet on the peg. He tossed his submachine gun on top of his cot and sat down behind his desk. His first instinct was to open his drawer and take out a package of cigarettes, but he stopped himself because he knew no cigarettes were there. His second instinct was to pull out his canteen full of white lightning and take a swig, but his canteen was full of plain old water now. He pulled it out anyway and drank some down.

Burping, he put his canteen back into its case and looked at the pile of correspondence on his desk. On top of the pile was the request for court-martial proceedings against Sergeant Bannon, signed by Lieutenant Jameson in triplicate, and Colonel Hutchins picked up the forms. Frowning, he read the charges against Bannon.

What a crock of shit this is, Colonel Hutchins thought, turning down the corners of his mouth. At the bottom of the form was a space where he was supposed to sign his name. He leaned back in his chair and his brow became furrowed with thought. He liked Bannon and didn't feel like signing the form.

"Fuck it—I won't," he muttered.

He tore up the forms and threw the scraps into his wastebasket.

The survivors of the recon platoon sat around in the village of Afua, eating C rations out of cans. It was two o'clock in the afternoon and Frankie La Barbara had found a huge aluminum pot two feet high, in which he was cooking something.

The Reverend Billie Jones looked at a mask he'd found hidden under some debris in one of the huts. The mask was painted black and had a long sloping nose with a small birdlike mouth.

"Lookit this," Billie said, chewing cold spaghetti and meat balls while holding the mask in the air. "It's some kind of pagan god, I bet. The natives probably bowed down and worshiped it, the damn fools."

"No, that's not what it was used for," said one of the newer men in the recon platoon. His name was Addison and his rank was private.

"How do you know what it was used for?" asked the Reverend Billie Jones.

"Because I studied anthropology before the war."

"What the hell's that?"

"It's the study of primitive cultures, and I've done a bit of research on the South Sea Islands."

"No shit," said the Reverend Billie Jones.

"I wouldn't shit you, buddy."

Bannon looked down at the mask. "What the hell was it used for, then?"

"I can't say exactly, but I believe it's the kind of mask that was used in the yam cult rituals."

"The what?"

"The yam cult rituals."

"What the hell's that?"

Addison paused to put his thoughts in order. He had straight brown hair that needed to be barbered, and sharp scholarly features partially hidden by his beard, filth, and grime. "The tribes on these islands lived by hunting, gathering food, and primitive agriculture," he said. "Food often was scarce, and long-term famine was common. Many tribes planted yams to supplement their diets, and elaborate rituals developed out of the planting and harvesting of yams, because a good crop meant they ate well and a bad crop meant they walked around hungry for a few months. They used masks like that one in their ceremonies, which consisted of chanting and dancing to invoke the assistance of their various gods. They also had a great number of other rules and rituals such as, for instance, only young boys who'd never had sexual relations were chosen to plant the seeds, because it was felt that men who'd had sexual relations contaminated the seeds."

"Dumb pagans!" the Reverend Billie Jones said. "Damned heathens!"

"Well," said Private Addison, "evidently it worked."

"The yams probably woulda grown the same way without all that pagan stuff," Billie Jones replied.

Bannon threw an empty C-ration can over his shoulder. "How do you know?" he asked.

"Because it don't make sense."

"Maybe not to you."

"That's right," Private Addison agreed. "We shouldn't look down on primitive cultures just because they don't do things the way we do things."

The Reverend Billie Jones refused to budge. "They was just pagans and heathens. They didn't know Christ so they was damned to hell."

Frankie La Barbara looked up from the potful of boiling water. "Aw, fuck you!" he said to the Reverend Billie Jones.

"Whataya mean—fuck me?" Billie Jones asked, getting to his feet.

"Just what I said: fuck you!"

Bannon cleared his throat. "Settle down, you two."

"He can't talk to me that way," the Reverend Billie Jones complained.

"Sit the fuck down."

"I don't feel like sitting down."

Bannon reached for his M 1 rifle. "I said sit the fuck down."

The Reverend Billie Jones sat the fuck down. Bannon pulled a can of fruit salad out of his pack and pried it open with his GI can opener. "What're you cooking over there, Frankie?" he asked.

"Nothing," Frankie replied.

"What're you mean—nothing? You're cooking something, aren't you?"

"Nope."

"Then what the fuck are you doing?"

"I'm boiling something."

"What're you boiling?"

Frankie La Barbara looked inside the pot. He drew his Ka-bar knife, stuck it into the pot, and came up with Colonel Sakakibara's head!

Everybody stared at the head in horror. Private Addison gagged. Private Wiley, another of the newer men, put his hand over his mouth and ran into the woods.

Frankie tossed the head back into the pot. "I'm boiling all the skin off it," Frankie said. "A good Jap skull like this can go for fifty bucks to one of them dopey sailors who's got more money than he knows what to do with, and this head belonged to an officer, so maybe I can get seventy-five."

Bannon looked down into his can of fruit salad, and somehow he didn't feel so hungry anymore. "Frankie, you're a fucking animal, you know that?"

"Fuck you," Frankie replied.

Bannon stood, slung his M 1 over his shoulder, and walked away, carrying his can of fruit salad in one hand and his pack in the other. The rest of the soldiers gathered their gear and dispersed to other parts of the village also, leaving Frankie alone with his pot of boiling water and Colonel Sakakibara's head floating around inside.

The bungalows were constructed only fifteen feet apart, and formed a three-sided rectangle with the open side facing the street. Each had a front porch that opened on a sidewalk that ran perpendicular from the street, and little children played on the sidewalk and porches as Lieutenant Norton parked the o.d. green Chevrolet across the street. A radio blared on one of the porches, and the Andrews Sisters were singing: "Don't Sit Under the Apple Tree with Anybody Else But Me."

Butsko pointed to the bungalows. "I think the address is over there."

Lieutenant Norton turned off the radio and flipped the ignition key. The engine coughed and died. "Well, let's go over there and see if your wife's home."

"I hope the hell she ain't home," Butsko said.

"You mean we came all the way out here to see your wife, and you hope she isn't home?"

"That's right," Butsko wheezed.

"Listen," Lieutenant Norton said, "don't worry about anything. If there's any trouble, I'll handle it. Just don't punch anybody, got it?"

"Yeah."

"I hope you do, because if you punch somebody you're going right back to the front."

"I think I'd be better off at the front than here."

"You're even dumber than I thought. Let's go."

"Lemme take a drink, first."

"You'd better not drink too much of that stuff."

"Just a couple swallows will set me straight."

Butsko opened the glove compartment and took out a brown paper bag. Inside the bag was a bottle of Philadelphia Blended Whisky. He removed the bottle, unscrewed the top, raised the bottle to his mouth, and threw his head back, his Adam's apple bobbing up and down.

"Take it easy on that stuff," Lieutenant Norton said.

Butsko moved his head forward and held the bottle up. The fluid inside the brown bottle was diminished by one-third. He returned the bottle to the bag and stuffed the bag into the glove compartment. Lighting a cigarette, he pushed open the door and stepped out onto the sidewalk.

He slammed the door of the Chevrolet and looked across the roof to the complex of bungalows across the street. The children on the porches and sidewalks wore helmets and carried wooden rifles. They were playing war, mimicking sounds like gunshots and machine-gun fire with their voices. Butsko flashed on his old recon platoon fighting with loaded guns somewhere in the jungles of New Guinea.

Lieutenant Norton got out of the Chevrolet and slammed the door shut. "Let's go," he said.

Lieutenant Norton crossed the street, and Butsko followed him. The children noticed them coming and stopped playing. One of the kids shouted: *"Ten-hut!"*, and all the other kids snapped to attention.

"At ease!" said Lieutenant Norton. "As you were!"

The children rushed forward and crowded around Lieutenant Norton and Butsko.

"Are you guys tankers?" one of the kids asked.

"No," said Lieutenant Norton.

"Did you ever kill a kraut?"

"We're in the Pacific Theater. That's where the Japs are."

"Are they really as sneaky as they say?"

"Sneakier."

Butsko looked at Dolly's address on the piece of paper in his hand. The numbers on the bungalows were close to her number. Evidently she lived somewhere in the bungalow complex.

A door opened and an elderly man appeared on a porch nearby. He wore a white Air Raid Warden helmet, tan slacks, and a dirty white tanktop undershirt that made him appear as though he was pregnant. He descended the steps in front of the porch, as a female voice came on the radio singing "There'll Be Bluebirds Over the White Cliffs of Dover."

The Air Raid Warden walked toward Lieutenant Norton and Butsko. "Can I help you fellers?"

"I'm looking for my wife," Butsko told him.

"You kids get lost!" the Air Raid Warden said. "Go on! Beat it!"

The kids scattered in all directions, hiding behind porches and bushes, looking at Lieutenant Norton and Butsko.

"What's your wife's name?" the Air Raid Warden asked Butsko.

"Dolly Butsko."

The Air Raid Warden smiled. "Dolly Butsko! So *you're* her old man!" The Air Raid Warden held out his hand. "I'm pleased to meetcha. My name's Ruby Pacheco."

Butsko shook his hand and introduced him to Lieutenant Norton. Pacheco's eyes widened when he saw the Congressional Medal of Honor ribbon on Lieutenant Norton's shirt.

"Where does my wife live?" Butsko asked.

Pacheco pointed. "That house over there, but I don't think she's home right now."

"She live alone over there?" Butsko asked.

"No."

"No?"

"No."

Butsko's face got mean. He looked at Lieutenant Norton, then turned back to Ruby Pacheco. "Who's she living with?"

"Her name's Muriel Hathaway."

"Muriel Hathaway?"

"That's right, and I believe Muriel's home right now. Why don't you go over there and say hello to her." Pacheco pointed.

"It's the house right there."

Butsko looked at Lieutenant Norton, then squared his shoulders, straightened his cunt cap on his head, and marched toward the house Pacheco had indicated. Lieutenant Norton slapped Pacheco on the arm and followed Butsko. The bungalows were made of wood and painted yellow. The radio now was playing "Pennsylvania 6-5000" performed by the Glenn Miller Orchestra.

Butsko ascended the steps to the porch. The entire bungalow shook as he crossed the porch and banged his fist on the door. "Anybody home?" he roared.

Lieutenant Norton caught up to him. "Who're you talking to: the mayor of San Francisco? Keep your voice down."

Butsko pounded on the door again. The children and Ruby Pacheco watched him. Butsko's cigarette dangled out of the corner of his mouth. He didn't know exactly what to expect, but he was going to tough it out anyway.

The door opened and revealed a willowy brunette in a white satiny robe. The brunette's hair was mussed and she looked as though she just got up. She looked at Butsko, blinked, and pointed her forefinger at him.

"I know who you are!" she exclaimed. "I seen your picture! You're Dolly's husband!"

"You're damn right I am," Butsko replied. "Where the hell is she?"

"She's at work."

"Where the hell does she work?"

"McBride Aircraft Corporation. She works days and I work nights this week. Next week she works nights and I work the days. We're on the swing shift."

"What the hell does she do?" Butsko asked.

"She's a riveter," the brunette replied. "She helps build bombers."

Butsko turned to Lieutenant Norton. "She builds bombers," he said incredulously.

"I toldja things weren't as bad as you thought."

"What did you think?" the brunette asked Butsko.

"I thought Dolly'd be shacking up with some guy."

"Do I look like some guy to you?"

"You sure don't, baby."

"My name's Muriel."

"This is Lieutenant Norton."

"Hi Lieutenant Norton."

"Hi Muriel."

Butsko snuffed out his cigarette on the heel of his shoe, and field-stripped the butt as if he was still in the jungles of New Guinea. "Where the hell's this factory where she works?"

"You can't go there now," Muriel said.

"The hell I can't. Where the hell is it?"

She told him the address. "But you can't go there now," she insisted.

"Oh yes I can."

"What makes you think so?"

"Because I go where the fuck I wanna go." Butsko turned to Lieutenant Norton. "Let's hit it," he said.

"Wouldn't you guys like a cup of coffee first?" Muriel asked.

"Maybe later," Butsko replied, "but right now I got things to do."

He turned around, walked across the porch, and jumped to the ground. The kids gazed at him in awe as he marched over the sidewalk to the street, followed by Lieutenant Norton.

Lieutenant Ono walked into General Adachi's office. General Adachi stood at his map table, looking down at geographical demarcations. "What is it?" he said to Lieutenant Ono.

"I regret that I must inform you, sir, that we've lost radio contact with the Southern Strike Force."

"When did you receive your last transmission from them?"

"At eleven hundred hours this morning, sir."

"In that case, we must assume that Colonel Sakakibara and his men have fallen in battle."

"Perhaps they've only fallen out of radio contact, sir."

"Extremely unlikely. Please direct General Kimura to report to me immediately."

"Yes sir."

Lieutenant Ono turned around and walked swiftly out of the

office. General Adachi gazed at his map for a few moments, sighed, and returned to his desk, sitting heavily on his chair.

It was all over now. That was clear to him. The attack by the Southern Strike Force had been the last sizable military operation that he could mount. He assumed that Colonel Sakakibara had killed many Americans before dying honorably for the Emperor. Now the Eighteenth Army could attack no more, except piecemeal here and there to irritate the Americans. General Adachi had no hope whatever of making a dent in the American defenses now.

General Adachi sighed and lit up a cigarette. He felt strangely calm, and his stomach didn't bother him the way it had in the past. He felt as though a great responsibility had been taken away from him. No one could expect any military victories from him now. The Americans would either advance and try to wipe out him and his men, or they'd stay where they were and let him and his men starve to death in the jungle.

The Eighteenth Army has been a tragic Army, he thought sadly. He recalled the many battles in which it had fought, and the many defeats it had suffered. He'd always been understrength and lacking supplies except at the beginning, but those battles had been lost too. Luck had not been on the side of the Eighteenth Army. General Adachi was convinced that he'd done his best. If he had everything to do all over again, he would have done it all the same way.

"Sir?" said a voice on the other side of the tent flap.

"Come in," said General Adachi.

A short officer with a deeply lined walrus face entered his office. He was Brigadier General Tatsunari Kimura, General Adachi's executive officer. General Kimura approached his desk and saluted.

"Please be seated," General Adachi said.

General Kimura sat on the chair.

"The Southern Strike Force has been wiped out," General Adachi said. "The time has come to move my headquarters farther west. I would like you to take charge of the move and determine where we should go."

186

"How far would you like us to move back?" General Kimura asked.

"You may make that decision yourself. It is possible that the Americans will push forward and attempt to annihilate our remaining soldiers, so I'd like my headquarters to be far enough back so that we won't be bothered by any of those skirmishes. On the other hand, I'd like to be close enough so that I can be in touch with my men."

"You may rely on me to find an appropriate position, sir."

"Excellent. Do you have any questions?"

"It is possible that you could be evacuated by submarine, sir," General Kimura said. "Would you like me to make the necessary arrangements?"

"I wish to remain with my Army."

"I quite understand, sir."

"These are difficult times, General Kimura. So many brave men have died. General Tojo has resigned. How the Emperor must be suffering."

"A great tragedy, sir. Everything has gone against us. But Japan is not a very large nation. The Americans and British drove us to war."

"We had no choice," General Adachi agreed. "If we didn't fight, we would have appeared to be a nation of sniveling cowards. Better to die than be a coward."

"The Americans and British are swine. They want to own everything."

"They will never own us. Only our Emperor owns us. Please return to your office, General Kimura, and plan our strategic relocation."

"As you wish, sir."

General Kimura arose, saluted, and marched out of the office. General Adachi puffed his cigarette and stared into space. *What a strange and terrible war,* he thought. *I wonder what history will say of it?*

Private Victor Yabalonka opened his eyes. He heard buzzing in his ears and felt as though he weighed a thousand pounds.

187

Where am I? he wondered. *Am I still alive?*

He focused on the top of the tent and realized he still was in the Eighty-first Division Medical Headquarters. That meant he was alive, although he didn't feel alive by much.

He moved his head to the side and saw soldiers lying on the ground inside the tent. The walls of the tent were rolled up and it was gray and damp outside. Yabalonka felt a deep pain in his chest, and his head was spinning. He could barely move his arms and legs. He realized the buzzing was a man's voice nearby. Turning to the other side, he saw a chaplain saying a prayer over a wounded soldier.

Yabalonka blinked and recognized the chaplain as Father Sheehy, the Catholic priest assigned to the division. Father Sheehy was in his forties, bald on top of his head, with his sidewalls graying. He had a long thin nose like a finger and his skin was pink. Yabalonka couldn't hear exactly what he was saying, but it sounded like a religious ceremony of some kind.

Yabalonka remembered the Bible he'd carried in his shirt pocket, and how it had stopped two Japanese bullets on two separate occasions. But it hadn't stopped the bullet that got him. The first two times he'd been lucky, but the last time his luck had run out.

I wonder if I'm gonna die, he thought. He felt alone and miserable, not aware that Lieutenant Breckenridge and Private McGurk had visited him while he was unconscious. He wanted to live but somehow didn't think he had the strength to pull through. He felt as though Death was defeating him a little more every moment. *I'm gonna die,* he thought. *I wonder what it's like to be dead?*

"Are you a Catholic?" asked a voice above him.

Yabalonka looked up and saw Father Sheehy hovering above him, looking like a strange friendly buzzard.

"Can you hear me, soldier?" Father Sheehy asked gently.

Yabalonka took a deep breath. "I can hear you," he replied in a rasping whisper.

"Are you a Catholic?"

"I used to be."

"Would you like to receive Holy Communion?"

"I've fallen away from the church," Yabalonka said laboriously.

"You can always fall back," Father Sheehy told him. "It's as easy to fall back as it is to fall away."

"I don't believe in God, Father."

"Then who made the world, soldier?"

"The world made itself."

"How can anything make itself? Did you make yourself?"

"No."

"Nothing can make itself. Only God can make things."

"I can't believe that, Father. I'm sorry."

"I can offer you communion anyway."

"That'd make me a hypocrite, wouldn't it?"

"I don't know. I'm only here to offer you the body of Christ. Are you familiar with the argument of Pascal?"

"Who?"

"He was a French theologian. He said that if you pray to God, and he doesn't exist, you haven't lost anything except a little of your time, but if you don't worship God, and he does exist, you just might lose eternity. So from a practical point of view, it's better to worship God once in a while. Do you get my point?"

"I don't know, Father," Yabalonka said in a quavering voice, "but I think I'm gonna die."

"That may be so, my son. I'm not a doctor and I don't know. But if you think you're going to die, it might be best to make your peace with God, just in case."

Yabalonka was overcome by sadness. It was as though he had no strength left, and all he had to give the world were his tears.

"All right," he said, "I'd like to receive communion."

Father Sheehy took a roll of white satin fabric out of his knapsack, kissed it, and hung it around his neck. Then he pulled out his little black book, opened it up, and crossed himself.

He muttered in Latin, and Yabalonka wondered why he'd agreed to receive communion. He really didn't believe in God, and Pascal's argument sounded like bullshit. But Yabalonka felt lonely and frightened. He was happy to have the human warmth that Father Sheehy was giving him, and the ceremony was somehow comforting. It reminded him of when he was a young boy in Chicago, where he'd been raised, and his mother had made him attend church regularly. He'd even been a choir-boy for a while; those had been good days.

Father Sheehy intoned the prayers, and Yabalonka recalled how happy he'd been when he was a child. His father had a good job and everything had been fine, but then the Depression struck and the bottom dropped out of his world. His father lost his job and Yabalonka had to quit school. He left home and bummed around the country, riding the rails, and finally wound up in San Francisco, where he managed to get a job as a longshoreman.

He heard Father Sheehy's voice, and looked up at him. The old priest seemed to really believe in what he was doing. *How can he believe that superstitious stuff?* Yabalonka wondered. *If there was a God there wouldn't be any wars.*

Yabalonka had a dizzy spell, and lost consciousness for a few moments. When he opened his eyes he saw the holy wafer in front of his face. The wafer was in Father Sheehy's hand.

"Can you hear me?" Father Sheehy asked.

"Yes Father."

"The body of Christ," Father Sheehy said.

Yabalonka stuck out his tongue and Father Sheehy placed the wafer upon it.

"May the body and blood of our Lord Jesus Christ bring us to everlasting life," Father Sheehy said.

Yabalonka closed his mouth on the wafer, and Father Sheehy muttered more prayers. He made the sign of the cross over Yabalonka, smiled, squeezed his wrist, and gathered up his equipment.

"Good luck, soldier," Father Sheehy said.

Yabalonka nodded. Father Sheehy stood and stepped out of Yabalonka's field of vision. Yabalonka was alone again, with the wafer melting on his tongue. *The body of Christ,* Yabalonka thought. *How can anybody believe that piece of bread is the body of Christ?*

Then he became aware of a strange phenomenon. He realized that he felt a little better. It wasn't anything big, he hadn't been completely cured; no tremendous miracle had occurred, but he did feel a bit lighter and a little happier. He analyzed his feelings and realized it wasn't his imagination; he actually did feel perceptibly better.

Now why is that? he wondered. He didn't want to be superstitious and say that God made him feel better, but he didn't want to be a stubborn idiot and try to convince himself that he didn't feel better when he knew that he did.

Again, he had to remind himself that it was no tremendous healing. He didn't feel as though he could get up and return to full frontline duty again, but his spirits had improved somehow. That was an empirical fact that he couldn't ignore. *Maybe it was just the ordinary human contact with Father Sheehy,* Yabalonka thought. *Maybe what I'm feeling has nothing whatever to do with religion.*

He closed his eyes and savored the wheaty wholesomeness of the sacrament on his tongue. It tasted earthy and sweet, chasing the awful bitterness of medicine out of his mouth. He went limp on the ground and relaxed, not bothering to fight the pain and weakness that threatened to drown him. *I'm tired of fighting,* he thought. *I'm just gonna let anything happen that happens.*

He took a deep breath and exhaled air out of his lungs. Then he sucked in a fresh draft of air. The pain seemed diminished now that he was more relaxed. *What the hell am I fighting for all the time?* he asked himself. *If I'm going to die, I'm going to die, and there isn't a fucking thing I can do about it. And if there is a God, at least I've received Holy Communion.*

Somehow that thought amused him, and he laughed. It wasn't a great uproarious laugh because he was whacked out on a variety of drugs and chemicals, but it definitely was mirth and it raised his spirits even higher. *What's the use of worrying?* he thought, remembering the old patriotic World War One song. *It never was worthwhile. So pack up your troubles in your old kit bag and smile, smile, smile.*

He smiled as he lay on the ground. The pain didn't seem

so terrible anymore. It existed, but it was almost as if it had nothing to do with him. It was just there, like the tent, the ground, and the gray day outside.

The sacrament continued to melt on his tongue, and his saliva carried it down his throat. *What if there really is a God?* he thought. *Maybe He really does exist. Nobody can say for sure that he doesn't. All I know is that Father Sheehy made me feel better, and if he comes around again I'll take that biscuit again. What the fuck. Why not?*

The face of a woman appeared above him, and for a moment Yabalonka thought she was the Virgin Mary.

"How're you feeling, soldier?" she asked. She wore Army fatigues and evidently was one of the nurses in the medical headquarters, but Yabalonka had never seen her before.

"I think I feel a little better," he told her, speaking thickly because part of the wafer still was on his tongue.

"Good for you," the nurse said. "It's time for you to get another shot."

"Shoot away," Yabalonka mumbled.

The nurse wiped his forearm with a swab of cotton that had been soaked in alcohol. She jabbed the needle in, pressed the plunger slowly, and watched the morphine enter Yabalonka's vein.

"Didn't faze you at all, did it," the nurse said.

"No ma'am. I'm getting used to it now."

She pulled the needle out. "Get some rest, soldier."

"Hey tell me something," Yabalonka said.

"What do you want to know?" she asked.

"Am I gonna pull through?"

"I haven't got your medical records in front of me," she said, "but you seem to be doing all right. You just said you were feeling better, didn't you?"

"Yes ma'am."

"Always trust your instincts, soldier. They'll never let you down."

The nurse walked away and the morphine hit Yabalonka's brain. He felt dizzy and closed his eyes. His breath became

192

regular and he swallowed the remaining bits of the wafer that had been on his tongue. The morphine carried him away and he felt as though he was floating in the air. *Who knows*, he thought. *Maybe she really was the Virgin Mary.* Then he went slack on the ground, drifting off into a deep drugged slumber.

The big sign on top of the factory said:

MCBRIDE AIRCRAFT CORPORATION

Smoke hooted out of chimneys on top of the roof, and a terrible clatter issued forth from inside. The factory was surrounded by a wire fence, and soldiers stood in guardhouses next to the gates.

"Pretty soft duty, I bet," Butsko said, as Lieutenant Norton drove the o.d. green Chevrolet into the parking lot.

"What's soft duty?" Lieutenant Norton asked.

"Them guards over there."

Lieutenant Norton glanced out the corner of his eye. "Yeah I guess it is."

"You know what I'd be doing if I was one of them guards?"

"What?"

"I'd be fucking every dame who works in the factory."

Lieutenant Norton found a parking spot and steered the Chevrolet into it. Butsko realized what he'd just said, and his face turned red. He thought one of those guards must be fucking Dolly. He knew somebody was fucking her. Dolly just wasn't sitting on that thing. She was using it, unless she wasn't the Dolly he used to know.

"A leopard never changes its spots," Butsko said.

"What was that?" Lieutenant Norton asked, hitting the brakes.

"I wasn't talking to you."

"I don't see anybody else around here."

"I was talking to myself."

"I always knew you were a psycho case." Lieutenant Norton pulled up the emergency brake, turned off the ignition key, and looked at Butsko. "You've been good up until now, but I don't

193

want any trouble when you see your wife. If you lay a hand on her or anybody else in there, I'm gonna put you in the stockade and throw away the key."

"Oh yeah?" Butsko said.

"Yeah."

Both men got out of the car. Lieutenant Norton walked around to Butsko's side, and together they made their way to a sign that said: GATE 17. The sun shone brightly in the sky and in the distance Butsko could see the San Fernando mountains. The closer they came to the factory, the louder the racket became.

"How can anybody work in a place like that?" Butsko asked.

"Beats the hell out of me, but it's not as loud as an artillery bombardment."

"Artillery bombardments don't go on every day around the clock the way this place does."

"I sure do feel sorry for those people in there," Lieutenant Norton said.

They strode toward Gate 17 and saw a sign that said: POLICE POST. The sign was fastened to a wooden guardhouse painted white, beside a wire fence fourteen feet high. Butsko wondered who that fence was supposed to be keeping out. A simple pair of wire cutters could make an opening big enough for the entire Twenty-third Regiment to pass through.

Lieutenant Norton walked toward the guardhouse and knocked on the door. It was opened from the inside, and a second later somebody inside shouted: *"Ten-hut!"*

Lieutenant Norton looked inside the tiny guardhouse and saw two soldiers and two chairs. The soldiers stood stiffly at attention, and they were older men, the kind who performed duties on the home front while younger men went to the real front.

Lieutenant Norton cleared his throat. "Sergeant Butsko and I want to go into the factory," he said.

"You got a pass?" asked one of the guards.

"No, but I got I.D."

"You'll need an escort."

"Get one."

One guard made a telephone call, while another guard examined Lieutenant Norton's and Butsko's I.D. cards.

"What're you gonna do in the factory?" the guard asked Lieutenant Norton.

"Sergeant Butsko here wants to see his wife."

"Why can't he wait until she gets out of work?"

"Hey!" Butsko said, stepping forward. "I'll punch you right in your fucking—"

Lieutenant Norton held out his hand and stopped Butsko. "Calm down."

"Who does that clown think he's talking to?"

"Shut up!"

"Yes sir."

Lieutenant Norton turned to the guard. "Sergeant Butsko here has just returned from the front, and he's on his way to Washington to receive the Congressional Medal of Honor. He's here to see his wife because he doesn't have much time."

"I see," the guard said.

"If I ever see you alone someplace," Butsko said to the guard, "I'll blouse your fucking eyes for you."

"I thought I told you to shut up!" Lieutenant Norton shouted.

"Yes sir."

A few minutes later a patrol of four guards showed up. Lieutenant Norton identified himself and Butsko to the leader of the patrol, and they were escorted onto the factory grounds. They passed through a huge proscenium door and entered the factory itself. It was one immense room, bigger than twenty football fields, full of bombers in various stages of construction. Welders sent sparks flying in showers through the air and riveters hammered away at the seams. The building was six stories high, and cranes carried wings and fuselages over everyone's heads. The male and female workers wore blue denim uniforms, and some of the women wore colorful bandanas to keep their hair in place.

Lieutenant Norton and Butsko climbed a flight of metal stairs and made their way along a catwalk. All the executive offices were near the ceiling, and the guards stopped in front of the office door stenciled with: PERSONNEL.

Lieutenant Norton and Butsko were escorted into an outer office where women pounded on typewriters. Against a wall were private offices, and one of them was marked with: DIRECTOR OF PERSONNEL. The sergeant in charge of the guards opened the door to that office, spoke with the secretary inside, and then opened another door that said: CLARENCE P. WHITTAKER.

Clarence Whittaker was in his fifties, short and slim, with a bald head and a salt and pepper mustache. His eyes were sad.

"What can I do for you, Lieutenant?" he said in a businesslike manner, as if he was being disturbed, and then he noticed the Congressional Medal of Honor ribbon on Lieutenant Norton's shirt. His voice became more ingratiating. "What can I help you with?"

The office had photographs of airplanes on the walls. Papers were piled high on Clarence Whittaker's desk. Behind the desk was a photograph of President Franklin Delano Roosevelt, who was running for re-election that summer against Thomas E. Dewey, the former governor from the state of New York.

Lieutenant Norton introduced himself and Sergeant Butsko. He explained that Butsko was on his way to Washington to receive the Congressional Medal of Honor, and wanted to say hello to his wife, who was a riveter at the factory, before he left Los Angeles.

Clarence Whittaker shook Butsko's hand. "A pleasure to have soldiers like you come to visit us," he said. "How long since you seen your wife?"

"About two years," Butsko said.

"What's her name?"

"Dorothy Butsko."

Clarence Whittaker picked up his telephone and asked his secretary to find out the section in which Dorothy Butsko was employed. He stood with the phone next to his ear for a few moments, and then the secretary told him that Dorothy Butsko had been assigned to Section 14.

Clarence Whittaker hung up his telephone. "Mind if I bring our company photographer along?" he asked.

"What the hell for?" Butsko asked.

"The press might be interested in the picture."

"I don't think I—"

Lieutenant Norton interrupted him. "Of course it's all right, Mr. Whittaker."

"Who asked you?" Butsko said.

"I'd like to talk with you in private, if you don't mind, Sergeant Butsko."

Lieutenant Norton grabbed Butsko by the arm and dragged him out of Mr. Whittaker's office, through the outer office, and to the catwalk overlooking the factory.

Lieutenant Norton pointed his finger at Butsko, and his finger was so close it almost touched Butsko's nose. "You talk too fucking much," Lieutenant Norton said.

"Get your fucking finger out of my face."

"You'd better start keeping your fucking mouth shut, you idiot."

"What'd I do wrong?"

"I just told you—you talk too much. From now on keep your mouth shut and let me do the talking."

"What do we need a fucking photographer for?"

"To sell war bonds. To make people feel patriotic about America. I can see the headline now:

RETURNING WAR HERO
SEES WIFE BUILD BOMBERS

It's the kind of headline that's good for the war effort. So shut up from now on and let me take care of everything, because that's my job, got it?"

"What'm I supposed to say: 'Yes sir'?"

"That's exactly what you're supposed to say."

"Yes sir."

"That's better."

Lieutenant Norton and Butsko went back to Mr. Whittaker's office, leaving the clanging and banging behind them.

"Have a seat," Mr. Whittaker said, dropping into his chair behind his desk. "It's a real honor to have men like you here.

197

You're the men who're saving the world for freedom, and we're all very grateful. I wish I had something appropriate to offer you, but alcoholic beverages aren't permitted in the factory."

"Shit," Butsko said.

"What was that?" asked Mr. Whittaker.

Lieutenant Norton cleared his throat. "Sergeant Butsko just said that he doesn't drink."

Finally the photographer arrived with a Speed Graphic news camera.

"I think we're ready," Mr. Whittaker said. "We might as well get started."

He led them out of the office and onto the catwalk. Butsko looked down and saw a completed bomber being hauled by a tractor toward an opening at the far end of the building. Butsko didn't know much about aircraft, but he'd seen bombers just like that one over Bougainville and New Guinea. They'd bombed the shit out of Japs that otherwise would've had to be killed by him and other GIs with bullets and bayonets. Butsko always had been overjoyed to see American bombers and fighters arriving in his combat zone, and now he could see where they came from: factories like this all over America where women built them alongside men who weren't fit for duty in the military. *I wonder which one of these guys she's fucking*, Butsko thought darkly.

Mr. Whittaker led them down a steel stairway. The din on the floor of the factory became louder. Riveting guns sounded like machine guns, and terrible clanging and slamming came from all directions. They reached the floor of the factory and walked down the center aisle. On each side of the aisle was a row of bombers in various stages of completion. The noise was terrific and Butsko wondered how the workers could handle it day in and day out. Components of planes were suspended in the air by chains and moved about by a crane apparatus overhead.

Butsko saw signs that said SECTION 9 and SECTION 10. He realized he was getting closer to Dolly. Looking around, he saw women in blue overalls and bandanas, riveting, hammer-

198

ing, and twisting in screws. He saw men who looked healthier than he, and wondered which one of them was screwing Dolly.

Midway down the line was a sign that said SECTION 14, and Butsko felt a lump arise in his throat. Butterflies flew around in his stomach. That's where Dolly was supposed to be working, and he hadn't seen her since before he left for New Guinea. They'd argued at their last meeting, but that was nothing new because they always argued.

They came to Section 14 and nobody paid any attention to them because everybody was building bombers. Mr. Whittaker called the foreman over, to find out which worker was Dorothy Butsko, but Butsko already was conducting a reconnaisance, and his eyes came to a stop when he saw the back of a woman in blue coveralls and a red bandana, leaning against a riveting gun. He looked down at her big fat ass, and he'd know that ass anywhere. It was Dolly.

Mr. Whittaker pointed at her. "That's her!" he shouted.

Butsko nodded. He didn't know what to do. Lieutenant Norton grabbed his arm.

"Easy now," Lieutenant Norton said.

"I'm okay," Butsko replied.

But Butsko didn't feel okay. He felt weird. There was his wife standing in front of him, and he couldn't believe she actually was working, because all she'd ever wanted to do was sit around in saloons, drink booze, and flirt with guys. It was amazing to see her working like a man, and it didn't look like easy work either. It was real man's work. Butsko always thought that Dolly was a lazy worthless bitch, yet here she was doing her part for the war effort.

Butsko put one foot in front of the other and walked toward her. A woman carrying a bucket of rivets walked between him and Dolly. Butsko continued to advance. He wondered what to say to Dolly. Maybe she'd hit him over the head with her rivet gun. He stopped, looked back, and saw Mr. Whittaker and Lieutenant Norton looking at him. The photographer had his camera raised to his eyes, ready to snap a picture. *How did I get into this mess?* Butsko asked himself. Lieutenant Norton grinned and gave him thumbs up. Butsko turned toward Dolly again and moved toward her. He came up behind her and tapped her shoulder.

She continued to shoot rivets into the tail assembly of the bomber. Butsko tapped her shoulder again. She pulled the gun away from the tail and turned around. Her goggles covered her eyes, and she stared at Butsko. A flashbulb exploded. Her jaw dropped open. Butsko winked at her, but he was so nervous both of his eyes closed and he looked like a dope.

Dolly wore big thick canvas gloves, and she pushed her goggles up. "What're you doing here?" she asked Butsko.

"Which one of these guys are you fucking?" Butsko asked.

"All of them," Dolly replied.

Another flashbulb exploded. Everyone in the area turned to look at what was going on. Riveters stopped riveting and hammerers stopped hammering.

"What're you doing here?" Dolly asked again.

"I came to see you, baby," Butsko said.

"This is a helluva surprise, Johnny."

"I went to your house and you wasn't home."

"Why didn't you answer my letters?"

"I was busy," Butsko said.

"Are you all right?"

"I think so." A mist came over Butsko's eyes as he gazed at her. She wore a bit of makeup and still looked as perky as when he'd first picked her up in that bar near Fort Campbell, Kentucky. "It's really good to see you again, Dolly," he said.

"It's good to see you too, Johnny."

Their eyes met and the old fires burst into flame. They held out their arms, leaned toward each other, and embraced. Their lips touched and their bodies pressed against each other. Another flashbulb exploded and another photograph was snapped of the hero who'd just returned from the war, greeting his wife, a riveter in a bomber factory.